AN UNSETTLED GRAVE

Also by Bernard Schaffer

The Thief of All Light: A Santero and Rein Thriller

Superbia

Guns of Seneca 6

Grendel Unit

The Girl from Tenerife

Whitechapel: The Final Stand of Sherlock Holmes

AN UNSETTLED GRAVE

BERNARD
SCHAFFER

KENSINGTON BOOKS
www.kensingtonbooks.com

KENSINGTON BOOKS are published by

Kensington Publishing Corp.
119 West 40th Street
New York, NY 10018

All Kensington titles, imprints, and distributed lines are available at special quantity discounts for bulk purchases for sales promotion, premiums, fund-raising, educational, or institutional use. Special book excerpts or customized printings can also be created to fit specific needs. For details, write or phone the office of the Kensington Special Sales Manager: Attn. Special Sales Department. Kensington Publishing Corp, 119 West 40th Street, New York, NY 10018. Phone: 1-800-221-2647.

Library of Congress Card Catalogue Number: 2019932237

Kensington and the K logo Reg. U.S. Pat. & TM Off.

ISBN-13: 978-1-4967-1725-2
ISBN-10: 1-4967-1725-2
First Kensington Hardcover Edition: August 2019

eISBN-13: 978-1-4967-1726-9
eISBN-10: 1-4967-1726-0
First Kensington Electronic Edition: August 2019

10 9 8 7 6 5 4 3 2 1

Printed in the United States of America

To Bill Thompson,
the first to say author,
and
to Cliff Laing,
an uncle when one was needed.

I

ROAD DOGS

CHAPTER 1

*O*ut in the long stretches of road beyond the lights of the super-markets and shopping centers, she drove. True darkness waits in the places with no streetlights. Her high beams dissolved into the fog. Monica Gere wiped the inside of her windshield with her palm, doing nothing but smearing wetness across the glass, and turned up her defroster. It was fall. The days were still warm but the nights turned cold. Sweat cooled on her bare arms and legs and left her shivering. She turned up the heat on the defroster, hoping it would help her see better. It didn't.

Monica went slow. Her headlights connected with eyes along the side of the road. Deer turned their heads, staring as if they might leap in front of her car at the last second to make a run for it. She had a fear of hitting a deer at high speed. A friend of hers hit one and it came barreling through the windshield. The damn thing kicked and thrashed, all antlers and hooves, destroying the car and slicing her friend into a bloody mess. Deer were stronger than they looked. They were large, powerful animals. She passed two others and slowed down even more.

She crossed over the double-yellow lines into the oncoming lane, giving the animals a wide berth. It was ten o'clock at night and she hadn't passed another car since she left the gym. Out here in the woods, cruising under a canopy of thick nighttime cloud and fog, she thought she could have driven in the left lane the entire way.

Unknown to her, the vehicle behind her moved as she moved, changing from lane to lane and closing in. Its engine whined as it raced to catch up to her, never turning on its headlights as it cut through the fog. Monica squinted into the rearview mirror, trying to see what was making the noise. As she looked, brilliant white light blossomed inside the glass and blinded her.

The car behind her activated its high beams, and a light bar mounted across its roof spun to life with dizzying red and blue LEDs. The driver aimed a spotlight at her side mirror, and its glare reflected straight into her face. Monica raised a hand to shield her eyes and skidded to a stop.

She put her car in park and heard someone coming up behind her. She could not see him. Only a shadow, the shape of a man, blocking out the light between his car and hers. In his silhouette, she saw the bright crimson flare of a cigarette. The man flicked it away, sending it into the grass beyond Monica's car.

She rolled down her driver's side window. A flashlight activated inches from her face, the LED burst of a thousand lumens blinding her. Even when she flinched and clenched her eyes shut, all she could see was its white halo.

"Please," she said, but he spoke over her, commanding her to hand over her license and registration.

Monica reached across to undo her glove compartment and fumbled for the paperwork. "I've only had this car a few months," she said. "I'm not sure where anything is."

She could see the flashlight waving around the interior of her car, checking, no doubt, for drugs. It lingered over her chest and stomach, shining against the droplets of sweat above her sports bra. Looking to see if I have my seatbelt on, she thought. Good thing I do. The hand holding the flashlight came in through the open window and aimed downward, straight down at her lap, so bright it revealed the fibers of her yoga pants. The stitching of the seam that ran up her crotch. She closed her legs together, telling herself he was checking to see if she'd tried hiding any weapons.

Cops, she knew, had every reason to be cautious. Night after night, in some part of the country, a police officer was murdered, just because he was doing his job.

Monica handed over her license and the pink registration paperwork marked *temporary*. She smiled politely and said, "I've never owned a new car before. Is this because I went into the other lane? I was trying to go around the deer. They're everywhere."

The officer stepped out of view, his flashlight still aimed at her face while he read her information. "Have you been drinking tonight?"

"No, I'm coming home from the gym," she said.

He went behind her car, standing off to the side of the road, out of view. She heard him say, "Can you check that again for me? Make sure you have the spelling right. Monica Gere, with a *G*."

She couldn't hear anyone respond, but then he came back to her window, his flashlight back to her face. "Ma'am, are you aware there's a warrant for your arrest?"

"What? That's impossible."

"It may be just some procedural error," he said. "Sometimes the computer gets mixed up." He read her info back to her, making sure he had the right name and date of birth and address.

"Yes, that's all correct."

"Well, apparently, there's a drug warrant out for you. Did you get any paperwork in the mail?"

"What kind of paperwork?" Monica asked. Had there been? She normally threw out anything that looked like junk mail. Would she have even recognized an envelope from some kind of court appearance? "No," she said. "I don't think I did. Listen, this is crazy. I've never done drugs in my entire life. There has to be a mistake."

He reached for her door handle and opened it. "Ma'am, step out of the car."

"No, wait a second," Monica said. "I run marathons and work out five nights a week. Do I look like I do drugs?"

"Ma'am, don't make this any harder than it has to be."

He reached for her arm and she yanked away, saying, "Listen to me, sir. Just listen for a second. I respect the police, and I know you have a job to do, but this doesn't make sense. I do not have any warrant."

"Get out of the car now!" he shouted.

It was the tone of absolute authority. An angry school principal. An irate father. A boss with his employee's financial security in the palm of his hand. She got out of the car.

He spun her around and pressed her, face first, against the door. "Spread your legs," he said, pulling her hands behind her back. "Do not move. Understand?"

"Yes, I understand," she said, trembling. "I didn't do anything wrong."

He grabbed her by the back of the hair, making her gasp. "Say that again. Say that one more time, and see what happens."

She felt the handcuffs cinch down, crushing her wrists until she cried out, begging him to let her go.

He kicked her feet apart wider with his boot. His hands went to her hips, fumbling with her waistband, coming up along the sides of her ribs, rubbing across her chest. He yanked her sports bra up, exposing her breasts to the cold air, and squeezed them. "What are you doing? You can't do that!" she shouted.

He smacked her across the back of the head, cracking her so hard she felt dizzy. He shoved her toward the back of the car. She stumbled, trying to get away. He threw her down on the road, holding her handcuffed wrists and twisting. The metal cuffs ground against her bones.

He grabbed the back of her yoga pants at the waistband and yanked them down from her backside, revealing her, and spread her open. She screamed, her voice echoing through the woods, but the road was empty and the fog was thick. He raped her while pressing her facedown into the dirt, telling her he was the cop and he had the power and it was what she deserved.

She lay in the darkness, unable to move, not remembering when the man had left. The night air was cool against her bare, exposed flesh. She heard a car coming and couldn't lift her head. The car stopped. Doors opened. People came running toward her, their voices panicked.

What happened to her?

My God, I think she's been raped.

Someone dropped a sweatshirt on top of her half-naked body, and someone else said, Call the police.

"No," Monica moaned, forcing the sound from her throat. She could hear the police dispatcher on the other end of the phone asking, what's your emergency?

"No!" she screamed, trying to roll over and get away, but they held her down and told her it was going to be okay, the police were already on their way.

CHAPTER 2

*N*o matter how early Carrie Santero went to bed, the phone call in the middle of the night jarred her. It angered her, always intrusive and surprising, when it came. She'd lie on her pillow, staring in confusion at the brightly lit, vibrating thing on the nightstand, unable to comprehend why it was making so much noise. Sometimes, one of her arms would be numb from the way she slept, and she'd struggle to get it to move.

The question on the other end was always the same, no matter which of her new coworkers called. "Are you awake?"

"I am now."

She'd done four weeks straight of being on call, covering for the older, more senior Vieira County detectives. She'd covered during a fishing trip to Alaska. A real illness brought on by strep throat. A fake illness brought on by the oldest county detective being denied four days off and calling out sick. They called that The Blue Flu. As the youngest and most inexperienced cop ever brought over to the county dicks, and the first female ever bumped up to so lofty a position, she would cover a hundred on-call shifts and never complain. A thousand, even.

The extra on-call pay wasn't bad, either. She'd taken a pay cut to leave her uniform police job at Coyote Township.

As a patrol officer, she'd dreamed of the day when she'd get to work big cases. Being a cop in a small town meant you did every-thing from covering school crossings to settling arguments be-

tween neighbors about someone's tree dropping leaves on the other person's front lawn. "Someday, I'll be a detective and not have to handle this bullshit," she used to tell herself.

No one warned her what it was going to really be like.

For one thing, the county detectives' area of responsibility extended far beyond the limits of Vieira County itself. There were vast unincorporated areas far away from the municipalities she was familiar with, places out in the mountains that extended toward West Virginia and forests that stretched across the Ohio border.

The Vieira County District Attorney's Office covered that region under a wide-spanning mutual aid agreement. The few small police departments scattered throughout those places were generally not worth a damn. The DA preferred sending his county detectives out to handle important investigations out there, rather than let the locals screw them up.

The position had its benefits, though. A take-home car. Top-notch training. And most importantly, they were the elite investigative agency in the county, given the most serious Part One crimes: murder, rape, and robbery. Major investigations were theirs for the taking. For everything else, it was on a request basis. If the local chief of police had an investigation that was too much for his team to handle, he could contact the newly appointed chief of county detectives, Harv Bender, and ask for help.

At least, that's how it was supposed to be. Two weeks ago, Carrie had been called to a burglary scene at four in the morning. She drove out to a farmhouse at the outer edge of the county, deep Pennsyltucky country, she called it. When she got there, the owner was flapping his hands on the front porch, weeping, "They got Bertha! Oh, they got her! Those sons of bitches!"

She went around the side of the farmhouse and found a local cop standing in the backyard, his enormous gut hanging over his zipper. Wearing his Smoky the Bear campaign hat with the circular brim bent and crinkled, he was taking pictures of a chicken coop in the rear of the yard, trying to get the camera to focus in the dark.

"Hey," Carrie said.

"Hold this," he said, handing her his flashlight while he worked the camera.

Carrie looked at the empty chicken coop while he snapped photos. She started to get a sick feeling. "Tell me you didn't."

He spat a mouthful of black tobacco juice on the ground, splattering some of it on his gut. "What?"

Carrie pressed her fist against her forehead. "Tell me you didn't call me out here for a goddamn burglary of a goddamn chicken coop."

"But they got Bertha," the cop said.

"Is that right?" Carrie asked. She held the flashlight upright like a runner's baton, cocked it over her head, and hurled it as far into the field beyond as she could throw it.

"Hey!" the cop said, watching her turn around and head back to her car. "What you do that for?"

"If you ever call us out here for something like this again, the next time, it's going up your ass!" she shouted.

The next day, she was ordered to write a letter of apology to that department's chief and reimburse them the cost of the flashlight. The next time anything like that happened, she'd be fired. She wrote the letter, wrote the check, and scribbled *Fuck Bertha* on the check's memo section. Before she dropped it into the envelope, she crossed that part out.

Twenty minutes after the latest phone call, Carrie stumbled into Wawa, yawning against the back of her hand as she made her way toward the coffee island. The heavyset, dark-skinned cashier's head shot up. "My blond-haired American princess! Back again tonight?"

"Hi, Gangajat," she said, waving over her shoulder.

He hurried down the aisle, snatching the pot of hazelnut away before she could grab it. "That's been sitting out for too long," he said. "I'll make it fresh."

"I can just get something else," she said, looking down the row of other coffees.

"No! It won't take more than a few seconds. Are you in a hurry?"

"Not, like, drive a hundred miles an hour through the fog hurry, but I have to get somewhere," she said.

"Another case? One of the bad ones?"

"Can't a girl just come in here to see her favorite Wawa guy?"

His round face stretched into the widest smile she'd ever seen, and he said, "My mother would not let me ever bring home a white girl, no matter how beautiful."

"Well, that's too bad," Carrie said. "I guess I'll just have to settle for your wonderful coffee, then."

He brought over the fresh pot and poured it for her. "But then again, my mother is sick, so both of us must be strong and patient, okay?"

Carrie laughed as he handed her the cup of steaming coffee, and she fixed it with milk and sweetener. From the corner of her eye, she could see Gangajat wiping the counter, singing to himself in Hindi, his voice low and strong, dancing between each note.

She knew he wouldn't take her money, so she stuffed a few dollars into the Fight Childhood Leukemia donation bin next to the register. He kept singing, his voice following her out the door like lengths of luxurious colored fabric in a Bollywood movie. Gangajat waved to her through the window, holding his hand to his heart, still singing, his face filled with warmth and softness for her.

Carrie backed her car out of the parking lot, reaching down to double-check the pistol on her hip. She did not wave back, because the time for singing and soft things was done now.

The visitors' parking lot was crowded, but she drove into it anyway, avoiding the open spaces in front of the emergency room doors reserved for police. God forbid she park her unmarked county car there to do a rape investigation. Security would harass her until she proved to them she was a cop. Then any cops who showed up would harass her for taking up one of the spots, when they had DUIs to drag in and out of the hospital.

She knew cops who made four or five DUI arrests a night. They did it for the plaques handed out at the state capitol and annual free steak dinners sponsored by MADD. They'd sit outside bars cherry-picking the patrons as they left, or drive up and down their one stretch of highway following cars until they found any infraction that let them stop the driver. The slightest waver over a double-yellow line. A missing license plate light. Anything.

Of course, the people who lived in the towns they were protecting and serving weren't made any safer by this practice. What they needed were cops patrolling their neighborhoods and stores, making sure none of the meth freaks and heroin addicts were stealing everything that wasn't nailed down.

But the papers made a big deal about it, and the chiefs of police crowed high and low whenever one of their guys got a new award for traffic enforcement. In Carrie's mind, there were two kinds of police officers. The first kind were the road dogs, and the others did traffic.

Road dogs had no problem arresting a dangerous DUI, but they'd just as quickly give somebody a break and call for someone to pick them up. They stopped to talk to the kids on the street corners, finding out what was what and who was who. They checked doors to businesses after hours. They knew what cars belonged on the streets in their sector, and what ones didn't.

The older road dogs might bust you in the head if you deserved it. A good old-fashioned ass-kicking, but a fair one. Then they'd drive you home and let you sleep it off. The next day, they'd knock on your door and make sure you were all right.

Traffic cops, though? Different animal. A traffic cop gets off on writing the most tickets in his agency. He smiles when he recounts the story of how he pulled over a tractor trailer and wrote the driver an eighteen thousand–dollar ticket, and son of a bitch if that fucker didn't start crying right there on the side of the road.

If Carrie had to put her money on it, if she had absolutely had to gamble, even if it meant all the money she'd made being on call for so many weeks straight, she'd put every last cent on it not being a road dog who raped Monica Gere. If it was a cop, Carrie would bet the house that it had to be some traffic asshole.

She slung her work bag over her shoulder as she walked through the ER's sliding doors and waved to the nurse at the front desk. "I'm here to see the SANE nurse."

The nurse looked bored, cracking a piece of bubble gum between her front teeth, the tip of her finger hovering above her cell phone's screen. "Your name?"

"Carrie Santero."

The nurse cocked an eyebrow at her, the gum paused between her teeth. A decision was made behind the dark, unsympathetic eyes, as they looked Carrie up and down. The nurse picked up her desk phone and said, "One to admittance." She put the phone down again, set her phone aside, and said, "The SANE nurse is with another patient right now, but someone will take you back and talk to you. Are you injured? I mean, besides, you know."

"No," Carrie said. "That's not what I meant. Hang on."

This is what I get for throwing on jeans and a T-shirt to get here as fast as I could instead of taking my time getting ready and milking it like everyone else does, she thought.

She reached into her coat pocket, searching for the slim black wallet tucked inside. Even after six months, she still wasn't used to being out of uniform. She pulled the wallet out and opened it, revealing the gleaming golden badge within. "I'm a detective with the DA's office."

The nurse leaned forward, squinting to read the writing engraved on the badge. "I didn't know they had any female detectives. None ever came here before."

"I'm new," Carrie said, setting her coffee down on the desk as the nurse slid a visitor's pass toward her.

Sgt. Dave Kenderdine was standing outside of the Sexual Assault Nurse's Examination room, chiseled arms folded across his wide chest. Dave was only a few inches taller than Carrie, but twice as wide. He tipped his head to her as she walked down the hallway, saying, "Congrats on the gold shield. Looks fancy."

It was perfunctory. Everyone congratulated her, but no one ever said she'd earned it. Or deserved it. They never said the county couldn't have picked a better person. At least they respected her enough to not lie to her face, she thought.

She liked Dave. He was a good cop, with more than twenty years on the job, and an even better sergeant. They'd worked together on the task force several times, and they knew each other from her days in patrol. She'd always been able to rely on his judgment. He was one of the few guys on the job who never bull-shitted her. But that changed when she got moved up to the county. She was now no longer one of the team. She was one of *them.*

Carrie looked past him at the closed SANE office door. The windows were covered by curtains. The faint murmur of voices came from within. She slid the long, narrow notebook out of her bag. "Did you get a chance to talk to her?"

"Yeah, right," Dave said. "She took one look at the uniform and started screaming. I backed out of the room and stayed in the hallway. This chick's nuts."

Carrie sipped her coffee, still looking past him. "How did you get the call?"

"It came in as a nine-one-one from a passing motorist. They found her facedown on the side of the road with her bare ass hanging out and figured she'd been sexually assaulted. As soon as she heard them talking to dispatch, she started freaking out about the police. The witnesses said she'd been attacked by a cop, and that story seems to have spread." Dave eyed Carrie to see what she made of that. Testing her. "Obviously I don't need to tell you what I think of that claim."

Dave passed her the county dispatch sheet with the name and phone number of the person who'd called it in. Carrie read the location and said, "This didn't happen in your jurisdiction, Sarge. How'd you get stuck with it?"

"I was dumb enough to answer the radio," he said. "Dispatcher heard them saying it might be a cop and was smart enough to ask for any available supervisors. That should have been my first clue not to get involved."

"Has she said anything else?" Carrie asked.

"Besides screaming and telling me to get the fuck away from her? Not that I know," Dave said. "Listen, you understand this is most likely bullshit, right? I mean, I get that you only had a few years on the street before going to the county, and I'm not saying that factors into this, but come on. A cop did this? On duty? I know all the guys out here. Some of them might not be the sharpest tools in the shed, but they aren't rapists."

Carrie pulled out her notepad and wrote while he talked. "Does anybody know the victim? Any previous contacts?"

"I ran her through our system. She called in a road hazard two years ago. Nothing since."

Carrie kept writing. "No mental health issues?"

"None that involved the police. Doesn't mean there weren't any."

"Understood," Carrie said. She looked up at him. It was time for the real question. Everything else had just been passing time waiting. "Who else is working the street tonight in the area. Besides you, I mean."

Dave stared at her. "You're kidding me, right?"

"You know how this goes, Sarge. I need to know where everyone was at when she says it happened, so I can start clearing guys. Anyone on a call, or a business check, or meal break, that's all good stuff that helps me say they don't have anything to worry about. The first part of internal investigations is eliminating good cops from bad accusations."

"Is that what they teach you at internal affairs school now?" Dave said. "They tried to send me to that shit a few years ago and I walked out. It probably cost me a promotion, but I guess I just sleep better at night knowing I'm not a scumbag."

Carrie swallowed the last of her coffee and tossed it into the trash. "You know what's funny, Dave? We all act like anybody out there is still giving us the benefit of the doubt. Meanwhile, cops are getting caught every five seconds shooting people in the back or planting evidence. Do I think a cop might have raped this chick? God damn, I hope not. But if he did, I will drag his ass to jail through a fucking F.O.P. fundraiser if I have to. And I would hope good guys like you would be right there with me."

She pulled a manila envelope from her bag and held it toward him. The top was stamped *DNA Kit*. "Swab the insides of both cheeks with the Q-tips inside the packet, then seal it, and sign the waiver saying you gave it to me voluntarily."

Dave looked down at the envelope without moving. "It's not voluntary if you tell me to do it. Maybe I should talk to my union rep first."

The door to the SANE room opened and the nurse looked at Carrie with relief. "I was afraid they'd send a male detective."

"Now even detectives are suspect?" Dave shot back. "What, maybe the bad guy changed out of his police uniform and suddenly put on a suit to come here? Maybe he's some kind of evil genius with a costume for every occasion, right?"

Carrie went through the door and closed it behind her. Monica Gere was sitting on the bed with her knees tucked under her chin, muttering to herself. Leaves and pieces of grass were still tangled in her long hair. Carrie made a few quick notes. Monica's bare arms and legs stuck out through the hospital gown. They were muscular and trim. Early thirties, she wrote. She's in good shape. Not an easy target.

Pieces of gravel were stuck in the raw scrapes covering the woman's forearms and knees. Carrie inspected her knuckles and fingernails, seeing no bruises from punching her attacker or blood from trying to rake his flesh. Whatever had happened to Monica Gere, she hadn't fought back, Carrie thought.

"Monica?" Carrie said, leaning down next to her.

The SANE nurse, a stout woman with short, white hair, patted Monica on her shoulder. It wasn't affection. "Come on," she said, rubbing the woman's arm briskly. "It's time to talk."

Carrie leaned forward to read the nurse's name tag, making sure she spelled it right. "Miss Pritchett?" she asked, holding up her hand. "Maybe just let me try it my way." She leaned down again, closer. "Monica, I'm Detective Santero. Can you tell me what happened?"

Monica stared at the wall beyond them, still muttering.

"I want to help you," Carrie said. Still nothing.

Nurse Pritchett rolled her eyes. "I've got some notes from what she said when she came in. I'll write up my report and get it to you first thing in the morning."

Carrie reached out to touch Monica's arm, but she swatted Carrie's hand away, then scurried to the far side of her hospital bed, flailing her hands and feet. "Don't touch me!" she screamed.

"All right," Carrie said, standing back and holding up her hands. "I'm sorry. Jesus. I'm just trying to figure out what happened."

Monica thrust her head up, eyes gleaming with hatred, and screamed, "It was a cop! He had on a uniform! He pulled me over in a car with red and blue lights! Get the fuck away from me!"

Carrie backed off. Monica lowered her head into her arms, half screaming, half sobbing. "Monica?" Carrie tried again, and the woman thrashed out with her arms and legs, screeching and bashing her fists against the blanket.

Nurse Pritchett snatched the call box from the side of the bed and mashed its red button. Nurses and doctors rushed into the room, bearing restraints and a syringe full of pale liquid.

"Is there anybody we can call for her?" Carrie shouted above the din.

Nurse Pritchett latched on to one of Monica's arms, pinning it down. "Somebody from victims assistance is on the way. Clear the room and give us some space, okay?"

Carrie pulled a business card out of her bag and laid it on the counter. She left the room and shut the door behind her, muffling the screams, and worked her jaw to make her ears pop. Dave Kenderdine was leaning against the wall, looking amused. "Batshit crazy, right?"

"I don't know," Carrie said. "Maybe. Doesn't mean it didn't happen."

"Well, that must be why I'm just a glorified patrolman and you're a big shot county dick."

Carrie slapped the DNA envelope against his chest, right against the badge. He didn't move. "My report is going to say me and you talked, you immediately agreed to cooperate and provide the county detectives whatever assistance we needed in order to get to the bottom of this."

She pulled another handful of DNA envelopes from her bag and stuffed them down in the crook of his folded arms. "After that, I need you to make a list of all the cops working tonight, and their patrol logs. If you see any who have unaccounted time during the two hours prior to the nine-one-one call, go ask them for a voluntary DNA swab."

He looked down at the stack of envelopes. "And why exactly would I do that?"

"Because I asked you. And we go back. And I trust you, even if you're being an asshole right now."

"I'm not comfortable going after my own kind, Carrie."

"Whoever did this, cop or not, he's not our own, Dave. You know that." She started down the hallway. "Anybody with long stretches of time where they weren't doing anything, starting with you, okay?"

He called out after her, "Hey, what makes you think I wasn't doing anything?"

She shrugged. "You're a sergeant."

She looked back at him, grinning as she went through the door.

"Oh, real nice," he said but couldn't help grinning back.

CHAPTER 3

A group of men in orange hunting vests stood in the gray dawn. Mist rolled off the mountains like a slow river, snaking through the trees and caves and swirling around the men's dirty boots and camouflage pants. Sitting among them was a large black dog, so old its snout showed white and its eyes looked glazed over. The dog panted and whined, staring into the mist. The man beside it shifted his shotgun onto his left shoulder and patted it on the head, saying, "Quiet, now, Butch."

Two police officers headed up the hill, toward the men. The older officer's wool-lined collar was pulled up against the cold. The gold star pinned to the front of his brown Stetson glinted in the emerging light. Not many cops wore Stetsons anymore, even that far out into the western parts of Pennsylvania.

Decades ago, when there were no local police departments, the state police covered the hundreds of miles of unincorporated country with just a handful of troopers. The state police had a long and storied tradition of sending only their most serious fuck-ups that far out into the middle of nowhere. It was a good place to bury their sins in the purgatory of dirt roads and farms and coal mines and a populace with no interest in coming into contact with the law.

Back in the old days, the state troopers were known for their wide-brimmed campaign hats. They were also known for being drunk in their cars and firing their duty weapons into the air when they came upon a fight and were too outnumbered to do anything but watch. A farmer named Franklin Hayes had once been shot in the leg by a police bullet from two miles away. Hayes never even heard the gunshot when the trooper pulled up to a group of drunks fighting in the local bar's parking lot and stuck his gun in the air and fired.

Hayes was sitting on his front porch, drinking coffee, his aching legs stretched out in front of him after a hard day in the field. He heard something sizzling through the air, coming right down on top of him. By the time he looked up, the bullet had already punched through the porch's thin aluminum roof and sunk deep in the meat of his right thigh.

The farmer hollered so loud his wife came running. He laughed the whole way to the hospital, saying he'd been struck by a meteor and that they were lucky. Meteors were rare and expensive things. He'd read they might even be made of pure gold or diamond, and once the doctors dug it out of his thigh she would have to make sure none of them ran off with it.

Much to Franklin Hayes's dismay, the doctors pulled out a chunk of deformed lead instead. The story made it into the Pittsburgh newspapers several days later. The state police maneuvered its infinite tentacles to pay off his hospital stay and erase the speeding tickets messing up his car insurance. The trooper who'd fired the gun was quietly transferred to a barracks back east.

After that, the local towns decided they needed their own police departments. As a way of differentiating themselves from the Staties, Walt Auburn, Liston's first chief, opted to outfit his men in cowboy hats. The eastern parts of Pennsylvania with the big cities and counties are about as far from the Old West as possible. That changes out past the Poconos. Beyond the Allegheny Mountains, going toward West Virginia, western Pennsylvania people are frontier folk, rednecks and hillbillies stranded north, tied to odd religions and conspiracy theories about the government. They live that far out from civilization for a reason.

Forty years later, Chief Steve Auburn carried on his father's tradition. It was the same style Stetson, but not the same one. All that remained of Walt's hat was the warped metal star he'd worn pinned to the front of it. It still smelled like smoke, whenever Steve opened the ornate cedar box he kept it in.

Auburn cupped his hand across the gold star pinned to the front of his own hat and tipped it forward, lifting it off the top of his bald head. "Morning, boys." He breathed through his nose, trying to catch his wind after the long trek up the hillside and not show it. Sweat ran down the sides of his face. "I heard you think you found something up here."

The hunter holding the dog by the leash was named Willie Oaks. He swatted the dog across the backside, trying to get it to quit whining. "I set Butch after a down bird, and he come back carrying it, Steve," Oaks said. "At first I hollered at him. Thought he picked up a damn rock and lost the bird. He started covering it up before I yanked him away. I didn't want to touch it or go anywhere near it once I saw what I thought it was."

The man next to him laughed. "You drunk idiot. I told you it was just a deer bone."

"That weren't no deer bone," Oaks said. "I know what I saw."

Auburn asked him where it was. The man turned and pointed at a dead tree, with black bark that was crackled and peeling away like burnt skin. Auburn started toward the tree, waving for his officer to follow. "Be careful not to touch anything else we find, Paul," he said.

"What good's it going to do?" Paul replied. "Anything out here's been rained on, snowed on, and shit upon by every living thing under the sun, especially if it's sat long enough."

"You never know," Auburn said, eyeing the tree and the fresh uncovered dirt all around it. Roots poked through clumps of upended earth, writhing with fat worms and grubs, where the dog had ripped up the ground to bury its find. Laying at the center was what looked like a fossil, some kind of ancient artifact covered in soil. It was gray, with long thin bones connecting its toes and knuckles to the length of the small foot. It was no bigger than a dog's chew toy, or the carcass of a small game bird. But it was unmistakable. The moment Auburn's eyes set upon it, all the air left him like he'd been punctured.

"I'll be goddamned," Paul whispered.

"Be quiet," Auburn hissed, feeling the trickle of sweat thicken. He wiped his face with the flat of his hand and dried it against his uniform shirt. He glanced back at the hunters, who had crept forward from where they'd been told to stay, trying to listen. Auburn waved to them and gave a thumbs-up. "I think you found the rest of that deer I shot when I was twelve years old, Willie."

The other hunters laughed, slapping Willie Oaks on the back. He rolled his eyes and laughed with them. "I swear to God it looked just like a child's foot."

"To be honest, I can't tell exactly what it is. Nothing to get excited about, though," Auburn called out. "You boys run on home now. Me and Paul will have a look around. I'll swing by the bar afterward and let you know what we find."

Auburn watched the men leave, then leaned in close to Paul and whispered, "Go back to your car and radio for the fire company. Get as many of them out here as fast as you can. I want lights up here, big as they can find. Then call the State Police. Tell them I need their helicopter in the air, helping us search."

Paul didn't move, unable to look away from the foot. Auburn smacked him on the chest. "Keep this whole thing quiet, you hear? Otherwise, these woods will be crawling with people before we know it."

"Okay," Paul said, blinking, his mind racing through the series of calculations necessary to make sense of what he was being told. "What do you need the fire company for?"

"To see if we can find the rest of the remains," Auburn said. "God knows if we don't, the Boy Scouts and everybody else will be out here looking. We'll have people bringing pieces of the body into our station for the next two years."

Paul looked down at the foot, face drained of light. "It's Hope Pugh, isn't it? I went to school with her. I was in her class when it happened. Christ, I thought she just ran off, like everyone said. I never believed any of it. It's her. She was just a little girl, Steve."

Auburn wiped his face again. The inside of his Stetson was soaked in sweat. He took it off, feeling the cool air blow across the back of his head. Paul was muttering a prayer. Auburn whacked him and told him to shut up. "On second thought, you just stay put. One look at your blubbering face and people will start thinking this actually was some kind of murder," he said.

CHAPTER 4

*I*t had been months since Jacob Rein's last operation, and he was still wearing the bandage around his hand and wrist. Carrie knew he didn't need it. Some days he covered the scar with a black neoprene wrist brace, switching the disguise the same way he wore baseball hats or pulled his hair back into a knot. All of the photographs used in the newspaper articles were from his days as a detective, or sometimes from the mug shot when he was arrested. No one recognized the bearded, long-haired man. Not unless they saw his hand, and the scars around his wrist. Everyone knew about that.

Carrie watched Rein come through the diner's door, then step out of the way as someone walked past. He lowered his head, using the baseball hat to cover his face. Carrie held up her finger for the waitress and said, "My friend's here now. Can you bring him a coffee?"

Rein made his way to the table and slid into the seat, keeping his left arm out of view.

"I tried to call you," Carrie said. "It said the number's no good now?"

"I ran out of minutes," Rein said. "I'll get more soon."

She knew better than to offer him money. "Are you hungry?"

The waitress set a mug of fresh coffee in front of Rein. He sat back against the booth, studying Carrie. "You look tired."

"You look homeless," she replied.

"I am homeless," he said.

"I've offered you a thousand times to come stay with me. There is no reason for you to be sleeping on people's couches."

Rein reached with his right hand for the nearest packet of sugar. He tried ripping it open with his teeth. "Give that to me," Carrie said, and took it from him. She tore the rest of the packet open and dumped it inside his coffee. "I thought you were supposed to be using that thing," she said, cocking her head toward his left side.

"It's sore today," he said.

She picked up a creamer and spilled it into Rein's coffee. "You still have to use it. The doctor said."

Rein brought his left hand out from under the table and looked down at his fingers, straining to force them to move. He forced them to curl inward, like he was gripping an imaginary ball. "There," he said. "Are you satisfied?"

"It's going to get easier," she said. "You just have to keep at it." She picked up a spoon and stirred the coffee for him.

"What was the case?" he asked.

"What case?"

"The one you went out on last night. Your eyes are red and your right eyelid is swollen, meaning you didn't get enough sleep. You're in jeans and a T-shirt, but you're wearing your gun," he said, indicating the weapon under her T-shirt. "Pretty obvious you went to work late last night and never made it home."

"Got anything else?" she asked.

"You're cranky. You're hiding it by smiling and appearing cheerful, but I can see it. You're always cranky when you don't get enough sleep. What was the case?"

Carrie sighed, defeated. "A woman claims a cop raped her last night. From what I can tell, he pulled her over and ripped her out of the car. She was freaking out at the hospital, screaming at me to get away from her. All I was trying to do was help."

Rein listened, running the tip of his finger around the mug's rim. "Go on," he said.

"I asked for DNA from all the cops who were working in the area last night."

"How did that go?"

"Like you'd expect."

"It's understandable why they weren't happy being asked to do that."

"Why?" Carrie said. "If they didn't do anything wrong, all I'm doing is helping them clear their names. For God's sake," she said. "Anyway, no cop could have done this. I know all the guys who were working last night. None of them are rapists. Maybe Kenderdine is right, this chick is just a whack job."

Jacob picked up the mug and took a long swig. He set it down, turning it on the table, watching the handle go past. "What kind of people seek to become police officers?"

"Going by the ones at this table? Crazy, pain-in-the-ass people," she said.

"I mean the majority."

"Former soldiers. Guys looking for a good-paying job that doesn't require much education. People who want to serve their community."

"Agreed," Rein said. "But there's another group who specifically seek out the job because of the power. The badge and gun. The ability to degrade and dehumanize others. We weed out a lot of them during the background checks, but a few slip through. They're like enemy insurgents."

"So you think it could be a real police officer?"

"Of course. Why wouldn't I? Because it's terrible? You're right, it is terrible. And terrifying. The same way when a teacher or doctor or celebrity or grandparent does something so horrific it is hard to even think about. That doesn't mean it's untrue."

"Listen, I know you don't want to get involved, but can you come with me to talk to this victim?" Carrie said. "Please, I think you'd be able to communicate with her. Crazy person to crazy person," she added, smiling.

"I can't," he said. "Not right now."

"Why not?"

"There's something happening," he said, looking over his

shoulder to make sure no one was listening. "Something I can't talk about just yet."

"Well is it good or bad?" she asked. "Are you sick?"

"No."

She leaned close. "Just tell me what it is. I won't tell anyone."

"I shouldn't even have brought it up," he said, moving back against the seat. "Forget I said anything."

The alert on Carrie's phone sounded. She pulled it out of her pocket and glanced at the screen. "Just give me one second. This conversation isn't over." She read the brief message on the bulletin's header, raised an eyebrow, and dropped it back in her pocket.

"What is it?" Rein asked, back to turning the mug in circles.

"Some chief out in Liston-Patterson is asking for any departments with a helicopter to give him a call, asap. I've never even heard of that place."

The mug stopped spinning. Coffee splashed over its sides and dripped onto the table, but Rein didn't notice. "It's over an hour away, out in the country. Why do they need a helicopter?"

Carrie grabbed a napkin and mopped the spill. "An hour away? I hope Harv doesn't send me out there. Did you and Bill used to get sent out into the boonies to cover bullshit investigations?"

He pointed at her phone. "What else does it say?"

Carrie scrolled through the rest of the e-mail. "Okay, hang on." She kept reading, then said, "Who does this guy think we are? Law enforcement agencies with actual resources? It says he's also looking for cadaver dogs trained in recovering skeletal remains."

Rein slid out of the seat and dropped a crumpled dollar bill on the table. "I have to go. Is this enough for the coffee?"

"Rein, what are you doing?" Carrie asked. She pushed the dollar out of the way. "I don't need your money. What's wrong?"

"I'll call you," he said, turning toward the door and making his way past the rest of the people leaving.

"I've heard that before," Carrie said, watching the glass door close behind him. She signaled for the waitress and said, "Check please."

"No breakfast?" the waitress asked.

"I'm not hungry anymore," she said. The only thing left to do was go to the office and see her boss. It was never a good idea to do that with a full stomach.

The framed front page of a local newspaper hung outside of Harv Bender's office. It was only a year old, and already going dull from baking in the overhead fluorescent light. The headline's typeface and the large color photograph beneath it were fading. Newspapers, the news they contained, the materials they were printed on. Cheap, fleeting, and disposable. Every day, some new scandal, wartime atrocity, or historic collapse of a once sacred institution spewed across the front page of every paper in the country.

The day the paper was printed, Harv Bender had gone to the nearest mall and bought the only frame he could find to display the article. It came from a sports memorabilia shop, the kind of frame local bars hung over the urinals so patrons could read the latest standings.

DETECTIVES DEFEAT OMNIKILLER

Under it was a photograph of Harv Bender, swarmed by reporters, flooded by lights. Framed beneath the article was a photograph that no reporters had ever seen. It was a picture Bender had shown off at every police conference along the eastern seaboard that year. The prize trophy photo. Bender raising the dead killer's head off the floor, leaning down next to it, smiling for the camera.

Carrie knocked on the open door, peeking in. "You wanted to see me, Chief?"

Bender's office hadn't been unpacked yet, with most of his things still in boxes. A stack of unreviewed cases sat piled in the far corner, behind his brand-new desk, angled to hold up a worn leather golf bag and clubs that had been presented to him on the night he was promoted. Fresh grass still stuck to the driver's blade from earlier that morning. The others were dull and scratched from hard use.

Bender folded his hands on his desk. "Have a seat."

Carrie picked up the stack of framed photos from the nearest chair and moved them to the floor. Harv Bender and the state governor shaking hands. Harv Bender and a famous retired athlete. She sat down. "Something wrong?"

"I heard you got called out last night. Some lunatic is claiming a cop raped her?"

"That's what it looks like," Carrie said.

"Let me guess. Oh, I didn't get a good look at him. Oh, I'm not sure where it happened. Oh, I'm not going to cooperate with the detectives. Typical bullshit. She'll be suing every department in the area, just trying to get them to pay her to go away. The sad reality is that most of the stories we hear about sexual assaults are phony. Some chick gets drunk at a party and hooks up with every dude there. Next thing you know her boyfriend hears about it, or somebody takes a video of it and posts it online, and she cries rape."

"This lady wasn't at a party, Chief," Carrie said. "She was driving home from the gym. She said a cop car pulled her over with red and blue lights, and the guy that did it was wearing a uniform."

"What's that prove? I can buy a uniform on eBay right now. Emergency lights, too," Bender said. "Hell, I can go to any police auction in the country and buy an actual police car if I want. They won't even unplug the lights or pull off the decals or anything. Just let me drive it right off their lot and be glad to get rid of it."

"I'll be happy to check to see if there's any reports on police impersonators in the area," Carrie said. "But that's not all we need to do. We have to pull every internal investigation from all the local PDs and see if there have been complaints against any of their officers. Inappropriate contact with women during car stops or arrests. They would keep that kind of thing quiet, but we need to get this guy off the street before he does it again."

Bender's interlocked fingers turned white under pressure from his squeezing them together. His eyes turned upward to the ceiling, like he was searching for help there. "You want to go digging through the internal affairs of every local police department?" he said in slow, clipped measures. "Do you have any kind of idea the shitstorm that would create? This entire county would erupt into open rebellion. And what do I tell the commissioners and DA when they ask me what I based my investigation on? The word of a girl with five whole years' police experience?"

Carrie looked down, keeping her mouth shut.

"You know, I got a call from the Hansen Township chief of police this morning about you. Apparently, you tasked one of his sergeants with obtaining DNA from his fellow police officers. Who in the hell gave you permission to order him to do that?"

"I didn't order, I requested it. I was trying to rule people out," Carrie said.

"Let me be real clear on this," Bender said. "You will not do a single fucking thing involving accusing or suspecting a fellow police officer in a criminal investigation unless I give you absolute clearance. Absolute! Is that understood?"

"Yes, sir," Carrie said.

"Listen," Bender said, rolling his head to loosen his neck. He stuck his finger between his tie and his throat, digging for room there. "You've got the makings of a good cop, Carrie. I know that. You had just as much to do with catching that psycho Omnikiller as anyone in this agency."

Carrie took a deep breath, staying silent.

"But there's a lot of people who think you don't deserve to be here," Bender continued. "They think you got here because you're a female. They think you got here because your name was attached to a big case. Most folks think you're here just because you and I are sleeping together."

Carrie's brow raised. "I never heard that last one."

Bender sat up and hitched his belt over the lower fold of his gut. "Seriously? That's all over the place."

"I would think they knew better."

"What you need to do is lay low. Learn the ropes. Let people know you aren't trying to make a big deal about every little thing, that you're not some sort of glory hound, you understand?"

"That's all I want to do, sir," Carrie said.

"Good," Bender said. "Listen, I like you. And unlike a lot of the guys around here, I think you deserve to be here, okay? So I'm going to do you a favor. I'm going to give you a real simple case that gets you out of the office for a little while. Something nice and easy." He slid his chair backward and turned, reaching for the top file on the stack behind him, and dropped it on his desk in front of her. "Did you see the bulletin that came in from Liston-Patterson? I want you to head out there, give those boys a hand with whatever they need, and show everybody you can handle a nice, simple call for assistance without turning it into an enormous shitstorm."

Harv Bender leaned back in his chair and spun around to look at his golf clubs. "It's a long drive, so get going. You'll thank me when this is over. Nobody trusts an animal that tries to eat its own kind, Carrie. Remember that."

CHAPTER 5

*I*n the deep country, they don't bother to mark the streets with signs. Gravel roads intersect with other gravel roads. Old horse trails covered with stone led to places no one needed to go anymore, where once important families or businesses used to be, but were now gone. The cornfields on either side of her were so tall with corn, they towered over her car. She took a narrow lane cut through the middle of a field, watching the green leaves slap her windows and mirrors as she drove. She wasn't even sure it was a road.

The GPS on Carrie's phone beeped, announcing it was off-line. She turned down the next dirt road she came to, following the path that seemed the most welltrodden. This was black bear country. Water moccasin country. As untouched as it was in the days when the Shawnee packed their homes and left for Ohio, abandoning the region and leaving nothing of themselves behind.

Like every lower-middle-class white girl she knew, Carrie grew up hearing she had Indian blood. Her father was Cuban and her mother was pearl white. Except for a baby book with a half-drawn family tree, nobody had bothered writing down the names and dates of birth of any relatives beyond two generations, but her mother would tell anyone who listened they were part Indian. Carrie's mom left when she was still young, but her father kept up the myth, often reminding Carrie she was a true child of America, and to always eat all her corn because her ancestors had been the ones who taught everyone else how to grow it.

It was bullshit. When she was twelve years old, she found an old trunk of her mother's belongings tucked away in the attic. Inside was an old Indian blanket. Carrie stared in wonder as she pulled it from the trunk and carefully peeled it apart, shaking dirt from its folds. The fabric was moldy and frayed, but more precious to her than spun gold, because she knew, she just knew, it had been passed down to her mother from some distant native relative. It was the answer to the mysterious connection to her mother, a connection denied Carrie since the day the woman left.

She laid it on the attic floor to examine it, running her fingers over the fading Navajo symbols, when she saw the tag at the bottom of the blanket, hidden in the fringe. Made in China. She folded the blanket and stuffed it back into the trunk.

Her best friend, Molly, had always claimed to be Indian too. Penny, Molly's mom, said an old family photo somewhere showed one of her great grandmothers dressed in buckskin, her long black hair done up in feathers. She wasn't sure where the photo went, but she'd seen it, or her mother had seen it, one or the other, she couldn't recall.

For all of eleventh grade, Molly wore around her neck a medicine bag, stuffed with things she called relics. A lock of her grandfather's hair. A bag of weed. A guitar pick from her favorite local band. None of it made sense. Whenever Carrie asked her, Molly said, "It's part of my religion. I'm Indian."

They'd sit in the woods and smoke weed and drink, and then Molly would burn sage and wave it around, chanting. She'd tell Carrie, "I don't need to know what I'm saying, it's about the feeling. I'm connected to nature, to the stars, to the universe itself. That's what being Indian is. Before the white man came, Indians were pure and peaceful, one with the land and guided by the Great Spirit. I'm going to live on a reservation someday, in a place where they still remember what that means. That's why it's okay if I smoke weed. I'm allowed to because it's part of my religion."

"Then it's part of my religion too," Carrie had said, reaching for the joint. "I'm part Indian."

"No you aren't."

"You aren't either, bitch. Pass it over."

Molly closed her eyes and inhaled, touching the medicine bag around her neck, then exhaled slowly. "You have to promise me something," Molly said. "If I ever die, you have to make sure I have this with me. I'll need it for my journey into the afterlife."

Carrie said that she would make sure of it, but that wasn't going to happen.

Molly handed the joint to Carrie and started drumming on her thighs with her hands. Carrie took a long drag, coughed, and threw back her head, singing fake Indian words until they both busted up laughing.

Molly had been dead almost a year now.

Carrie found the medicine bag in one of her jewelry boxes. She cut off a lock of her own hair and then cut off a piece of Molly's daughter Nubs's hair and stuffed them both inside it. At the funeral, she'd tucked the medicine bag into Molly's stiff hand and wept so hard people came up from their seats to keep her from collapsing.

Carrie stopped her car at the next intersecting road, if that's what it was, instead of just a flattened path run over so many times it had killed everything but the dirt. If it rained, she was never getting out of there. The dirt would turn to quicksand and sink her car up to the bumpers of the unmarked Ford Crown Victoria. People out in these parts drive trucks and Jeeps for a reason, she thought. The closest thing the county had were a few SUVs, and she was too low on the totem pole for one of those. The newest member of any police organization is always given the shittiest equipment, with all the good stuff going to the senior people. The kicker is, the FNGs get stuck with all the work.

Carrie had been the Fucking New Guy her entire career. Five years in patrol at Coyote Township, but she was the last one hired, so she was the Fucking New Guy. Promoted to county detective, an accomplishment nobody had done at such an early age, and to them, she was still just the Fucking New Guy.

Even if they didn't see her as the FNG, they saw her as something much worse. The Girl Cop. Hired in Coyote just because Chief Bill Waylon was afraid of getting sued. Protected and coddled because he thought of her like a daughter. Hired by the county because—and the very idea turned her stomach—she was supposed to be sleeping with that walking bag of chauvinistic shit Harv Bender.

It was always something, she thought. Maybe it always would be. Maybe it was like that all over the world, and always had been. No matter what you did, there was some group of assholes standing off to the side flinging shit at you.

She made a right turn onto another dirt road. Sooner or later, she was going to find civilization or she was going to drive off the edge of a cliff. At that moment, either one would do.

A large sign posted at the edge of the road read, LISTON-PATTERSON TOWNSHIP, ESTABLISHED 1982. Carrie stepped on the gas, glad to be driving on a real road. It was cracked and patched so many times it looked like a quilt made from different-colored pitch and tar, but it was wide and flat and she didn't care.

Abandoned shops and gas stations lined the road on both sides, their windows and doors boarded up, and the prices for the goods they once sold were so old they were comical. Cigarettes, a dollar a pack. Gasoline, seventy-five cents a gallon. The stores still in business had dull neon signs in their windows where the light gave out around the bends in their letters. Guns, beer, tobacco, and lottery tickets, in varying configurations, and several newer-looking shops proclaiming, We Buy Gold!

The We Buy Gold! shops were franchise operations. They'd popped up throughout the county over the past few years to capitalize on the heroin epidemic. Junkies stole whatever they could get their hands on, wedding rings, earrings, watches, it didn't matter. They stole it from anyone dumb enough to leave their car or house unlocked. Or gullible enough to believe the junkie had gotten clean and could be trusted. A bag of heroin cost ten dollars in the big cities and got more expensive the farther out you went. But nobody bought heroin by the bag. They bought it by the bundle. Tightly rubber-banded blocks of ten or twelve bags each, which normally cost a hundred bucks.

Enterprising fiends ripped off enough people to make a quick hundred dollars at the We Buy Gold! shop, raced to the nearest heroin dealer to buy a bundle, shot up what they needed, and came home. They sold half the remaining bags to their fellow fiends for a few dollars extra, and the next day, it all started over again.

One We Buy Gold! in such a small town meant they were testing out the market. Two meant they'd liked what they found. Any more than that was a clear sign of a robust and thriving heroin problem, and junkies were coming in from all over to sell their stolen shit. Carrie could see people standing inside the gold shops, biting black fingernails as the owner counted out their money. Others waited outside, staring through the front window, waiting for their cut of whatever was sold inside. The gold shop employees always smiled as they handed over money when they were buying six thousand–dollar wedding rings for $140. They always said, "Come again."

The area beyond the stores was a wasteland of gravel lots overgrown with weeds that grew up through discarded car wheels and glinted with the shattered glass of broken beer bottles. Narrow roads led past those lots, toward clusters of shanty houses, each one no bigger than the length of Carrie's car. Behind them a series of trailers sat on concrete slabs. Yellow "Don't Tread on Me" flags rippled in the wind. Jack Daniels blankets were draped across some front windows in place of curtains. Rusted charcoal grills and old cars propped up on cinder blocks covered the small patches of land in front of them.

She saw a sign for the Liston-Patterson police station and pulled into the lot. The station's front windows were yellowed. The protective covering applied to the windows to keep people from seeing in had cracked and peeled away in large strips, but no one had bothered to scrape them.

The lot was empty. Carrie draped her gold badge around her neck and walked to the station's entrance. She knocked lightly, then louder, and waited. She couldn't see anything past the film covering the windows. No doorbells or phones were mounted to the wall to allow a visitor to contact the dispatcher. She knocked again, then tried the doorknob, and to her surprise, found it unlocked.

She pulled the door open and called out, standing at the entrance, looking in. Open offices lay to the left, and beyond them a corridor led down to two jail cells. A framed portrait hung on the wall in front of her, the painted image of a smiling police officer in a wide-brimmed cowboy hat. Beneath the frame was a brass placard reading, "Liston Borough Chief of Police Walter C. Auburn. Killed in the line of duty, February 16th, 1981. Forever our Chief. Forever our Greatest Defender."

The sound of shuffling papers drew her toward the corner office. Stacks of papers were everywhere, scattered across old desks and bulky metal filing cabinets. The man inside the office had his back turned to her, showing a few long strands of white hair covering his liver-spotted scalp. He muttered in annoyance as he pulled a metal filing cabinet drawer out and grunted as he shoved the papers stacked inside it back, then stuffed a handful of new ones down in front of them. He had to use both hands to close the thing and was out of breath by the time he turned to see Carrie in the doorway. "Who are you?" he asked.

"Detective Santero. From the DA's office."

"Nobody's here," he said, moving to grab another handful of papers. He wore thick, plastic-framed glasses with lenses that magnified his eyes, making him appear like some sort of frog.

"Can anyone come back?"

"I don't know. Nobody tells me anything."

He looked through the papers in his hand, then turned away again, searching the faces of the filing cabinets. Old incident reports, Carrie realized. The kind they used to write up before we all had computers. The kind you needed a typewriter to fill out. How quaint.

The clerk scowled at one of the reports and slapped it with his fingers. "These idiots. I told them they have to put the day and the date, each time." He crossed the room in front of her, heading out the door toward an adjoining office.

"You guys always leave the station unlocked like that?" Carrie asked. "I was able to just walk right in here."

He tossed the papers onto a desk inside the next office and sat down, pulling the vinyl covering off a large manual typewriter. He leaned forward, squinting as he rolled the incident report into the slot and lined it up with the keys. "What's today?" he asked, without looking at her.

"October fifteenth."

He counted backward on his fingers, then typed. "How hard is it to remember to put the day and date in? We trust these people to carry guns, but they can't remember to do a simple thing like that."

Carrie waited for him to stop typing and unscroll the paper. "I really need to speak to someone. Can you call one of your cops back for me?"

"Chief's out in the woods. So's the other two. Radios don't work out there. You're welcome to go looking for them if you want, but I advise against it."

"So there's no one?"

"There's me. But I'm just a clerk. Name's Lou."

Carrie watched him use both hands to force one of the metal filing cabinet drawers open, grunting as he pulled. "Who's handling your calls for service?"

Lou furrowed his eyebrows. "If we get any, I'll let you know."

She slid a business card out of the back of her badge holder and laid it on the desk. "Tell your chief he needs to call me when he gets in. I'm here to help with the human remains they found out in the woods."

"All right," he said over his shoulder.

"You know anything about that, Lou?"

"Not much," he said. He grunted as he gripped a stack of reports stuffed inside the cabinet drawer and tried to pull them out. "Hot damn, they wedge these things in here so tight. From what I hear, they found a foot. Now they're looking for the rest."

"Any idea who the foot belonged to?" she asked. She bent down beside him and helped pull the reports free.

"Probably some little kid went out in the woods and got lost."

Carrie let go of the files. "They found a child's foot?"

"That's what I hear."

"Did any kids go missing around here recently?"

"Not for years," Lou said. He carried the stack over to another filing cabinet and pulled the drawer open. "Long time ago, back in 1981, a little girl named Hope Pugh vanished, never to be seen again. If I had to guess, I'd say that's who the foot belonged to."

"Jesus," Carrie whispered. "Is there a case file around I can look at, from when she went missing?"

"No case files that old around here," Lou said. His thumb flipped through the row of reports in the cabinet, searching their numbers. "Not since the two departments merged back in '82." He cocked his head at the portrait of Walter C. Auburn and said, "Just one of many things that got screwed up in the aftermath of his murder. Damn shame that was. Walt was a great man."

Carrie glanced back at the portrait on the wall, the smiling chief, Forever Our Greatest Defender. "I'm sure he was. Hey, do Hope Pugh's parents still live around here?"

"Sure, they go way back around these parts," he said, slamming the filing cabinet shut and going off in search of another. "Why?"

"I'd like to speak with them. Maybe they remember something that can help."

He pushed his thick glasses upward on the bridge of his nose. The wide frog eyes behind them focused on her. "I hope you don't intend on bothering them. They're good people."

"I told you," she said, "I'm just here to help."

She followed the clerk's directions, turning left to go the opposite way of the police station, into what used to be Patterson Borough. Along the main street stood a long row of well-kept stores, all of them old, but clean. The kind of place where the storekeepers swept the sidewalks in front of their businesses each day. She didn't see any chain stores or fast-food places. She drove past a few local bars, an ice cream shop, a diner called Ruby's, a

magazine and newspaper store, a compound pharmacy, a hardware store, a coin laundromat, even a vacuum repair store. A hu-
mongous John Deere tractor was parked on the street in front of
the shops, its fat tires sticking halfway out into the street. The drivers that had to go around it did so without complaining. Carrie
chuckled to herself as she steered around it too.

The houses in that area were small single homes with porches,
and rickety wooden steps going up to them. People sat on swings
or rocking chairs, watching her unfamiliar car turn down their
street. She counted the addresses until she found the right one,
and parked.

A metal handrail, made of what looked like crudely welded
pipes, rose alongside the steps to the Pugh house. It wobbled when
she touched it, rust flakes coming off in her palm. She brushed her
hand on her pants, smearing them with a dull brown streak. She
knocked on the front door, still brushing at her pants. When she
looked up, an old woman with sunken eyes stared back at her
through the door's screen.

The woman wore a high-necked shirt with a blue apron tied in
front of it, all of it simple material, except the apron had been
decorated with white lace around the edges, their slight uneven-
ness revealing their handmade origins. She opened her mouth to
speak, but could not seem to bring any words up.

"Mrs. Pugh?" Carrie asked.

The woman's eyes welled with tears, and she covered her neck
with her hand, stroking it, calming herself, as she saw the gold
shield draped around Carrie's neck.

"I'm Detective Santero with the Vieira County detectives," Carrie said. "Are you all right?"

"I'm fine," Mrs. Pugh said. "What can I do for you?"

"Can I come in? I'd like to talk with you and your husband if
he's around."

"What about?" she asked. She leaned forward, looking at the
street behind Carrie, and up and down it as far as she could see
without opening the door. "Is something wrong?"

"No, ma'am," Carrie said, forcing a smile. "I'm here about your
daughter."

"Who's there, mother?" a man's voice boomed from the rear of the house.

"A girl, says she wants to talk about Hope," Mrs. Pugh said over her shoulder.

"I'm a detective, sir," Carrie called out. "With the DA's office." She smiled again at Mrs. Pugh, doing her best to mean it. "Can you let me in, please? I'd hate to keep hollering about your personal business from out here on the porch."

The door opened and Carrie entered a small, cluttered living room filled with threadbare furniture. Mrs. Pugh vanished into the kitchen to fetch her a cup of coffee, ignoring Carrie's initial refusal. Mr. Pugh came in, a tall man, with sallow bags hanging beneath his eyes like loose chicken skin. His dark gray hair was slicked back against his head, and he wore a pair of loose blue overalls. He sat down on the worn reclining chair next to the couch and held out his hand for Carrie to sit as well.

"You're a police officer?" he asked, looking at her badge. "I'm sorry to hear that. Pretty girl like you, dealing with all the craziness in this day and age. The world's gone all wrong. I never thought I'd see the day when this country went wrong along with it."

Carrie slid her notebook and pen out of her jacket pocket. "I was wondering, Mr. Pugh, if you could answer a few questions for me about your daughter."

"What would you like to know?"

"Well, to be totally honest, I'm not exactly sure what kind of investigation was done when she went missing. I was hoping you could fill in some gaps for me. Did anyone ever come and talk to you about the investigation? Let you know how they were proceeding?"

"Oh sure. Right after it happened, the chief at the time was here. He went all over the house with a fine-tooth comb. Thought she might be hiding somewhere, I guess." He leaned forward in his chair, making sure his wife couldn't hear, and said, "I think he was also making sure we didn't do nothing to her. He didn't come right out and say it, but I read enough about these things to know the parents are always suspects." He held out his hands. "I didn't take offense, you understand. He was just being thorough."

Forever our Chief, Forever our Greatest Defender, Carrie thought. "I went to the police station," she said. "It seems the case file went missing after Chief Auburn died."

"It wasn't Walt Auburn who worked the case," Mr. Pugh said. "Walt was the Liston police chief. Back then, our towns were still separated. We live in Patterson, you see. It was after all the trouble that the towns decided to combine. Regionalization is what they called it. Taxes going up is what it was."

Mrs. Pugh returned, holding a steaming cup of coffee that she set down in front of Carrie on top of a saucer. Carrie thanked her and took a sip as the woman sat down on the couch next to her husband's chair. The coffee was boiling hot. Carrie set the cup down, feeling a raw place on the roof of her mouth with her tongue.

"Liston had a few officers at the time, but we only had one. He was called the chief, but really, it was just him," Mrs. Pugh said. "That poor man had to do everything. When people needed him, they called him on his house phone if it was after hours. It's no wonder he did what he did."

"That's enough, mother," Mr. Pugh said to his wife. "Let the past lie."

She lowered her head and folded her hands in her lap.

"Anyway," Mr. Pugh continued, "after the towns combined, they built a new police station and shipped all the records there. We heard some of them got misplaced, and apparently, one of them was Hope's."

"But no one ever followed up?" Carrie asked, writing on her notepad. "Or you never heard, if they did?"

"It doesn't matter, dear," Mrs. Pugh said, interrupting. "Hope's alive. She's alive and well."

Carrie dropped her pen on the table. "Excuse me?"

It was Mrs. Pugh's turn to smile, but this one was warm and wide and alive. "She lives on a farm. Out in Ohio, or West Virginia or such. She has at least two children, both grown, and maybe even a grandchild by now."

Mr. Pugh's eyes closed as his wife spoke, his hands braced against the armrests of his chair.

"Any day now, the phone is going to ring, or she is going to knock on that door and I'll see her standing there." Her eyes fell on Carrie once more, growing moist again. "At first, when I answered the door and saw you on the porch, I just," she said, swallowing, her voice fading away. "I guess you're too young to be her, anyway," she said, wiping her finger under her eye.

"We saw something on the news a few years back about a missing girl that got found," Mr. Pugh said, reaching over to lay his hand on his wife's. "Many years later, after she'd gone missing. They'd located her working out on some farm out in the Midwest. They reunited her with her parents on live TV."

"That's what happened to Hope, too," Mrs. Pugh said, tears streaming down her face. "I prayed on it, and that's what the Lord told me. She's alive, and someday, she's going to come walking right through that door."

CHAPTER 6

"*H*ey, Chief," Carrie said into her phone, leaning her head back against her car's headrest. "When you get this message give me a call. I'm out here on this missing person's case, and there's no way in hell I'm going to be able to find my way back in the dark. I'm going to use my department credit card to get a room. Hope that's all right," she said. She grimaced at the building in front of her and said, "I doubt it's going to be expensive."

She ended the call and opened up her text messages, going to the first name on her favorites list. The profile picture was of her and Nubs at the little girl's birthday, their faces pressed together, grinning with mouths full of cake frosting.

"Hey, sweetie, are you on your iPad?" she typed. She watched the bubble, hoping it would turn from Delivered to Read.

"Hi!" the response came.

"How was school today?" Carrie typed.

"Good."

"You just going to give me one-word answers now?"

"Sorry, Aunt Carrie," Nubs wrote back. **"Love you. Gotta go!"**

"Hey, what's the rush?"

"Grannie says I have to take a bath."

"'k baby. I love you too," she wrote, setting her phone aside.

* * *

The sign for the Honeysuckle Inn was red and bright, with the cartoonish image of a woman blowing a kiss. Carrie knew right away what the motel was for. It was the kind of place men brought hookers to, so far away from their families that there was no chance of getting caught. She'd learned about it from a waitress at Ruby's Diner, who talked while Carrie ate a greasy Reuben that was stuffed with so much corned beef she could barely fit it into her mouth.

"You go down to the end of the street, make a left at the stop sign. It's on the right side."

"Is it clean?" Carrie asked, feeling the sandwich's dressing spill out of her mouth. She grabbed a napkin and pressed it against her face.

"Since the bedbug thing last year, I didn't hear anything," the waitress had said, wiping the counter in long circular motions.

Carrie decided she didn't want the rest of her sandwich.

After dinner, Carrie parked her car in the motel's lot, making sure not to drive over any of the broken beer bottles scattered on the ground. She grabbed two bags out of her trunk. Her work bag filled with police gear, and a go-bag she carried at all times. She'd had to trek through enough filthy crime scenes and handle enough dead bodies that she knew to always keep a few spare changes of clothes on hand.

She pushed the button on her key fob to lock her vehicle, looked around the dark lot once more, and patted the gun on her side, making sure it was there. As she walked, she pressed the key fob in her pocket one more time, listening to it beep, just to be certain.

The clerk inside the small rental office was a heavyset woman with orange hair and green eyeshadow that went as high as her eyebrows. She cracked her gum and sneered at Carrie as she walked in. "Hi there. You're new."

Carrie said hello and reached into her purse for her wallet. "I need a room."

The clerk took Carrie's driver's license and credit card and wrote down the information in a ledger sitting on the desk in front of her. "There's a fifty-dollar charge to have any unregistered guests in your room, and I do mean any, so don't try and cheat us, because we'll know. Don't care how many you bring in, as long as you don't make too much noise, and as long as you pay the fee, understand?"

"It's just me," Carrie said.

The clerk cocked one green-shadowed eye at her and smirked. "Sweetie, you don't want to take any chances with us, believe me. My advice to you is to just pay the fee. Don't throw away all your hard work over fifty freaking dollars."

"Just give me the key, please," Carrie said, holding out her hand. "One guest. Me. Nobody else."

"Suit yourself," the clerk said, punching Carrie's credit card numbers into the machine on her desk.

The room was on the second floor. None of the rooms around it looked occupied. The air smelled like cheap carpet and bed linens and some kind of astringent used by the cleaning people. The first thing Carrie did was turn on all the lights and inspect the bed, sheets, and pillows, looking for any signs of insect life. The sheets were stiff and smelled of harsh cleanser, but they seemed clean.

She kicked off her shoes and unslung her gun and holster from her belt. She set them on the nightstand and collapsed backward on the bed's rough comforter. She closed her eyes and just as she felt her body settle, the phone in her pocket vibrated.

"Hello? Detective Santero speaking."

"It's Chief Auburn. Sorry for calling so late. I just got back into the office."

"That's fine, thanks for calling me back," Carrie said, sitting up. "Did you guys find the rest of the little girl?"

She could hear the hitch in Auburn's voice. She'd gotten the drop on him. "Who said we were looking for a little girl?" he asked.

"Hope Pugh, went missing back in nineteen eighty-one, right?" she said.

"Yeah," Auburn said. "You goddamn county people must have one hell of a time keeping track of everybody else's old cases."

That was a laugh, Carrie thought. Better to let him think that than get her new buddy Lou in trouble for blabbing. "Speaking of cases, I asked your clerk if I could see the case file. He told me it was lost."

"Actually, I've been thinking about that missing case file all day," he said. "There's one place we can still look. We're going to need those reports if we locate the rest of the body. Are you still out and about, or do you want to stop by in the morning?"

Carrie stood up, grabbing her gun and belt, while cradling the phone against her ear. "I'm on my way."

Steve Auburn was standing at the front door, holding it open, as she pulled into the police station lot. The dome light over the entryway reflected off the surface of his bald head, making it shine. She could see the outline of hair growing where he hadn't had the chance to shave it that day. It grew in a ring around his head, even across the front, leaving the top part bald and looking like the tonsure of a medieval monastic order.

Carrie hurried toward the door, clutching the front of her coat in her fist. The temperature had dropped with the sun, bringing a cold, cutting wind with it. She shivered inside the station's lobby, warming herself under a ceiling vent as Auburn welcomed her and thanked her for coming to help.

The portrait of the deceased Chief Walter Auburn loomed behind the man standing in front of her, and Carrie could see the resemblance in their faces. Walter died in '81, but he was younger in the face than Steve, painted without any blemishes or wrinkles. They'd done so much to beatify the man in the portrait that she was surprised the back of his head wasn't spouting sunlight surrounded by baby angels blowing trumpets. "Is that your father?"

Auburn nodded. "That's him."

Carrie pointed at the placard beneath the painting. "He got killed on the job?"

"He certainly did," Auburn said. "He didn't die alone, though. Took out a whole gang, all by himself. They killed him, but hell if he didn't kill every last one of them bastards in the process."

"That's amazing," Carrie said. "I mean, it must have been awful for you and your family, but still."

"It's all right. I was just a kid at the time," Auburn said. "I don't remember much."

"It's good you honor him like this, keeping his painting up."

"Gives me a lot to live up to, to be honest. Being the son of the town's most famous hero is no fun, I promise you that. I'm pretty sure they gave me the chief's job just because of my name."

"Well, maybe someday another gang will show up and you can wipe them out too, right? Like father, like son. I mean, except for getting killed in the process," Carrie said, letting out a small laugh.

Her laugh rose up between them like smoke, dying somewhere among the ceiling tiles and fluorescent lights. Auburn worked his tongue around the inside of his mouth, scraping something off his teeth with it, not responding. He found what he was seeking, swallowed it, then turned down the hall, saying, "Come on, we'll check some boxes in the basement. I think I remember seeing a few old case files in there."

Police departments, no matter where they are in the world, hate throwing things away. Old equipment that's long obsolete. Broken telephones. Leather holsters for weapons and gear no one carries anymore. The reason is simple: All police departments run on public funds. When those funds are spent, the public expects their tax money is being put to good use. No police administrator wants to get caught throwing anything away, because it's an admission, however slight, that money was spent on things that weren't really needed. It all winds up in some back room or utility closet or anywhere else it can be stored out of sight. As Carrie followed Steve Auburn through the basement door and down the steps, she knew they were in the right place.

She squinted in the dim light coming from the bare lightbulbs that hung from the rafters above them. There were damp crates of used traffic ticket booklets, being saved in case the State Police ever decided to do an audit. Boxes with ripped uniforms stuffed inside, being saved for their patches and buttons. Filing cabinets filled with every fingerprint card and mug shot photo ever taken by the department, from the days before digital photography and processing, and next to those filing cabinets, boxes of old cameras, dried-up fingerprint ink pads, crusty rollers, and yellowed ten-print cards that still listed "Negro" as one of the options under race.

These are the archaeological places of police departments, with boxes packed against each wall that are labeled with markers, in handwriting so faded it cannot be read. They are inherited from the people who came before and kept because no one wants to be responsible for throwing them away.

She walked next to Steve Auburn, reading him. A simple man. Wholesome. Overwhelmed. Unsure of why any of this had fallen on him, and wishing it hadn't.

Carrie knew if you asked Auburn why his police department did things the way they did, he would say the same thing as every other small-town chief: We do it this way because that's the way we've always done it.

A stack of molding boxes was piled in the farthest corner of the basement stamped with the words *Property of Patterson Boro PD*.

"I've been through these, and never saw anything related to the Hope Pugh case, but maybe there was something I missed," Auburn said. He shined his flashlight over the various boxes, searching behind them in the shadows. Most of the boxes contained artifacts from the old police station. Pens and used notepads and a beige rotary telephone sat on top of a stack of Pennsylvania Crimes Code books from the 1970s.

Carrie picked up the first box and set it aside, then the next, and the next. The closest thing they found to case files was a long cardboard banker's box stuffed with old handwritten accident reports. "I went through that box," Auburn said. "It's not in there."

Carrie set it aside and kept pulling things away until she reached the bottom. There, hidden behind the first row of boxes, sitting in an inch of brown basement water, was a large firesafe container. She heaved at it, inspected the lock, and called for Auburn to give her a hand.

"I never saw that back there," he said, helping her slide it away from the pile. "Damn."

"Do you have anything that can open it?"

"There's some old tools over here," he said, turning his flashlight to a metal cabinet beneath the staircase. "Let me see what I can find."

Carrie ran her hands over the container's metal lid. It was the size of a small beer cooler, made of rusted metal, and heavy. Why was it locked? she wondered. Maybe it held compromising photographs of some long-dead politician, saved by a long-dead police officer, just in case. She rocked the container back and forth, hearing the contents shift within. A policeman's version of Schrödinger's Box. Until it was open, it both contained the hidden treasure that would unlock the mystery of the missing little girl, and didn't.

Auburn returned with a crowbar. "Stand back."

He slid the crowbar's flat end between the lid and crate, heaved, but it didn't give. He jammed it in farther, stomping the length of metal with his boot, bending the crate's flaps, but not opening it. His boot slipped and the crowbar shot up, striking him in the shinbone with a dull thud. "I'm going to shoot this damn thing!" Auburn shouted, clutching his shin.

He worked the other side, bending that too, and then yanked the crowbar out, trying to fit it between the lock and metal sides of the crate.

Carrie found a sledgehammer leaning against the wall and grabbed it. "Look out, Chief," she said, gripping the sledge under the head of thick steel. Auburn was bent over, sweat dripping from his bald scalp. He slid back, watching as Carrie turned the firesafe on its back, the metal lock facing the ceiling. She raised the sledge high in the air, letting it rest against the wooden rafters and insulation above them, and swung it down hard.

The lock cracked in two, and the bent lid flopped open, spilling the safe's contents onto the floor. A file folder of newspaper clippings. Scattered documents. A large grocery shopping bag, stapled together, with the word *Evidence* written across it in black Magic Marker. On the first faded newspaper clipping, the smiling face of a little girl, twelve years old, stared up at Carrie from the basement floor, and from across the distance of four decades.

A school photograph of Hope Pugh.

CHAPTER 7

*C*arrie squatted down to pick up the safe with both hands, straining to lift it. Auburn reached to help her but she said, "I've got it."

Auburn moved to help her navigate her way toward the steps. He winced when her leg crashed into a box of tools, sending them scattering. "Why don't we put everything inside one of these boxes?" he asked.

"I'm good," she said, clenching her teeth. "Every envelope and bag in here is rotted and was never properly sealed. If we try moving it around in this basement, we could contaminate any piece of evidence that's left. Better to leave the whole thing intact."

"Do you want me to at least get it in your car?" he said, watching her mount the steps.

"It's not that heavy," she grunted.

Carrie heaved the safe up the stairs to her hotel room, moving it two steps at a time. She dropped it on every second step, slid it, gripped it by its edges, cursed as she lifted it, and dropped it again. At the bottom of the steps, the painted-face clerk stormed out of the front office, shouting, "What the hell is all that noise?"

Carrie cursed under her breath. She felt the bones in her spine compress as she shoved the safe over the top step and braced herself against it, trying to catch her breath. Once it was flat, she was able to push it across the worn carpet all the way to her room.

She plowed the safe across her hotel room, crashing it against the bed frame and chipping the cheap dresser, but it didn't matter, it was chipped in other places already. She got the safe under the table at the far end of the room and collapsed over it, resting her arms on its cool surface.

The lid squeaked as she pried it open, forcing it back on its bent hinges, until it was left hanging at an odd angle over the back of the frame like a dead animal's protruding tongue. From the floor next to her, she grabbed her bag, a tactical model made from sturdy nylon with multiple pockets, and undid the first one. A tangled mass of black rubber gloves spilled out. She picked out a pair and pulled them onto her hands.

She bent over the safe and sifted through its contents, assessing what was inside before she removed any of it. Several folders contained photographs and newspaper clippings. One held documents on official letterhead from the FBI and State Police, another was stuffed with handwritten notes torn out of a spiral pad.

Last was a large paper bag marked *Evidence*. There were no long-form investigative reports of any kind. No evidence forms. No chain of custody for anything. She took a photograph of the inside of the safe with her cell phone, pulled out a notepad and pen, and set them on the table.

Item: CS-1, she wrote. *File folder containing various photographs.*

She lifted the manila folder and laid it carefully on the table. Some of the photographs were stuck together. She did her best to pull them apart without tearing them. For the ones that couldn't be pulled apart, she bent and folded them as much as she could, trying to see what they contained, then let them be.

CS-1-A. School photo. Someone had written *Hope 5th Grade 1981* on the back. The smiling little girl's wild red hair was frizzy and pulled back. Her mother had applied some sort of straightener, but the girl's natural curls were too strong to be contained. Her eyes sparkled. Alert. Fierce. Intelligent.

Hope Pugh would be dead soon after the photo was taken, Carrie thought. Son of a bitch.

CS-1-B. An 8 × 10 black-and-white photograph of the front of the Pugh house. Carrie looked at the photograph, realizing it was the same place she'd been to earlier that day, and that it had been much better kept back then.

The next group of photographs showed the home's interior, including multiple pictures of Hope's bedroom, the basement, and backyard. Carrie remembered what Mr. Pugh had said about the investigator going over the house with a fine-tooth comb, thinking Hope might be hiding there. She found photographs of Mr. Pugh's tool shed and workbench, including close-ups of his tools, focusing on his saws and shovels. The cop didn't think she was hiding there, Carrie thought. He was making sure she wasn't cut up and buried there.

The first place to check in any missing child investigation was the house. Kids were always falling asleep in a crawl space or some closet or attic, getting into places adults never expected them to. The cop, whoever he was, had been smart not to let on that he suspected the parents. It was much easier to search someone's house with their permission than it was to get a search warrant.

She pulled out the last photo and laid it on the table. It didn't belong with any of the others. It was taken outside, at night, but wasn't in the Pugh backyard. It had way too many trees. It looked like some kind of makeshift campground out in the woods.

In the background stood an old brick fire chimney and stove, the basin filled with burnt sticks. Spread out in front of the stove was a blanket, with a few scattered leaves blown across it. Two things caught Carrie's eye. An overturned stuffed bear lay in the center of the blanket, and on the lower-right corner, what looked like a child's sock. It was dirty, but the smiling face of a cartoon character was visible, printed across the top.

She dropped each of the photographs into its own plastic bag, wrote their new numbers on the surface of the bag in marker, and set them aside. She reached back into the safe and unrolled the large paper shopping bag marked evidence, shaking loose decades of dirt that had dried to it sides. The bag wasn't sealed. She peeled it open, peering down at the contents, scowling at the intense stink of mildew.

Inside was a blanket, likely the same one in the last photograph, but covered in mold from years of storage inside the police station's damp basement. She lifted the fabric, keeping it far from her face, and laid it on the table. She picked at the blanket's edges with the tips of her fingers. Dead bugs and dirt were embedded inside each fold. Something was buried inside the blanket. She could feel it through the fabric. Its plastic wrapping crinkled each time she pulled another layer away.

As she undid the last flap, she found what was buried there, hidden away inside a yellowing plastic bag that had been stapled multiple times. She picked up her cell phone and took a picture. It was the same stuffed bear and child's sock from the photograph, perfectly preserved. The sock was light blue. Thick. Meant to be worn under boots in the cold weather.

Carrie reached into her left pocket for the knife she kept clipped there. She flicked the karambit's curved blade open with one hand, feeling the warmth of its metal handle in her palm. The weapon was designed to resemble a bird's talon. It was never intended to do anything but rend human flesh.

She'd inherited the blade from Jacob Rein and, like him, had put it to use against a man who preyed on the innocent.

Carrie used the karambit's razor-sharp point of the talon to slice the plastic bag open along the side. She slid the stuffed bear out of the bag and laid it on the blanket, then removed the sock and spread it out, placing it exactly as it appeared in the photograph.

She pulled off the gloves and scratched behind her ear, then ran her fingers up and down the back of her head, feeling the lengths of her hair sliding between them, staring at the items spread out in front of her, then back at the photograph. It was all an enormous puzzle. She wasn't sure she had all the pieces and had no real idea of what the finished picture was supposed to look like.

She put on a fresh pair of gloves, picked up the folder filled with handwritten notes, and spread them all out across the floor in front of her bed. Some of the notes were crumpled and stuck together, many with just names and phone numbers and no explanation. She sifted through them, making a stack of the useless ones, and a much smaller stack of the ones with any kind of narrative.

Spoke to neighbors. No one saw anything.

February 14th—Spoke to school Principal. No concerns with parents. Hope never spoke about running away. No distant relatives.

A phone number, with the words *Speak to pediatrician when he gets back from vacation.*

She came to the last handwritten note and stopped. It was folded in half and had mud smeared around the edges. *February 14th—Found kid's hiding spot. Collected blanket, sock, stuffed bear. Found knife.*

Knife? Carrie thought. She went back to the table and raised the corners of the blanket, making sure nothing was stuck to the underside. She looked down into the safe. The hotel light was dim and the remaining files had spilled their contents. She scooped them up and set them on the carpet, then tilted the safe to get a better view inside its dark belly. Something rattled when she moved it. Carrie reached in and found a filthy plastic bag, rolled up long and thin.

"Come on," she whispered as she peeled the bag open.

It was a switchblade handle, long and thin, and caked with dirt. The blade was still seated inside. It had rusted in places, but when she pressed the small silver button to click it open, the stiletto's steel flicked outward, bright and clean.

She walked the knife over to the lamp and held it directly beneath the bulb, leaning so close she could feel its heat on the tip of her nose.

"Son of a bitch," she whispered. There, on the polished surface of the blade, were the faded ridges and whorls of a fingerprint.

She set the switchblade down and photographed it, then marked and numbered it in her notebook.

* * *

It was dark by the time she pulled out of the motel's driveway and got back on the main road. She turned onto the main road and saw it was called Auburn Street. The lights of the stores that were still open made the town look more alive than it had in the daytime. People strolled along the sidewalks. She smelled pipe tobacco, sweet and rich, and a man holding a long-stemmed hickory pipe nodded to her as she slowed to let him cross the street in front of her car. He took his time in the road, not worried about oncoming traffic. It wasn't the kind of place where anyone moved fast.

Carrie checked her phone and saw two missed calls. Her first thought was that Nubs had finished her bath and tried to call her back before getting ready for bed. Instead, the calls were from an unknown number with no way to call back, and no message left.

The only people who used unlisted numbers were telemarketers and bill collectors. I'm lonely, she thought, but not lonely enough to talk to the likes of you.

It was after eight P.M. She pictured Nubs snuggled in her pajamas, surrounded by the dozens of stuffed animals Carrie had bought for her over the past year, warm and safe in bed. She was about to text, "You still awake, kiddo?" but stopped. If Nubs is in bed it would be selfish to interrupt that, she thought. No matter how much I could use another "I love you too" text right about now.

She slowed down as she drove past the Liston-Patterson police station. The lights were off again. "Stupid small-ass town!" she said, smacking the steering wheel in frustration.

The phone rang again. Another unlisted number. She put it to her ear and said, "Detective Santero. This is a police phone, and I swear to God if you're bothering me in the middle of an investigation just to sell me a warranty on my car or some bullshit, I'm going to come find you and rip out your eyeballs."

A pause on the other end, and then a familiar man's voice said, "That seems excessive."

"Rein?" Carrie asked. "Oh, thank God. I'm stuck in the middle of nowhere out here and there's no one at the station. This place is total hicksville. The goddamn motel lady thinks I'm a hooker, and—"

"Carrie?" Rein said.

"What?"

"Be quiet. I don't have much time."

"Okay," she said. "Why not?"

"Phone minutes are expensive, and I only have a few," he said. "The body that they found, have they identified it yet?"

"Almost," Carrie said. "Everyone seems to think it's from this little girl that went missing almost forty years ago. Hope something."

"Hope Pugh," Rein said.

"Right. Jesus, you're like Wikipedia for old criminal cases or something."

"Do the police still have any evidence?"

"Some. It was never packaged properly and isn't in great shape. I found one thing, though. An old switchblade that I might be able to get prints off of," she said. She raised a clenched fist in the air and shook it, saying, "Except the goddamn police station is closed and I don't even know if I have any powder."

"I wouldn't put powder on it if it's that old," Rein said. "The oils forming the print might be too degraded to bond anymore, and you'll ruin it. I wouldn't put any powder on it if it's that old until it's been glued."

"Oh sure, yeah," Carrie said. "That's great, except if I don't have powder, do you honestly think I have cyro . . . sierra . . ."

"Cyanoacrylate."

"Whatever! Cyrano de Bergerac, for all it matters, because I don't have any. No glue. No fuming chamber. No nothing."

"So make one," he said.

"Make one?" she asked.

"That's what a real detective would do."

Carrie made it to the hardware store just as the elderly owner was opening the register to do his final count for the night. He had yellow, stained-looking hair smeared back across the top of his head, and his baggy plaid shirt bunched at the shoulders under the straps from his overalls. "We're closed," he said.

"I need five minutes," Carrie said, pressing her hands together. "Please. I just need a few quick things, and I am spending money that doesn't belong to me, so I don't care what it costs. Please?"

He frowned and looked at the clock. He slapped the register shut and said, "I'll clean up while you look around, but don't dillydally, young lady. I've got a date tonight." He shuffled behind her and locked the door, flipped the sign around that said CLOSED, and waved her on. Carrie thanked him and hurried down the first aisle. She headed straight for the shelf displaying all kinds of tapes and superglue. She picked the strongest of both she could find, and bought several of them. "Who's the lucky lady?"

"What now?" the owner said, looking up at her from his broom. He cupped his left hand behind his ear and leaned toward her.

"Your hot date. Your wife?"

"Oh, no," he said, going back to sweeping. "She passed on more than ten years ago. It's one of the ladies from church. Mary, with red hair."

Carrie raised her eyebrows, impressed. She went farther down the aisle, looking through a display of flat cardboard that could be shaped into boxes, trying to figure out how big they'd be when assembled. She grabbed four of different sizes to be safe.

"Wait, hang on," the owner said, resting the broom against his shoulder. He reached into his back pocket and pulled out a worn black book that was secured by a rubber band. He pulled off the rubber band and flipped through the pages, licking his thumb each time he turned a page, and shook his head as he read the last thing he'd written. "Wilma. She wears a wig. She's from the bowling alley. Mary with the red hair is tomorrow night."

Carrie laughed, carrying the boxes and other supplies up to the counter and setting them down.

The old man eyed her. "How many nights are you in town for?"

"Just a few. I'm working on something."

"You like pinochle? I play in a league and we might have an open seat tomorrow night."

"I thought you had a date with Mary?"

He flashed a smile, more gum than tooth. "You just let me worry about that."

Carrie laughed again, heading down the next aisle. "That's the best offer I've had in a long time, mister, but I'm afraid I don't have time to socialize."

"Well, if something falls through, keep me in mind. I can show you around town."

She went past the hammers and mallets and screwdrivers, around the boxes of nails and screws of varying sizes and colors. Bins along the bottom of the shelves held piles of loose nails, under a handwritten sign marked USED NAILS—NICKLE A PEACE.

Lunchboxes and thermoses and lawn chairs were stacked along the back wall, along with ziplock baggies and other things a working man would need on a job site. Carrie grabbed a large roll of aluminum foil and searched until she found an electric coffee warmer, the kind that plugged in and was nothing more than a flat disc you could set your mug on to keep it hot on a cold day.

She checked the list she'd written on her phone of the items Rein said she would need. I hope that's everything, she thought. She carried the last items to the counter and set them down in front of the register.

The owner started tallying them up, writing in a notepad with a sharpened carpenter's pencil. "What do you need all this stuff for?"

"I'm doing a science project," Carrie said.

She reached for her wallet in her back right pocket and the owner's eyes snapped toward the black Glock holstered on her hip. She pulled out her wallet and covered the gun with her coat, then offered a county credit card.

He took it. "You a police officer?"

"That's right."

"I'm afraid I have to revoke my invitation, then. I can't date any more police officers. Not after the last one. You all are too crazy."

Carrie touched her heart over her jacket. "I'm hurt, but I understand."

He laid the credit card in an old-fashioned carbon paper press and wrapped his hand around the machine's lever. "You sure you got everything, right? Once I pull this, I'm closing up."

Carrie turned, looking around the store once more. She had everything she needed for the fuming chamber. The only other thing would be to try and process the blanket, sock, and stuffed bear, but she hadn't seen anything on the shelves remotely close to what she needed to do that. "That should be everything," she said, adding, "unless you have any luminol or an ALS."

"What's luminol?"

"Chemical treatment you spray on fabric to reveal old bloodstains." She waved the idea away. "Not important."

"No, I don't carry any of that. What's an ALS?"

"Alternate light source," Carrie said.

"Like, fluorescent bulbs? I got them."

"Ultraviolet light. The blue kind," Carrie said. "It's kind of a specialty item. Don't worry about it. I'm just glad you had all this stuff."

He squished up his lips, thinking about it. "I got an industrial bug zapper in the back. You hang it outside and it zaps the bejeezus out of any bugs that touch it. From what I recall, that's got a blue lightbulb. I'm pretty sure it says it's ultraviolet."

"How much is it?" Carrie asked.

"Well, I've only got one, and they're hard to come by right now," he said, scratching the side of his face. "Some kind of supply issue with the warehouse, or something. It's extremely powerful, though. Very high end." He glanced down at the credit card, stamped *District Attorney's Office, Vieira County, Pennsylvania.* He chewed the inside of his cheek, his right eye twitching with hesitation, before announcing, "Three hundred bucks."

"I'll take it. Long as it's ultraviolet light."

His face dropped a little as he realized he could have asked for even more money. He told her he'd be right back with it.

LUNATIC DETECTIVE USES BUG ZAPPER IN COLD CASE HOMICIDE. Now that's the kind of headline you frame outside your office door, Carrie thought.

Carrie spread the items across her hotel room floor, seeing what she would need. Someone had taken the room next to hers. A woman was talking: "You have to tell me you're a cop if I ask you three times, you know that, right?"

"Not true," Carrie said aloud. She used the karambit's tip to slice open the first roll of tape. It was like the older, stronger brother of duct tape. Clear, with threads woven through it, almost impossible to tear.

"How much if I don't want to wear a condom?" a male voice asked through the wall.

"Yikes. Bad idea," Carrie said, picking out the smallest cardboard box and assembling it. She covered any seams or gaps in the box with tape, sealing it up tight, except for the lid. She pulled the coffee warmer out of its packaging and plugged it in, keeping her fingers against the surface until it started to get hot. She set the coffee warmer down inside the box, decided it would be big enough to hold the rest of the items, and cut a small slot in the upper corner for the electrical cable.

She pulled off a length of aluminum foil and crumpled it into a small bowl, then set it on top of the coffee warmer. She grabbed a small paper cup from the bathroom, cut off everything except the lower rim and a half inch of its walls, and filled it with water. She set the cup in the opposite corner, careful not to spill it.

Now came the moment of truth. Carrie pulled on a pair of rubber gloves and went over to the table where her evidence lay. She picked up the switchblade, inspected its blade in the light once more, trying to decide if she really wanted to stick the thing inside a fuming chamber made out of a cardboard box.

She didn't need to tell herself that if she fucked this up, she was ruining a potentially vital piece of evidence. She didn't need to tell herself that if she fucked this up, and anyone found out, they might fire her for being incompetent. For not waiting until someone more experienced could take over.

"It's so big, oh my God, I can't stand it," the woman said, her voice flat. The headboard on the opposite side of the wall slapped hard and fast.

Carrie blew a length of hair out of her face, held the knife at both ends, and lowered it inside the box, tilting it at an angle so that the glue would get under it and around it and cover it from all sides. "Here goes nothing," she said.

She squeezed a puddle of superglue down inside the foil bowl and it immediately began to smoke. Fumes from the glue, evaporating, bind to the oils and acids left behind by a human fingerprint, clarifying it enough to be identified. It would bind to more than that, she thought, moving quickly to shut the lid. If she got her face too close to the fumes, she could accidentally glue her own eyeballs.

She sealed the lid with tape, covering any remaining gaps, and sat on the floor. Now was the tricky part. In a real fuming chamber, the walls were glass. The person processing the evidence could see how it was going, make sure the print was not being overdeveloped. If she waited too long, so much glue would bind to the print that it would be unreadable. If she opened the box up too quickly, she'd interrupt the fuming process, lose containment, and have to start all over again.

I'll take option number two in that scenario, she thought.

The headboard was slapping again, followed by a series of moans, male and female. Someone had gotten a second wind.

She made note of the time, thinking that she still had a few minutes. She looked at the bug zapper, still in its box, and thought it could wait. It said, in big bold letters, *For Outdoor Use Only.* She didn't want to deal with potentially burning down her motel room and overgluing the switchblade at the same time.

Carrie grabbed the last file folder out of the safe and sat down, leaning against the bed as she flipped through it. It was the one with the letters written on official Liston Borough Police Department letterhead. The first was written to the major in charge of the nearest State Police barracks, asking him for assistance with a missing child investigation.

I believe that something has gone horribly wrong for this child, the letter said.

"You weren't kidding, buddy," Carrie said. She scanned through the rest of the letter, and stopped at the bottom part, staring at the name of the man who'd written it.

Oliver J. Rein, Chief of Police.

Jacob, you bastard, Carrie thought. Who the hell is Oliver Rein to you?

There had been a look on Rein's face at the diner when she told him about the police bulletin, she'd just been too tired to pick up on it. He'd gone running out the moment he heard they were looking for a cadaver dog. He knew, she thought. He knew they'd found Hope Pugh. Hope Pugh went missing in 1981. She was twelve years old.

"Holy shit," Carrie gasped. "You two are the same age. You didn't know her name from some old case. You knew *her*."

She picked up the next letter and began to read. It said the same exact thing as the first, but was addressed to the special agent in charge of the nearest FBI office. *I believe that something has gone horribly wrong for this child.*

Oliver J. Rein. Chief of Police.

"It's no wonder he did what he did," Mrs. Pugh had said earlier that day, before her husband silenced her.

What did Oliver Rein do? Carrie wondered. What was the big secret?

This place has a bad record with chiefs of police, Carrie thought. *Right after Hope Pugh goes missing, Steve Auburn's dad gets killed in a shootout of some kind. That's a lot of drama for such a small area, and in such a short amount of time.* She didn't believe in coincidences. This puzzle was a pain in the ass. Something stung her nose, coming right up through her sinuses like a hornet, and her head shot up. Black smoke was leaking out of the corners of the cardboard box.

Carrie tossed the letters aside and scrambled for her knife. She had visions of the coffee warmer being engulfed in flames as she sliced the tape open across the lid. Luckily, it was just the glue melting through the foil bowl, burning on the surface of the coffee warmer. She grabbed the switchblade, pulled it out of the white cloud of fumes, and yanked the warmer's electrical cord from the wall. The other side of the wall had gone silent. Carrie hoped the woman didn't have any more clients that night.

She carried the knife over to the light and inspected the blade. The glue had bound to the fingerprint, sure enough, but done little to clarify any parts of it that she could not see before. Still, it was something, and now, if she tried to lift the print, she didn't have to worry about wrecking it. Its outline was locked on the blade, for better or worse, until the end of time.

She looked inside her tactical bag and pumped her fist when she saw a brush and tub of fingerprint powder at the bottom. She swirled a light sprinkling of black powder across the blade, and saw several more prints that had been developed by the fuming. They were smaller, and maybe just smudges, but they were something. She twirled the brush, adding a little more powder, then covered the length of the blade in one piece of tape and yanked it free. She laid the tape on a white glossy card and inspected it in the light.

Are you here? she thought, seeing the ridges of someone's fingerprints in several places across the surface of the card. Did I just find you, you bastard?

She did the other side of the blade, and the handle as well, finding nothing else that appeared of any value. She marked all of the index cards as evidence, recorded them in her log, and secured them in evidence baggies.

The stuffed bear, sock, and blanket were still sitting on the table. Carrie grabbed the box for the bug zapper and sliced it open, tossed aside the index cards warning *For Outdoor Use Only*, and pulled the fixture free. She plugged it in and turned off the lamp. "Okay," she said, taking a deep breath. "I'm going to turn this thing on now, and everything is going to go nice and smooth.

Nothing is going to burst into flames. It is all going to be fine. Just perfectly fine."

She lifted the bug zapper by its handle, holding it as far away from her and high above the table as she could, and pressed the ON button. It hummed to life, vibrating as it built up an electrical charge, until the large bulbs housed within it glowed hot with bluish purple light. The room hummed with electricity, and Carrie flinched as it flickered and popped across the surface of the glass bulbs. Her arms were shaking as she hoisted the lantern over the table, this hot and sparking contraption that was made out of metal and getting too heavy to hold, clearly meant *For Outdoor Use Only* and not cold case homicide investigations, and then she saw it.

A luminescent smear, glowing bright in the ultraviolet light.

Droplets were splattered along the stuffed bear's fur, invisible to the naked eye, but revealed in brilliant blue relief by the bug zapper. More, much more, appeared on the little girl's sock. Carrie knew that only organic fluids would react in such a way. Blood would glow, but unless it had been tampered with, it could be seen long after it dried. The sock was dirty when she'd inspected it, but she hadn't seen any blood.

Now, half of the sock looked like it had been painted fluorescent. Carrie knew of only one biological fluid in the world capable of presenting in such a way. "Motherfucker," she whispered.

Something buzzed near her hand, louder than even the humming of the bug zapper, and she saw a hairy black fly land on the surface of one of the bulbs. Electricity arced outward, filling the dark room with sizzling sparks that billowed the curtains back. Carrie screamed, nearly dropping the entire contraption, as the fly's dead body tumbled down in front of her, smoking and charred. She raced over to the outlet and yanked the cord out of the wall, set the zapper on the table, and bent forward, thinking, That is exactly why you shouldn't do this shit unless you have the right equipment.

Still, she'd seen what she needed to see. Serological residue was splashed across the child's sock and stuffed bear, and it was most likely semen. She looked at the photograph taken in the woods again. That's the crime scene, she thought. A rape, then a murder, and if the finding of her foot in the woods was any indication, maybe even a dismemberment to hide the body afterward.

Show everybody you can handle a nice, simple call for assistance without turning it into an enormous shitstorm, she thought. Yeah, right.

CHAPTER 8

*C*arrie put on fresh gloves and lowered the sock inside a fresh paper evidence bag. She sealed the bag with tape and wrote her name and the date across its fragile red surface without tearing it. Evidence tape is designed to split apart easily, so that anyone trying to tamper with it is caught. All it really does is break into pieces between your fingers when you're trying to seal something, or tear in half when you're trying to sign it. Maybe the true purpose of fragile evidence tape is to sell more goddamn evidence tape, she thought.

She took off that pair of gloves and tossed them in the trash, then slid on a new pair to safeguard against any cross contamination. She put the stuffed bear inside a larger paper bag and sealed it the same way, running multiple strips of evidence tape across the flaps to keep them from breaking open. She repeated the same process to secure the blanket.

When all was packaged and secured, she stepped back and looked it over. She had the fingerprint on the knife, she thought. Potential serological evidence on the stuffed bear and sock. Whatever they could find on the blanket. They could search that for semen and vacuum it for hair fibers, she thought. With all of that, they should be able to get something.

If the bad guy's ever been fingerprinted, and the fingerprint on the knife has sufficient ridge detail, he's done. If he's a convicted felon, and his DNA is on file, and the semen on the sock hasn't degraded so much it's useless, he's done. He's arrested.

The entire process could take sixteen to eighteen months, once the State Police crime lab got around to analyzing everything. That was if they decided to take all of the evidence she gave them. More than likely, they'd refuse to take so much at one time. Just give us one piece, whatever you think has the most potential, and we'll work on that for you. Sorry, that's policy. Only one lab for the entire state, and we can't just shut everything else down for your investigations, detective.

Then, after they got around to analyzing the bear and found nothing, she'd be allowed to send in the sock. After they got around to analyzing that, she'd get to send in the blanket.

With her luck, all of the evidence would come back either unreadable or with no match. The bad guy had probably been so filled with shame after the murder, he'd turned over a new leaf and never gotten in trouble again. Or he'd moved to another country, one that doesn't share its criminal databases with the United States. Or, fuck it, maybe he was just dead. It's been forty years, after all. People get old, or maybe crash their cars, or get drunk one night and blow their brains out.

She cleaned up her supplies and sat back down on the floor, stifling a yawn with the back of her hand. Her arms and legs and lower back hurt. She was tired from the long drive earlier that day and then running around this crappy small town, talking to all the weirdos who lived there. She felt zeroed out. Too tired and cranky to even bother taking a shower. Screw it, she thought. I'll take one in the morning. Maybe a layer of the day's grime will protect me from whatever kind of hepatitis is living in the sheets of this bed.

She picked up the stack of letters from the file on the floor and flipped through them once more. They were all to various agencies and department heads, federal, state, and local, in the surrounding area, all bearing the same Liston Police Department letterhead, all containing the same plea for help, all signed by a man named Oliver Rein.

The file did not hold a single response to any of the letters. If the men Chief Rein had appealed to had come racing to render aid, she found no record of it, and Carrie doubted she'd ever be able to track down anyone from any of those agencies willing to dig through their archives to find out.

As she stuck the stack of papers back into the file, gold leaf lettering on the last page caught her eye. She pulled it out and saw it was from *The Liston Borough Office of Chief of Police—Chief Walter C. Auburn.*

It was dated February 16, 1981. That was the same date on his plaque, Carrie thought. The day Auburn was killed.

> *Dear District Attorney and Chief of County Detectives:*
>
> *It is my sad duty to report that Chief Oliver Rein has died as a result of suicide, and I am temporarily assuming command of the Patterson Borough Police Department's jurisdiction, in addition to my own. I anticipate this will soon become a permanent position.*
>
> *Chief Rein is survived by his older brother, Benjamin, whom I have spoken to. If you should choose to call their house to pass along your condolences, I advise you to speak to Benjamin's son instead. I have known Ben Rein a long time, and he is an unstable man. His son was very close to Chief Rein, and you will do better talking to him. The boy's name is J.D.*
>
> *I do not wish to cast aspersions on the character of Ollie Rein. He was a good man, and I considered him a friend. We do not require any assistance with the matter. It was obvious what occurred, and we handled it accordingly, making sure to keep it as quiet as possible. I owed Ollie that much.*
>
> *Sincerely, Chief Walter C. Auburn*

Carrie reread the letter several times, then tossed it aside. A boy called J.D. Rein. His uncle dead of suicide in the middle of a child abduction investigation. Another chief dead on the day the letter was sent.

She leaned her head back against the bed and muttered, "What the fuck is going on?"

The house was a small two-story affair, with rotting shingles on the roof and two flags hanging from rusted poles, mounted to the porch. One, an American flag, was so faded it was translucent, and the other was a tattered US Army flag. The railing on the porch had once been white, but the paint had cracked and peeled away long ago, leaving bare wood along most of its lengths. The second step was split in two. Carrie stepped over it, coming up to the house's screen door. She knocked and waited. An old, creaking voice within the house barked, "Who the hell is that?"

A dark-skinned woman in a pair of bright purple scrubs answered. "Can I help you?" She was a head taller than Carrie, with flabby arms that jiggled as she held the door a few inches open.

Carrie raised her wallet, letting the flap fall to reveal her golden badge. "Is Mr. Benjamin Rein home?"

"He's sick," the nurse said.

"Who is it?" the man inside the house shouted, his voice swallowed by a fit of gurgling coughs.

"I need to speak with him," Carrie said.

"Well, I'm sorry, but that's just not possible," the nurse said. As she moved to close the door, she said, "He's at the end of his care. It's only going to be a few more days, and I can't let you disturb his rest."

Carrie put her hand against the door, barring it from closing on her. "I have to speak with him. It's important."

Before the nurse could push the door shut on Carrie's hand, an enormous crash of metal against glass was followed by another shout, "I asked you who the hell was at the door, you goddamn useless shit!"

The nurse charged back into the house, roaring, "If you broke that IV, you are paying for it! I told you about that last time. I wasn't fooling!"

More gurgling, another crash, and Carrie let herself in. She looked around the living room, scowling at the overwhelming stench of antiseptic, menthol vapor, and human waste. A portable commode was folded and leaning against the wall, and someone had draped a coat over it. Carrie saw a stack of adult diapers by the stairwell leading upstairs.

Above the diapers, covering the wall leading into the kitchen, were framed photos so old they were bleached by sunlight. In some, a uniformed, handsome young man stared at the camera. In others, that same young man, in a field with no shirt on, was surrounded by other young men, also shirtless, all of them holding large machine guns. In the center of the wall was a large shadow box with medals piled up from the bottom, like a slot machine tray after someone hit triple bananas. Hanging above the medals was a battered green beret, and beside it, a faded patch. The patch displayed a bird of some kind, spreading its wings, with the words *Phung-Hoa'ng* embroidered across the top.

Carrie picked up a framed picture sitting on an end table near the sofa. It was covered in gray dust, nothing more than an old Kodak print that was never meant for framing. A little boy flanked by two men stood in front of an older-model police car, which bore a large star on the door with the words *Patterson Borough Police* in large block letters across the top. The taller, older-looking of the two men was the same one in the photographs hanging on the wall. His face had changed. Something was wrong with the man and it showed. He looked unkempt, with long hair and soiled clothes.

The younger man was in a police uniform, handsome and smiling, with his hand draped over the boy's shoulder. And the boy had a face she recognized. His face, not yet lined with age, and eyes that were not yet haunted, unmistakably belonged to Jacob Rein.

Past the nurse, she could see a withered man lying in a metal-framed hospital bed centered in the otherwise empty kitchen. He was gripping an IV stand that was connected to his arms, refusing to let go of it while the nurse tried to keep it from falling.

They were screaming at each other, the nurse telling him to let go, and the man shouting at her that she didn't know what the hell she was doing. Carrie waved from the kitchen entrance and said, "Hi, Mr. Rein."

Ben Rein looked at her, still clutching the IV stand. "Who the hell are you?"

The nurse glared at Carrie, but she moved past the woman into the kitchen, gently took the metal IV pole, and set it upright. "I'm a detective with the DA's office. I have a few questions for you. But first, I believe I know your son."

"Who?" he said.

"Your son, Mr. Rein," the nurse said, tapping him on the outside of his leg through the blanket draped over him. When the IV was free, she lifted the stand and carried it out of his reach. "You know who she's talking about. Don't pretend like you don't."

"What about him?" Ben said. "Is he in jail again?" He coughed several times, hawking a ball of green phlegm into a bowl lying at his side. "I don't have any money for him, so don't ask. When I'm dead, you can sell the damn house and take whatever you get to pay his bail or whatever, but you'll have to wait."

"No," Carrie said, "he's not in any trouble. I'm actually here to speak about something else. A case I'm working on. I was hoping you might be able to help me with it."

He leaned back against his pillow, his large, purple-veined ears sticking out sideways through tufts of white hair. "You must be pretty desperate to come here, thinking I can help you with anything."

"It's about your brother, Ollie. I want to know what happened to him."

"Ollie," the old man said. The hard lines around his eyes and mouth softened. "I don't know what you mean."

Carrie put her hand on Ben's arm. She could feel his bones beneath the desiccated muscle. "Please, sir. I know something happened to him. Before he passed, he was looking for a missing little girl."

"Hope Pugh," Ben said. His eyes reddened and began to run.

"That's right," Carrie said. "Was she friends with your son?"

His eyes burned clear and bright then, as if the fog of illness and medication and being trapped in a bed wearing adult-sized diapers had lifted. "You said you know him?"

"That's right."

"He always knew what I did. That's why he never came back. He always knew, and he never told anyone. He's a good boy. You tell him I said that." His eyes fluttered. He was struggling to breathe.

Carrie moved closer, making sure she didn't miss a word of the old man's strained voice. "What did he know, Mr. Rein?"

"It was me," Ben said. "I'm the one that killed them."

The nurse swept Carrie aside and draped a blanket over Ben's chest. "You hush now, Mr. Ben. You need to get some rest. You're talking all crazy."

He swatted her hands away. "Get the hell away from me! I've been waiting almost forty years to say this, and I'm going to say it. I'm not ashamed of what I done." He glowered at Carrie. "It was me."

The nurse withdrew from the bed, scowling. "It ain't right bothering this man when he's sick and saying stuff he don't mean. I think you need to leave."

Carrie's heart hammered in her chest as she reached forward, wrapping both of her hands over the old man's. His hand was nothing more than a thin sheet of skin, softer than silk, covering gnarled bones and blue, worn-out veins, and it was shaking. "Who did you kill, Mr. Rein?"

"All of them. I killed them all."

II

PEOPLE WHO DIED

CHAPTER 9

*T*he last snow had fallen hard and thick that year, packing tight the moment it hit the ground. It was better than the other snowfalls, which had either been dry powder or wet goop. But this last one was a good one and the boys made use of it.

Adam Kraussen lived less than a mile away from the house where J.D. lived with his father. The Kraussens' place had two floors, with a finished basement, and two bathrooms. Both of Adam's parents had cars. Both of his parents worked. Mr. Kraussen was an engineer, but he spent of most of his free time accumulating things he rarely used. He was the only person in that part of the state who owned a Betamax machine and he swore by it. He would tell anyone who would listen that VHS was inferior. He got in such a huge fight with the people who owned the local video store because they refused to carry Betamax that they banned him for life. After that, Mr. Kraussen purchased every Betamax cassette released, many of which he never watched.

During sleepovers the boys always had a brief argument over which movie they would watch. The animated version of *The Hobbit. Scanners. Star Trek: The Motion Picture.* And when they couldn't decide, they picked *The Empire Strikes Back* and sat next to one another reciting the dialogue, taking turns being different characters, both of them skipping the lines for Princess Leia. They'd watch movies until the sky turned light blue outside, and slept only a little while before Mrs. Kraussen woke them up for a full German breakfast.

During that last snowfall, the good one, they'd taken all of their Star Wars action figures outside and set up an enormous battle in the snow. It had taken hours. Their ritual was to first pile all of their figures and vehicles on the floor of Adam's room and select them for their armies, one at a time. Adam owned nearly all of the figures, possessing his father's knack for collecting. He made lists of everything he owned, and hung pages from the Sears Wish Book on his wall with any of the figures or vehicles he was still missing circled.

J.D. Rein owned two action figures. One of them was a gift from Adam, who'd gotten doubles of a bounty hunter for his birthday. His other figure was a cheap army soldier he'd found in the woods. They'd agreed to allow the soldier to be included in the Star Wars battles, because they were always in need of more bad guys.

After the selection process, they carried their armies outside and set them up. They built snow forts and turrets and dug trenches, placed each figure in the best possible position, and hid them so that they could not be seen by enemy forces. By the time they were ready to start their toy war, it was getting dark. Mrs. Kraussen called them inside for dinner, and as they sat inside eating, Adam glanced out the window and had to adjust his thick glasses at what he saw. He cried out in despair. It was snowing, harder than before. Both of their armies were buried.

It took a full week for the snow to melt enough for them to hunt down their figures. By the time they finished, all of them were accounted for, all tossed back in a pile on Adam's floor, except for the second robot bounty hunter, the only true Star Wars action figure that J.D. possessed. J.D. said the one they'd found was his, because he remembered finding it on his side of the yard. Adam said he remembered which one was his, because it had a specific scratch on the bottom, the same as the one sitting between them.

They argued, until both of them were so angry they were yelling. Mr. Kraussen called upstairs, "Boys, is everything okay?"

"We're fine," Adam called back. He pulled his asthma inhaler out of his right pocket and stuck it in his mouth. He pressed the button and took a deep breath. "You take it," he said, looking down at the pile of toys. "It's not like you have any others, right?"

J.D. snatched his cheap army figure out of the pile, stuffed it in his pocket, and left.

It warmed up on his walk home, in the way that forty-degree weather feels tropical after a long stretch of twenty-degree days and zero-degree nights. J.D. took off his coat and woolen hat, wearing just a T-shirt, enjoying the sun's heat on his neck and exposed arms. He took the main road toward the woods leading back to Patterson, wishing he had brought his Walkman.

It wasn't an official Walkman. It was a cheap Japanese version with a cassette lid that had snapped off long ago. He used a rubber band to keep cassettes from falling out and had to keep switching the batteries around because the tape would start playing slower as they ran out. Switching them around helped for a little while. He'd tried leaving them in the refrigerator overnight, but that had only made it worse. The batteries would have to last, though. It was always a long time before he'd be able to find new ones.

He'd left the Walkman at home because he had more need of it there, where he could cover his ears with his headphones and turn the volume up as loud as it would go, to help block out everything else. Here on the road, where it was quiet, he didn't need music. He just wanted it to keep him company, to make him forget the hurtful thing his friend had said, to help him ignore the stupid, deformed action figure in his pocket and the better one he was now missing.

J.D. crossed to the other side of the street to go around the last house on the main road, keeping his head down as he walked. A group of boys was gathered around a tall oak tree. Several were up high in the tree, hidden by its branches, and two others clung to the bottom, trying to make their way up. J.D. did not see either of the Eubanks boys, the ones who lived there, but he kept moving anyway. Not running. That would have been too obvious and would draw attention. He lowered his head and walked fast.

He made it halfway past the house before they saw him. "Hey, faggot, where's your girlfriend, the Four-Eyed Freak?" Little Ritchie Eubanks, the younger brother, cried. He made wheezing sounds like he was choking to death, feinting one of Adam's asthma attacks, and the others cackled.

J.D. scanned the road ahead, assessing how far he was from the woods. The boys were on the other side of the street. Most of them were high enough up in the tree that if they tried coming after him, he had time to run. He would toss his jacket and hat and break for the woods. There was going to be hell to pay if he came home without either item, and even greater hell to pay if he admitted he'd tossed them while running from a fight, but he decided it was worth it. He'd come back and look for them after it got dark. Or maybe he'd get lucky and the warm weather would last and he wouldn't need them again.

Someone high up in the tree called out to him in a deeper voice that silenced all of the others. "Hey, J.D., come over here." Fred Eubanks was fourteen years old and already had the beginnings of a mustache. He was muscular, taller than the other boys in his grade, let alone the ones he hung out with, who were closer to J.D.'s age. He wrestled for the school team and had been so good at such a young age that other parents wouldn't let their children wrestle him. In sixth grade, his junior high coach had to send him to practice with the high school's junior varsity team. He'd heard stories about Eubanks threatening to break people's necks with a chokehold, and with no adults around to intervene, J.D. had no doubt he could do it.

J.D. looked at him from across the road, peering at his massive form in the upper reaches of the tree. "What's up?" he said. The other kids had stopped laughing, even stopped moving, doing nothing but stare at J.D.

"I just want to talk to you," Eubanks said, spreading his thick arms across the branches. "Come over here. I want to ask you about something."

"About what?"

"How about you stop being such a little chickenshit and get over here, before I come down and drag you."

Little Ritchie laughed his high-pitched, squealing laugh, and the rest snickered. J.D. turned his head, looking at the woods.

"I'm just messing with you," Eubanks said, smiling at him, spreading the layer of black silky hair across his upper lip. "You walk past here all the time, always going to hang out with Adam, but you never stop and say hi to us. What's wrong, we not good enough for you? Come hang out with us for a minute. I need to ask you something."

J.D. scratched the side of his face, looking at how many of them he could see; tucked his coat under his arm; and crossed the street toward them. The boys at the bottom of the tree climbed upward, pulled up by their friends who reached down to give them a hoist.

They were assembled in the branches like bats by the time J.D. made his way to the base of the tree. Looking up, he covered his eyes to shield them from the overhead sun. He could see Fred Eubanks standing on a branch high above him, and raised his head to say, "What did you want to ask me?"

In the glistening sun, he saw it before he realized what it was. Eubanks had his fingers wrapped around his penis, bulbous and reddened, sticking out through the zipper of his jeans. "Think it's going to rain?" Eubanks snickered as a hot stream of piss sprayed down in a wide arc, aimed at J.D.'s face.

J.D. managed to raise his hand and look away in time to keep it from going in his mouth. He felt the side of his face and his arm and the side of his shirt and back go wet. The laughter above him was loud and screeching. They choked on it. They clung to one another and nearly fell out of the tree, screaming, "Piss Face" as he ran.

By the time he reached the edge of the woods, J.D. was shivering with cold. His entire body ached from running. Every time he inhaled, he was overwhelmed by the ammonia stench of urine soaked into his clothing. Worse, the rest of him was wet now too, from running through the damp woods. His socks squished every time he walked, and his sneakers and his jeans from the knees down were covered in mud.

He didn't dare put on his coat and hat and contaminate them, too. He ducked behind a tree, made sure no one was coming after him, and scooped up two handfuls of dirty snow from the ground. He ran the snow through his hair and smeared it down his neck, then used a pile of wet leaves to clean off his arm and hand as much as he could. The leaves left streaks across his skin and smelled of damp earth, but he didn't care. It was better than the alternative.

The leaves blew away from his fingers in the rising wind. His whole head was wet now. He shook it and ran his fingers through it, trying to brush away as much of the snowy slush as he could. He shivered, clutching his arms around his body for warmth.

He walked around the back of the houses near his, having nowhere else to go. He was less than a mile away from home, but there was no way he could go there. He thought about his uncle's house, which was not far away, either, but that was also an impossibility. Ollie Rein would take one look at the boy and ask questions the boy did not want to answer. Even if he was somehow convinced not to tell J.D.'s father, he would most definitely go find the boys who'd done it and deliver them a reckoning.

As much as that idea warmed him inside, he knew that would not be the end of it. Fred Eubanks wasn't the type to be humbled by a reprimand, no matter how severe, and especially one that came in front of his friends or parents. The next time, he would hurt J.D. permanently.

A woman who was cooking dinner in the back of her house saw J.D. in her backyard. He leapt behind the nearest tree and hustled deeper into the woods, getting out of sight of her windows. It was getting dark, and he could see his breath frosting in the cold air with every breath. He was miserable with cold, constantly blowing into his hands. He would have tucked them inside his T-shirt if it weren't still wet and stinking.

He walked until he saw a clearing ahead. Some bricks, piled into a makeshift chimney. Branches were stacked across the bottom, wound with cords of rope that would help them burn when lit. He considered trying to make his own fire using sticks and dry grass like they did in the movies, but as he looked around, everything was damp.

He sat on the wet earth next to the chimney and lowered his head to his arms, no longer caring about the odor soaked into his clothes. A few feet away, a branch snapped against the ground, and J.D.'s head shot up. Someone was coming toward him. He struggled to get to his feet, fearing the boys had followed him, but before he could run, a girl, the same age as him, stepped into the clearing.

Her bright red hair was like a flame in the darkness sticking out from under the hood of her winter coat. J.D. scrambled to get behind the chimney, trying to put it between himself and her. Hope Pugh stopped on the other side of the chimney, looking down at J.D.'s coat and hat that he'd forgotten in his rush to get up, and folded her arms against her chest. "J.D. Rein, what are you doing out here lurking around in the woods, in the cold, with no coat and hat on?"

"I was too hot," he said, feeling the goose flesh riddled across both of his arms.

"You are soaking wet!" She bent down to pick up his coat and hat and thrust them out at him. "Put these on before you catch pneumonia."

He didn't reach for them. Hope came around the corner to insist again, only to stop, curling her nose in disgust. "Did you pee yourself?"

"No, I didn't pee myself. You see my hair and shirt's all wet, you think I peed all over my shirt?"

"It smells like somebody peed," she said, sniffing the air. She raised his coat and pressed it to her nose.

"Just give me those," J.D. said, snatching the coat and hat out of her hands. He was shivering, but still not putting them on.

Hope looked at his dirty arms and muddy clothes and shoes. "Was somebody chasing you?"

"Nobody was chasing me, you dumb girl," J.D. said. "Get on home."

"You get on home. This is my property."

"I can't, okay?" he said. "Can't you just go away, please? I won't touch anything."

"Okay, then, wait here a minute." Hope ran off, going back the way she'd come. Through the trees, J.D. saw a light come on in the back of her house and heard a screen door slam. Moments later, the light went off, and the screen door slammed again. She hurried back, carrying a laundry basket filled with items.

She dropped the basket at the chimney and said, "Put these on," reaching inside it for a gray sweatshirt and a pair of sweatpants. "They're my dad's so they're going to be big on you. Just roll them up." She handed him a balled-up pair of white socks after that, then pulled out a thick green military blanket. She spread the blanket out in front of the chimney, then reached in her pocket and pulled out a plastic lighter. She bent down to the pile of sticks, about to light them, when she looked over her shoulder and saw that he hadn't moved. "What are you doing? Get out of those wet clothes," she said.

"Am I supposed to just take off my clothes with you right here?" he said.

"I'm not looking, idiot," she said, turning back to the branches. She stuck her lighter under them and flicked it, letting the flame scorch one of the ends of rope until it began to smolder.

J.D. went around back of her, slid into the shadows, and pulled off his T-shirt as fast as he could, trying to get it over the top of his head with as little of it touching him as possible. He found another patch of snow, scooped it up with one hand, and smeared as much of it along his sides and stomach and back as he could endure. It was freezing cold, running down his skin like razor blades. He gasped when he got the sweatshirt on, feeling its immediate warmth.

He pulled off his pants and socks, standing on them in his bare feet as he hurried into the sweatpants and pulled on the fresh pair of socks. He stood there, arms buried inside the sweatshirt's long sleeves, still shivering, but no longer in pain from the cold.

The fire in the chimney took, a ball of flame forming inside its open brick belly. Hope came over to him, pulling the blanket close enough that he could stand on it instead of the bare ground. "Get over by the fire and warm up," she said.

He wrapped his arms around himself, standing so close to the fire he could feel it searing his skin, and watched her kick his clothing around in the snow. She stomped on them, squishing them under the snow, then dragged them with her foot into even more snow, making sure they were soaked completely through. She picked up his shirt and pants and socks and shoes and carried them over to the chimney and draped them across its back, hanging them to dry.

She came up beside him on the blanket and sat down, watching the flames. J.D. lowered himself to sit next to her, feeling the fire's warmth spread across his cheeks and outstretched hands. Hope reached into the laundry basket for the last thing, a stuffed bear. She pulled it out and tucked it under her arm, then looked at J.D. and held it out toward him. "Do you want it?"

"No," he scowled. "Why would I want that?"

"Are you hungry? My mom made pot roast and we have leftovers."

"I'm okay."

"I don't like it. That's why we have so much of it left. Do you like pot roast?"

J.D. shrugged. "I don't know. What is it?"

"What do you mean what is it? You never ate it?"

"Sure," J.D. said. "All the time. I just wasn't sure what you meant. That's all."

Hope frowned at him, then looked back at the flames. "What do you like to eat for dinner?"

"Sometimes we order pizza. When my dad gets his check."

"I wish we ordered pizza," Hope said, "instead of that dumb pot roast."

J.D.'s stomach growled loud enough that they both heard it. They looked at one another, and both of them laughed.

Hope got to her feet. "I'm going to get some food for us." She tucked her bear into J.D.'s lap without giving him a chance to resist. "Hold that. Be careful with him."

He watched her vanish into the darkness again. It was so warm by the fire his hair was drying. His clothes smelled like burning wood now. Cleansed by heat and smoke. He looked at the distant light of Hope's house when it came on. When he was sure no one would see, he picked the bear up and squeezed it tight.

CHAPTER 10

*I*t was noon before Ollie Rein got his first radio call of the day. He'd had his usual breakfast at Ruby's—toast and sausage and runny eggs—and managed to not spill any on his uniform. Like every morning, the customers at the counter greeted him by name, and he'd spent an hour drinking coffee, talking to the local truckers and out-of-work union men.

After he ate, he drove his police car, a 1980 Plymouth Gran Fury, painted bright blue with a gold star on the side, through the town's main strip, waving at everyone he saw. They knew it was him, because both of Liston's police cars were tan, and their chief made his officers wear their cowboy hats at all times. The poor bastards even had to wear their cowboy hats in the car. Ollie loved to hit the siren whenever they drove past. It always made them turn their heads to look, and they'd whack the stiff brim of their hats against the car window. The way it made their heads bounce made Ollie laugh.

The police radio squawked. Ollie picked up the microphone, holding it close to his face. "Well, good morning, Pretty Lady, I thought you forgot about me today. What do you got, something good?"

The woman's voice in the speaker purred, "Good morning, handsome. Just a two-car fender bender at the beer store. No injuries."

"Copy that," he said, hanging the microphone back up.

It squawked again. "We're getting another call on this, from inside the store. Stand by."

He reached forward, pressing the microphone's button while it was still holstered, "Received."

"One of the customers inside the beer store heard the crash and got spooked."

Ollie looked at the radio without touching it.

"Owner says he started yelling and grabbed one of the employees and dragged him into the back room. Now the door's shut and he won't come out."

Ollie closed his eyes, cursing under his breath. He hit the Plymouth's overhead lights and spun the car around, kicking up road dirt as the people on the sidewalk leaned back, waving the cloud of dust from in front of their faces. "Sorry," Ollie called out to them, spinning the heavy wheel to get the car righted, and stepped on the gas.

The beer store was at the other end of town. He made it there in less than a minute, swung into the lot and jumped out of the car, then walked toward the building. Two people ran toward him from the place where their cars were smashed together. He could see shattered glass from one of their busted-out rear windshields. Hot radiator fluid hissed onto the parking lot stones.

"This moron came out of nowhere and hit me!" the woman said.

"Give me a minute," Ollie said, still walking.

"She was backing up and didn't see me in her rearview mirror," the man protested. "She hit me! Hey!"

"I said give me a minute!" Ollie snapped, thrusting his finger in the air. He pulled the beer store's door open and reached down to quiet the heavy brass bells clanging against its glass surface. He stood at the entrance looking around the store. A stack of six-packs had been knocked over near the office door. A few bottles were broken and leaking on the cement floor.

"Help!" the owner cried, waving his hands in the air. "This crazy bastard's got my boy in there. Kick the door open and shoot this

son of a bitch." He slammed his fist on the door. "Open up, you psycho looney! I'm going to kill you when I get my hands on you."

Ollie grabbed the smaller man by the shoulders and pulled him away. "Shhh. That's enough. Let me handle this."

"My boy!" the owner protested. "That maniac has him!"

"It's going to be all right," Ollie said. "Just go stand over there and let me talk." He walked the smaller man backward toward the front counter and showed him where to stand. He made his way over to the office and pressed his ear against the door. "Ben?" he said through the door. "It's Ollie. You okay in there?"

He could hear the owner's son inside, pleading to be let go. He could hear another voice saying, "Don't make a sound. It's almost over. Everything's going to be all right."

"Ben?" Ollie said again. "We're ten-four out here. It was just a car crash. That's what made the loud noise. It wasn't a bomb or any kind of explosion. Just two people who don't know how to drive. Open the door and come out, and I'll show you."

"This fucking maniac can never come in my store again!" the owner shouted from across the room.

Ollie glared back at him, making a fist. He turned back to the door. "Ben, that kid in there is the owner's son. He works here. He's not someone you know. Listen, that kid's dad is worried about him. You're scaring people. You need to open this door and come out. It's me, Ollie. I promise, everything is all right."

Nothing except the sound of more pleading inside. Ollie hung his head, racking his brain. There was only one thing left to try. He stepped back, hiking up his gun belt with both hands, and stuck out his chest, shouting, "Now you listen to me you wet sack of raw recruit shit! Soldier, you will get your sorry ass out of that goddamn office before I personally put you on twenty-four-hour bathroom detail after franks and beans Friday! Do you read me, you lily-livered pissant?"

After a soft mechanical click of the door handle, the door burst open. A young man came sprinting out past Ollie, racing toward his father's open arms. Ollie ducked his head inside the office, peering beneath the large wooden desk. His older brother was squished beneath it, his knees tucked under his chin, shivering, sweat dripping off his chin and the long, loose strands of hair dangling over his face. Ollie bent down, gentle once more. "You okay now?"

When Ben didn't move, Ollie reached forward, slowly, and touched him on the arm. "Come on, let's get you home."

As Ben came out from under the desk, he blinked rapidly, like a man coming to out of a trance. Ollie helped him to his feet and led him out of the office, past the owner, who was now shouting, "Who's paying for all this?" He waved his hands at the broken six-packs. "I want to press charges!"

"I'll come back and we'll sort all this out," Ollie said, leading his brother toward the front door. "Just give me a little bit."

He opened the door, and the people near their cars shouted at him once more, each trying to tell him it was the other's fault. Ollie put his hand up. "I'm dealing with a medical emergency here. Start writing down each other's information, and I'll come back and take some pictures." He added, "I'll only be a few minutes," then opened the passenger-side door to sit Ben down, closed it, and hurried over to the driver's side.

When Ollie got in and started driving, Ben closed his eyes. "I still need beer."

"Well, you can forget the beer," Ollie said. "You won't be going back there anytime soon."

"Take me to the liquor store, then."

"I'm taking you home," Ollie said.

Ben ran his hand through his long, unevenly cut hair, feeling how wet it was between his fingers. He ran his hand along his eyes, rubbing them, and stared out the window. "You'd have made a pretty good drill instructor," he said.

"You think so?" Ben said.

"If you hadn't been a secretary instead."

Ollie rolled his eyes. "Here we go again."

Ben kept staring at the window, watching the outside world sweep past. "It's all right. Lucky for you, they needed people who knew how to type. I wish I'd known how to type."

* * *

Ollie followed Ben through the front door, steering him by the shoulder, making sure he didn't stumble. "Get off me," Ben said, swatting his hand away. "I'm not some goddamn invalid."

Ollie surveyed the living room. Trash was everywhere. A line of empty beer and liquor bottles circled the couch, from the back wall to the soiled throw rug under the table. "Have a seat," Ollie said. "I'll make you some food."

Ben staggered to the couch and sat. "Find me a beer. Check the bottom drawers."

"Where's the kid?"

A bottle emerged from between the couch cushions in Ben's hands. Ben tipped the dregs of amber fluid into his mouth, working his lips until he drained the bottle.

Ollie walked into the kitchen. Dishes were stacked in the sink, covered in sauce that looked glued to their surface, sitting in filthy water. He opened the refrigerator door and saw bare shelves.

He slammed the door shut so hard the wall rattled. "What the hell is this?" he shouted.

Ben was slumped over the side of the couch, checking the rest of the bottles. Ollie kicked a whisky bottle out of his hand, sending it spiraling under the couch. Ben's eyes narrowed as he looked up at his younger brother.

"Where is all the goddamn food in this house? What are you feeding J.D.?"

Ben pressed himself up from the couch, glaring. "You mind your own business about my house and my boy."

Ollie touched the badge on his shirt. "This is my business. I'm the chief of police around here. One word, I'll have social services yank him out of this house. You understand me?"

"Good," Ben said. "Take him."

"You really are a son of a bitch, you know that? And it's not the war, or your wife dying. You were a son of a bitch before any of that, even when we were kids."

Ben sat back down on the couch and searched through the rest of the bottles, one or two weren't completely empty.

Ollie went toward the stairs, stopping at the hallway to call out, "J.D.? You up there?" Faint music came from one of the bedrooms. As he walked up the steps, the screen door slammed and he saw Ben heading outside, walking toward the street. Ollie kept going up the steps. "J.D.? It's your favorite uncle."

The music shut off. Ollie heard something drag across the hardwood floor. Something heavy was slid from behind the door and pressed up against the wall. The door opened. J.D. stuck his head out. "You're my only uncle."

Ollie pressed the door open with the tips of his fingers and looked down, seeing the deep groove marks in the floor that led to the heavy wooden clothes dresser. It was cockeyed from not being pushed back into place properly. "Just because I'm your only one doesn't mean I shouldn't also be your favorite," Ollie said. Seeing a stack of books on the dresser, all of them from the school library, he picked up the first one and looked at the cover. It showed a knight on horseback with his sword drawn. "*Le Morte d'Artur*?" Ollie said, feeling how thick it was. "They make you read this at your age?"

"It's not for school," J.D. muttered, sitting down on his bed. He was surrounded by comic books, all of them with the covers cut in half. Any paperback books in the room had no covers. That was the way the used book store sold them.

"Is it any good?" Ollie asked.

"Not as good as *Once and Future King*, but pretty good," J.D. said.

Ollie scruffed his hair. "You're such a weird kid. That must be why I like you." He nudged the dresser back against the wall, getting it into place. "What are you doing tonight?"

"Nothing," J.D. said. "Just hanging out. Reading."

"Wrong. You're coming with me. Get dressed."

J.D. looked down at his clothes. "I'm already dressed, and I have school tomorrow."

The boy's pants were stained and showed his bony ankles in the space between the hem and his ragged sneakers. Ollie pulled open the first dresser drawer and saw it was empty. He didn't bother checking the rest. "Come on, kid. We're getting out of here."

Ollie picked up the police radio's microphone and was about to press the button when he looked at J.D., sitting delighted in the front seat, staring at all the buttons that worked the lights and siren and radio. He handed the microphone to the boy and said, "Here, you try."

J.D. took the microphone. "What do I say?"

"Well, first you have to make sure someone is there, so you call in. When they answer, that's when you know it's okay to talk."

J.D. pressed the button and the microphone beeped. "Hello?" he said hesitatingly. He looked at Ollie. "Like that?"

"Not quite," Ollie said. "For one thing, you have to let them know who you are. Say something like, Chief Rein to Dispatch. But here's the thing. My dispatcher, she's kind of finicky, so you have to sweet-talk her a little."

"How?" J.D. scowled.

"Call her Pretty Lady."

"No way."

"I'm telling you, that's how you do it. Chief Rein to Dispatch, come in, Pretty Lady. Go ahead, you can do it."

J.D. swallowed uncomfortably, then pressed the button on the microphone and repeated his uncle's words, giggling at the end so hard he could barely spit them all out.

"Attaboy," Ollie said, grinning.

The radio beeped on the dashboard and a woman said, "You sound a whole lot younger, handsome. Must be all that clean living. By the way, that beer store owner's been calling nonstop and those two people from the car crash are still waiting on you to come back and take their report."

Ollie looked at his nephew. "What do you think? You want to come do some police work with me?"

"Yeah!"

"Hell no," Ollie said, taking the microphone from him. "Trust me, kid, police work sucks." He pressed the button and said, "Afraid

I won't be able to respond, Pretty Lady. Something else came up. Put the State Police on call for the rest of the night, including those two calls we have holding."

The radio beeped again. "State Police are going to take a while to respond. I'm guessing you don't want me to ask Liston PD to handle the beer store and the crash?"

"Nope," Ollie responded. "You go ahead and have yourself a good night."

"You do the same, handsome. And you tell that little passenger you got with you that if he keeps on talking sweet like that to the girls, he'll have them chasing him around in no time."

Ollie hung up the microphone and clapped his hands together. "We got the rest of the night to ourselves, my man. You hungry? I'm hungry. Let's go get something to eat, but first I have to stop by my place. That all right with you?"

"Is that your girlfriend?"

"Who?" Ollie said. "On the radio?"

"Yeah."

"Nah," Ollie said, scowling. "That's just play talk. For all I know, she could be a hundred years old."

"You've never met her?"

"Never," Ollie said. "She works at the county radio, and we're the only borough too cheap to pay for our own dispatcher. I think she gets bored up there, so we kid around. Keeps the day going by for both of us, I guess."

"She called you handsome. Maybe she's seen a picture of you or something."

Ollie looked at himself in the rearview mirror, running his fingers down his chin. "That's because I am. Look at this face. You don't think so?"

J.D. looked out the window. People took notice of the police car. Some of them looked worried to see it. Others waved and told their children to wave too. J.D. waved back at them.

They drove across town to Ollie's house, a small rancher on bare dirt. It was out past the steel mill, where most of the people in town worked, but the lot was only half filled with cars anymore.

Every year, more people were getting pink slips, and the employ-ees who remained were told to do more with less or they'd be next.

Ollie parked his police car in the driveway and said, "When's the last time you were here?"

"Before school started," J.D. said, closing the car door.

"Didn't we agree you'd be coming over on the weekends more often?" Ollie asked, unlocking the door and holding it open for the boy. "We did, and then I had to work a few times, and you had things going on a few times, and it just got away from us. That's what life is like, I guess. The important stuff gets away from you when you are busy worried about all the other shit. Hey, look at me."

J.D. didn't pull away when Ollie cupped him under the chin. "We are going to do a better job of this from now on, okay?"

"Okay," J.D. said.

"Let me get changed, and then me and you are heading into town. You want Chinese? Pizza? Steak? You name it. We'll hit the arcade, see if there's any movies playing, whatever you want. How does that sound?"

"I told you, I have school tomorrow."

"So what? Let's live a little."

J.D. could see his uncle pulling off his leather gun belt and hanging it on his bedpost in his bedroom. Ollie unbuttoned his police shirt and tossed it into the hamper, then slid off his pants and let them lie on the floor. He grabbed a pair of faded blue jeans and a flannel shirt and sat down on the bed, sliding his feet into a pair of worn cowboy boots.

He stood up, ran his fingers through his brown hair, and snapped his fingers. "I'd say this is a special occasion, me and you getting to hang out on a school night. Wouldn't you?"

"I guess so," J.D. said.

"Come in here a second."

J.D. went into the room and stopped at the door. Ollie's bed-room looked different from the rest of his house. Every other room was clean and sparse, but the bedroom was packed with clothes and boxes.

A stack of books on the nightstand caught the boy's eye. Second-hand textbooks with titles like *Basic Criminal Investigations* and *Survive Your Shift.* J.D. picked one up called *Homicide 101* and flipped through it. The first picture was a dead woman with both her breasts chopped off. He gasped and slammed it shut, slapping it back down on top of the other books, then deciding it belonged farther down, buried it where no one could see it.

Ollie was rummaging in his closet and reached up to grab something hidden behind a stack of clothes on the highest shelf. He pulled down a shoebox and laid it on the bed, looking down at it. When he pulled off the lid, it was stuffed with bundles of cash.

Ollie pulled up a stack of twenties, fanned it with his thumb, counting off two hundred dollars, and set the money on the bed. "What do you want to be when you grow up?" Ollie said.

"I don't know. I'm only twelve."

"You must have some kind of dream. You want to be a business-man? An accountant? A lawyer? What interests you?"

"My dad says I'm going in the army as soon as I turn seven-teen."

"What about finishing school?"

"He says it's not important."

"And what do you say?"

"I guess army's okay." J.D. shrugged. "You get a cool uniform, and you defend your country."

Ollie stuffed the loose cash into his pocket and set the lid back on the shoebox, then placed it into the closet once more. He bent down on one knee to face J.D. and said, "I'm gonna tell you something nobody admits to, but it's true, so listen up. The entire thing is a goddamn lie. The army loves to tell people they're pro-tecting American freedom. That when a soldier gets killed, he's protecting American citizens. Absolute bullshit. When I was in Vietnam, there wasn't a single goddamn Viet Cong getting any-where close to the United States. Not in a million years. Neither were any of the Koreans in the Korean War. Or anywhere else in any of the dozens of shitstorms we've been involved with over the past ten years. Soldiers aren't protecting anything except the interests of people with money. You understand that?"

J.D. said he did, but his uncle could see that he didn't. "It's like this," Ollie said. "Some rich guy decides he needs a particular hill because it has gold, or oil, or whatever. Now, they need young men willing to take that hill, even if it means most of them getting blown up and mutilated. The only way to get those young men to do that is fill their heads will all sorts of horseshit. So, you, my friend, are not joining the army. You're too smart for that."

J.D. followed his uncle outside, heading for the beat-up Ford pickup parked around back. "You were in the army. You're smart," J.D. said, climbing in.

"That was different. I wound up working in the clerical department for a command unit. Typing up all their orders." Ollie turned the key, making the engine sputter and cough. "Come on," he said, turning the key and stepping on the gas. "Every day I'd see them telling the field officers to send boys out to infiltrate some village, knowing it was suicide. I'm talking about kids. Eighteen years old. Kids who hadn't lived long enough to ever come off their family farms, or kiss a girl, all of a sudden getting blown up in some rice paddy in Vietnam, all because some goddamn colonel wants a village, or some rich guy wants a hill. I'll be goddamned if they'll ever do that to you, J.D. That box of money in there, you know what that is?"

J.D. looked at the condition of the truck they were sitting in. "Money for a new truck?"

Ollie laughed. "Smart-ass. That's your future. I've been saving it for you. Every week, I put some in there so I don't spend it. You want to go to school, you want to be a plumber, you want to become a master carpenter, whatever it is, you'll get to do it. There's only one thing I ask. Do something you love and be the best you can be at it. The worst sin in this whole world is having a talent and not using it, especially if it's something the rest of us need. Understand?"

"I understand," J.D. said.

"All right," Ollie said, cranking the engine once more and getting it rumbling. "Now, enough of all that. Let's eat."

Ollie dropped the gearshift into drive and pulled out onto the road. "Look out, world. The night is young, we've got money in our pocket, and the Rein boys are coming!" Ollie rolled down his window, stuck his face into the gust of cool air, then threw back his head and howled like a wolf.

J.D. laughed, then rolled down his own window, feeling the blast of wind blowing back his hair, chilling his gums around his wide, gaping smile, and he howled and howled as loud as he could, his thin wolf voice ringing out into the night sky.

CHAPTER 11

*T*he school bus rocked side to side through the morning fog. It was dark and the woods all around swirled with the kind of mist monsters sprang forth from. J.D. leaned his head against the cool window, imagining what monsters were creeping through the fog alongside the bus, sniffing the children inside it, hungering for them. His new coat was thick and warm and cushioned his body against the window's metal frame. He swung his feet under the seat in front of him, looking at his new sneakers. Their thick laces were tied in double knots.

The song in his head would not stop playing. He could imagine knights in brightly polished armor racing after the bus, their horses thundering while *Carmina Burana* boomed throughout the woods. The monsters in the woods snapped their jaws and whipped their shaggy heads, but it was too late. The knights ran them down, swords and lances flashing, spraying the fog with bright red mist.

The bus hissed to a stop in front of Adam's house. Adam climbed up the steps, searching the open seats as he made his way down the aisle. The seat next to J.D. was empty. Others were open, but Adam slid into the seat beside him, and neither of them spoke.

The front door closed and the bus rumbled forward. Adam reached into his coat's front pocket and pulled out his inhaler, taking as deep a breath as he could.

J.D. waited for him to recap his inhaler. "I saw *Excalibur* with my uncle last night."

Adam's eyes went wide behind his glasses. "You're kidding. Lucky!"

"It was radical," J.D. said.

Adam slid his inhaler back into his pocket and came out with something else, cupping it with his hand. "Here," he said, holding up one of the bounty hunter action figures.

"You found mine?" J.D. said, taking it into his hands.

Adam pushed his glasses back up to the center of his nose and ignored the question. "So tell me about *Excalibur*. What was the best part?"

J.D. waved the figure like a sword, made sound effects with his mouth, and described the battles and grandeur. For both of them, it was as if they were surrounded by those knights riding alongside the bus, or even among them, clad in armor, rushing toward great evil.

Oliver Rein slid into the front seat of his police car, leaned his head back and groaned. The sun was too bright. He lowered the visor and put on his sunglasses, still needing to squint as he picked up the radio mic. "Good morning, Pretty Lady," he said.

"Good afternoon, I think you mean," she replied. "I wasn't sure we'd hear from you today. I thought maybe you'd hand things over to the State Police permanently, and we'd set up a taco stand."

"Tacos," Ollie said. "I'd give anything for some tacos right now. They got them out where you are?"

"There's a place not far from the radio room. We go there after work sometimes. You ought to stop by if you're ever out this way."

"I'll keep that in mind," Ollie said. "You got any calls holding?"

"Mr. Duggan called in to say his horses got loose, again, but then he called back and said he'd been able to round them up. That was it."

"Another day in the big city," Ollie said, putting the car in gear.

"Should I log you on as in service?"

"Not yet. I'm going to swing by Ruby's and see if they can

round me up some tacos. I doubt it, but it's worth a shot. Want me to bring you anything?"

"What do they have that's good?"

"Ruby makes her own cakes and pies, fresh, every day. She's famous for them."

"I'd kill for a slice of pie," she said.

"Someday, you're gonna look up from your radio and see me standing there holding a whole pie, just for you."

"You do that, I might have to marry you."

Ollie laughed and said, "Don't tempt me. You aren't that far away from here."

He hung up his microphone and turned up the volume on the local police scanner, housed beneath the county radio. It scanned the surrounding areas, and all of them were silent. That was all right, he thought. If there was any radio chatter, it would be from Liston police pulling over trucks along the highway. Nothing those cowboy hat–wearing nitwits liked better than wrecking the life of some poor, dumb trucker who was hauling too much weight. A single ticket for an overweight truck could be hundreds of dollars. Most times, the trucker had no idea what was being loaded on. Their bosses told them, "Haul this," and they hitched it up and drove off.

Ollie had seen Walt Auburn high-fiving other cops like they'd just scored a touchdown on the side of the road, after giving out tickets that wrecked hardworking men's lives. He'd seen truckers sitting in the dirt, heads down, trying not to let anyone see them cry.

That wasn't Ollie's type of police work, and he'd made no secret about it. He loved to remind Walt of all the times some cop had been getting his ass kicked on a car stop, and a random trucker jumped out to help. Not that it made a difference to Walt Auburn.

Ollie tapped his fingers on the door's armrest, singing to himself. He did his best singing alone in the patrol car. The borough had been too cheap to put an AM/FM radio in the police car when they bought it, but that was all right. Radio stations didn't get much out that way, except for a gospel station and talk show channels about agriculture and the weather. Ollie liked country music. Not the slick, tasseled, sequined shit coming out of Nashville, either. He liked what they called outlaw country. Songs about robbing banks and liquor. Low-down women. Gunfighter ballads and songs about the wide-open spaces on the trail and road.

Ollie drove down the main strip into the center of town, waving at the people who waved to him and also at the ones who didn't. He pulled along the curb in front of Ruby's Diner, behind a beat-up black motorcycle with ape hanger handlebars. Four more bikes were parked in front of it. None of them were the shiny weekend warrior bikes ridden by accountants and lawyers who wanted to feel badass in between business meetings and tennis matches. These were hard-use bikes, with fat gas tanks and saddlebags, designed to haul ass over a long period of time, carrying whatever could be stuffed down inside those bags.

Ollie looked through the diner's front window and saw five men in filthy denim vests, all bearing the same design on its back. A grim reaper with red eyes holding an M-16. Over the head of each grim reaper, an arch bearing the words *The Disgraced,* and underneath each one, another arch that said *Pittsburgh.*

"Shit," Ollie muttered to himself, walking past the bikes and opening the diner's door.

The voices inside the diner ceased as he entered. The bikers were seated in front of him at the counter, with stools open on either side of them. The normal diners who'd have been there were scattered around the rest of the tables, each of them looking at Ollie, while he looked at the bikers, trying to get a feel for them before they did the same to him. Ruby looked up from behind the counter and said, "Good morning, Chief. You want breakfast?"

The bikers glanced back, peering at him over their shoulders. A few wore full beards. In the middle was a dark-skinned one, completely bald from the collar up, without any eyebrows or even eyelashes, staring back at Ollie. The biker seated to the left was the only one who turned completely around. His stool squeaked as he spun, holding his mug of coffee under his narrow, braided beard. He had short, spiked hair, and tattoos up and down both arms. "Look out, boys," the man said, his voice a slow, measured drawl. "It's the law." He raised his mug to Ollie and smiled.

The rest of them chuckled, then turned back to their food, lowering their heads and eating.

Ollie studied the patches on the front of the man's vest, reading them like the language they were meant to be written in. The lowest patch was a US Army insignia, followed by a large letter *C* and one that read *20th*. It was all biker bullshit, as far as Ollie was concerned. They always used infantile codes, important to no one but themselves. Ollie told himself to be cool. It wasn't uncommon for veterans to come home and join motorcycle clubs. Especially after the war. Hell, the very first motorcycle clubs had been founded by World War II fighter pilot veterans.

The *President* patch on the man's right side explained his calm demeanor. He was in charge, and comfortable with it, unbothered by Ollie's appearance as he sipped his coffee. When he lowered his hand, Ollie saw the patch he'd been looking for. The only one that mattered. A small diamond-shaped emblem that read *1%*.

The story had been repeated at every single Outlaw Motorcycle Gang training seminar Ollie had attended. Back in the forties the head of the American Motorcycle Association was asked about the bad apples infesting the burgeoning motorcycle enthusiast scene. He had replied that 99 percent of riders were law-abiding citizens. From that point on, the remaining 1 percent made it their business to let you know they weren't.

The president set his coffee back down on the counter and wiped his hands on his greasy jeans, still looking at Ollie. "Am I in your spot?"

"No," Ollie said. He moved toward the empty stool, not sitting on it, and said, "I'll just take a coffee."

"You want that to go?" Ruby asked, seeing that he wasn't sitting down.

The rest of the men in the diner were watching him, wondering if he'd leave them alone with the newcomers. "No," Ollie said, looking at the narrow distance between his stool and the biker. His holster and gun were going to be right under the man's arm, close enough to grab, and even easier to lean down on, making it impossible for the gun to be drawn if needed. "Of course not. I'm sure these gentlemen won't mind if I sit next to them."

"Not in the slightest, sir," the president said, inching over in his stool so Ollie could sit.

Ollie laid his right hand over the handle of his revolver and the holster strap, keeping it secured, and used his left hand to pick up the coffee mug Ruby set down in front of him. "You boys on your way somewhere?" he said.

"Just taking in the sights," the president replied.

"Afraid there's not much to be seen around here," Ollie said, looking at him.

The man extended his hand. "I didn't catch your name, Chief."

Ollie looked at the offered hand, still keeping his own over his gun. "I apologize, friend, but I caught some poison ivy, and you don't want it."

"Hell of a thing, catching poison ivy in February, ain't it?"

"Hell of a thing," Ollie agreed. He set his coffee down and wiped his mouth with his napkin. "I'm Chief Rein, but mostly everyone calls me Ollie."

The man smiled, his teeth sharp and misshapen. "Pleased to meet you, Ollie. Everyone calls me Wombat."

Ollie saw the rest of them were wearing US Army patches on the front of their vests, alongside American flags, some of them upside down, and their arms were heavily inked with wartime tattoos. "Were all you boys overseas?"

"That's right," Wombat said, and the others nodded. "How about you?"

"I was there from '67 to '69," Ollie said.

"You don't say. Army? Whereabouts? Hell, we might know each other and not even realize it."

"I doubt it," Ollie said.

"Why's that? Were you some kind of hotshot?"

"No. I was at Long Binh. Command staff support," Ollie said. The men were all looking at him. "I was basically a secretary."

Wombat was the first to snicker, which set off a chain of laughter from the rest of the bikers, until they were doubled over, holding their stomachs. "I'm sorry," Wombat said, shielding his mouth with his hand, still laughing. "Ollie, it's good to meet you, man. We gotta get going." He turned in his stool and waved for the others to follow. Some left behind only half-eaten meals. The bald one reached into his vest pocket and threw down a fifty-dollar bill, telling Ruby to keep the change. As they walked behind him, Ollie kept his hand on his gun, not taking it away until the roar of their motorcycles was in the distance.

The last bell rang and the school doors burst open, releasing a flood of children into the parking lot. Little Ritchie's cackle could be heard over all the other voices, a slobbering hyena's laugh, when he snatched a girl's schoolbag and hurled it into the street. The boys he hung around all laughed with him, surrounding the taller, muscular form of Fred Eubanks, who leaned against a signpost, watching.

Fred hadn't gone to that elementary school in three years, but on occasion he came by to pick up his brother. Now he watched the little girl race into the street and bend over to pick up the schoolbag, the hem of her dress coming up just beneath her panties, and then watched her hurry off. He reached down and adjusted himself through his jeans, watching the rest of the smaller kids going wide around his posse.

A fourth-grader in a bright orange traffic vest raised a metal whistle to his lips and blew, holding up his hand, making all of the kids stop at the edge of the sidewalk and look both ways.

J.D. tapped Adam on the arm and pointed away from the buses. "Let's go this way."

"Our bus is right here," Adam said.

"We can walk home."

"It's too cold."

"Come on," J.D. said, pulling his friend's arm.

Adam refused, the fabric of his jacket sliding free of J.D.'s hand as he pulled his arm back. "What's wrong with you?"

J.D. looked at Fred Eubanks and the rest of the boys, standing near the buses, and said, "I just feel like walking today."

Adam took out his inhaler, gave it a shake, and stuck it in his mouth. He pressed the button, took a good look at the woods where J.D. wanted to go, then back at the bus, and said, "I'm getting on the bus."

The traffic safety kid blew his whistle again. J.D. watched Adam head into the crowd lining up for the bus but hung back, keeping his eyes on the Eubanks brothers and the other kids around them. No one had noticed him yet. He turned to go around the buses, toward the trees, when someone leapt in front of him, blocking his path. Hope Pugh's hands were outstretched, her cheeks red with cold, and curls of her long red hair spilled down over her face from the butterfly barrettes on top of her head that could not contain their mass. "Where are you going? Buses are that way," she said.

"I'm not taking the bus today," J.D. said, adjusting his schoolbag strap.

"How come?"

When he didn't answer, she turned. Her eyes narrowed on Fred Eubanks. "What's he doing here?" she said.

"You know him?" J.D. said.

Hope didn't have time to answer. Little Ritchie had seen Adam coming up through the crowd and shrieked, "It's the Four-Eyed Freak!" He leapt forward and snatched the inhaler from Adam's hands, holding it up like a trophy. He pressed it to his mouth and staggered around, sputtering and choking, pretending to take a huge dose of it, making the others laugh.

Adam grabbed for the inhaler, but watched in dismay as it was tossed to someone else in the crowd. He tried to catch it when it was thrown again, but it was useless. He was too slow for them. Too bogged down by his schoolbag. Too uncoordinated. He leapt and swept with his arms, shouting for them to give it back, but his cries were drowned out by their laughter. They kept laughing, even as his face turned purple, and he started to wheeze.

Little Ritchie jiggled the inhaler, holding it high in the air as Adam sank to his knees, clutching his chest. "If you can reach it, you can have it," he said. He never saw what was coming.

J.D. Rein raced up through the crowd, sidestepping onlookers and breaking through their lines, rushing the group of boys who were standing with their backs turned. He raced up behind Little Ritchie, swinging his schoolbag in a wide arc aimed square at the side of the laughing boy's head.

It hit with the sound of a baseball bat against a metal mailbox. The plastic pencil case inside the schoolbag cracked, backed by several dense and hardbound textbooks, against Little Ritchie's unprotected temple and cheek. The force of it sent him sprawling across the sidewalk, leaving him clutching his face, writhing on the ground.

J.D. picked up the inhaler and handed it to Adam, then helped him guide it into his mouth so he could take a deep blast from it. "You okay?" J.D. said.

"I'm good." Adam panted, readying himself for another quick dose.

Both of them looked up as the kids around them backed away. As the crowd parted, they could see what was coming toward them. A seething hulk in the form of Fred Eubanks. His eyes glowered. The veins on the side of his neck were tight as steel cords. Both of his hands were clenched into fists as he stepped over his brother's squirming form. "You're gonna die, Piss Face."

J.D. leapt up, swinging his schoolbag as hard as he could, the last assault of the slingshot toward the towering Goliath. Eubanks threw up his left arm as it swung, knocking it away and into the crowd. J.D. backed up. He had nowhere to run. They'd been encircled by kids, who'd abandoned their lines waiting for the buses and come to watch him get his teeth knocked out. Or worse, the life choked out of him.

He had no doubt he was going to die. Eubanks was going to throw him to the ground in some kind of expert choke hold and start squeezing. The rest of the kids were going to think J.D. was faking it. Or that he was knocked out. He was going to die on the sidewalk, kicking and scraping his new sneakers on the cement, unable to breathe, and by the time anyone realized it, it would be too late. Adam grabbed him by the hand and pulled himself up.

"Run," J.D. said, nudging him. "Get to the bus."

Adam pulled out his inhaler and took another deep drag. He puffed out his chest, ingesting as much of the medicine as he could, then stuffed it back in his pocket and said, "No way."

"You should have listened to Piss Face," Eubanks said. He snatched Adam by the shirt collar, twisting it in his hand until the seams ripped. J.D. latched onto the massive arm with both of his hands, trying to pull it away. Eubanks swung his free arm, clubbing J.D. across the back and upper shoulders. J.D. cried out at each blow but wouldn't let go. Adam kicked Eubanks in the side, his gray Velcro sneakers little more than swiping against the larger boy's coat, screaming for someone to help.

Someone was helping. Everything was a blur of panic and struggle, and J.D. felt someone collide against him, landing wrapped around the upper torso of Fred Eubanks.

J.D. twisted his head around in time to see Hope Pugh, latched onto Eubanks like a monkey, one hand clutching the side of his face and the other digging through her coat pocket, coming up with a piece of glinting metal, dangling from a chain. He watched Hope thrust the tip of the traffic safety whistle into the larger boy's ear and blow as hard as she could.

Eubanks screeched in agony. High-pitched pain. Not the little kid kind with blubbering tears. The kind of disturbing pain that made everyone's blood freeze. He dropped to his knees, clutching the side of his head.

"What did you do?" J.D. cried.

"Let's go," Hope said, pulling J.D. by his arm. "Come on."

She ran toward the crowd of kids, hurled the whistle back at the terrified-looking fourth-grade traffic safety director she'd taken it from, then looked back at J.D. and Adam. They hadn't moved. Adults were coming from the buses then, and even a few running up from the school. "We have to go!" she shouted.

The fire within the brick chimney in Hope's backyard warmed them, but Adam shivered anyway. He kept his hands stuffed in his pockets, teeth chattering, as Hope set a steaming mug of hot chocolate on the blanket in front of him and another in front of J.D. Hope and Adam picked up their mugs and blew on them, making steam rise into the cold air. "Are the two of you nuts?" J.D. said.

Both looked at him, their mouths still perched around their mugs.

"You are gonna die," J.D. said, pointing at Adam. "That maniac lives right down the street from you. He is going to come to your house and mess you up." He turned to Hope, "He's probably going to get you too. What were you thinking?

She sipped her hot chocolate and said, "I was thinking you needed help. He was going to kill you."

"Exactly," J.D. said. "A nice, easy death. Not the long, slow, painful one that he has planned for me now."

"This is really good hot chocolate," Adam said.

J.D. smacked him on the arm. "Are you listening to me?"

"Oh, stop," Hope said, rolling her eyes. "He won't do anything. He's just a big bully."

J.D. picked up his hot chocolate but felt too sick to drink it. "Well, you can't walk home," he said to Adam. "You'll have to call your parents to come pick you up."

"From your house? Is your dad home?"

"We'll have to check," J.D. said.

"You can call from my house." Hope sighed. "Why are you boys so dramatic about everything?"

They sat, listening to the woods all around them. A distant branch fell, sending an animal skittering across a patch of wet leaves. "Why did he keep calling you Piss Face?" Adam asked.

J.D. felt his cheeks burn hot. He raised the mug close to cover his face and said, "I don't know. He was just being a jerk."

Over the steam, he could see Hope staring at him. She knew. She said nothing. The wind rose, making the fire flicker inside its chimney housing. Hope moved away from it, coming up beside J.D. The two of them stared at the fire, sitting so close their arms and legs were pressed together. He could smell her. The back of her hand touched the back of his hand, and neither of them pulled away.

CHAPTER 12

*T*he rolling wave of orange flame was taller than the forest of trees it consumed. Its fire engulfed their lush foliage, turning it into black smoke. Ben Rein tried to scream, but the heat had sucked all of the oxygen out of the air and he was left gasping. The stench of the burning jungle was all over him. Smoke and charred flesh and the chemical smell that would linger for days after the bombs dropped.

He ran as fast as he could, diving for the nearest muddy trench and digging his way through the thick reeds covering its entrance. He clawed the earth like a desperate, wild dog. The flames licked his feet, melting the soles of his boots to his flesh. All around him men were screaming, some in English, some in Vietnamese. It didn't matter what language you spoke or what country you came from or what color you skin was when the world caught on fire. Burn enough of a man away and everything becomes the same.

The ground gave way beneath him and he tumbled through the hole, landing hard in the muddy pit below. He smacked his head when he landed, and everything was spinning. The field was on fire above him, and the flames were seeking a way inside the hole after him. He staggered to his feet and ran blind into the darkness, racing down tunnels, taking whatever turn he came to, splashing through piles of rotting food and human waste, until he tripped over a pile of blankets spread across the floor. He stopped to catch his breath, pressing his face against the cool, earthen wall. He could hear someone talking.

"Đó là cái gì?"

He sunk down against the wall, holding his breath. No, *he thought.* This isn't right. There wasn't anyone in this tunnel. *He felt something wet grab his arm and refused to look. He could smell the blood smeared across the hand gripping him, like the taste of copper inside his mouth. "Ben?" the hoarse voice whispering in the darkness, the hand refusing to let him go.*

Ben clenched his eyes shut, shaking his head.

"They took my eyes, Ben," the voice said in his ear, the stench of rotting flesh overwhelming. "I wouldn't tell them where you were, and they cut out my fucking eyes!"

"Ben?" Ollie Rein said, knocking on the door, pressing his face against the screen door. "You awake?"

Ben blinked, seeing the television set in front of him, two long rabbit ear antennas sticking out of it. He saw the *TV Guides* and newspapers scattered across the coffee table and the empty bottles set on top of them. The morning sun was streaming through the house's front windows, glinting off the glass rims and curves of each bottle. He looked at his own front door, trying to make sense of it.

"Open up," Ollie said. "It's your brother."

Ben closed his eyes and groaned, pressing his hands against the sides of his head. "What do you want?"

"Get dressed. We gotta take a ride."

"Where?"

"The beer store," Ollie said. "The owner filed a complaint and wants to press charges. We need to go down there and apologize and find a way to make some kind of payment arrangement. Let's go."

Ben closed his eyes and covered them with his fists. "Fuck off."

"Okay," Ollie said, resting his arm against the door frame. "Have it your way. Hope you don't like the taste of beer, though. That's the only store that sells it for twenty miles, and if they press charges, you ain't going back in there anytime soon." When Ben didn't move, Ollie said, "It's supposed to get warmer soon. Perfect weather for sitting outside, cracking open a cold one. I got this cooler and freezer packs that we can use, put a whole case of beer inside and make it so cold they'll all be just about frozen. So cold the cans'll hurt your hand when you take them out. That's only if you like the taste of beer, though. I'm not sure if you do or not. Course, if you like the taste of ice-cold beer, I suggest we can go apologize to the man. Maybe we can even grab a six-pack while we're there."

Ollie watched through the door as his brother rolled off the couch and stumbled toward his bedroom to get dressed.

Ben slumped in the front passenger seat, covering his face from the sun. The police radio cackled, making him wince. Ollie turned it off and rolled his window down, preferring the cold, crisp air blowing across his face to the stale alcohol sweat seeping through his brother's pores. Ben's olive drab army jacket was faded gray and worn out at the elbows. It smelled like old car motor oil. Ollie's patrol car was going to smell like that for a while now too, he thought.

He peered at the parking lot in front of the beer store, instinctively hitting his turn signal, when his foot stamped the brake. Ben slammed against the dashboard, hollering, but Ollie barked at him to be quiet. Five motorcycles were lined up in front of the store. One of them was blocking the entrance. "What the fuck," Ollie muttered, turning the wheel and rolling the car into the lot. He put it in park and let himself out, looking back at Ben to say, "Just stay here a minute. I'll be out in a little while."

Ben was crumpled in his seat, arms wrapped tight around his chest, like he was trying to pull himself inside of himself.

Ollie closed the door with a soft click and moved diagonally across the parking lot, trying to get a look through the front windows. It was no use. The windows were tinted, meant to better display the neon beer signs hanging from them. He stopped next to the entrance and pressed his ear to the glass window. Voices were muttering inside. As he pressed close, he could see the outline of the design on their jackets. The Disgraced's Grim Reaper stared back at him with red eyes.

"What do you mean in case anything happens?" the owner said. "I already have insurance."

"Not like this," Wombat replied. "See, what we provide is protection against the unforeseen. What you might call preventative insurance."

"I don't know what you are talking about. Get the hell out of my store."

"Now see," Wombat replied, stepping forward. As he moved, the bald, dark-skinned one moved with him, both of them closing around the owner. "That's the wrong attitude to have, especially when you got your family working here. Your boy, how old is he?"

"You stay the hell away from my son!"

Ollie pushed the door open, letting the bells clang hard against its glass.

"We're closed," Wombat said, without turning his head.

Ollie laid his hands on his gun belt. "Well, that's funny. It looks open to me."

The bikers turned to face him, spreading out, as Wombat smiled at the sound of Ollie's voice. He stroked the length of his braided beard as he leaned back against a tall stack of beer cases. "If I didn't know better, I'd say you're either following us around or you're thinking about becoming a member, Ollie," he said.

Ollie felt rooted in place at the entrance. His heart hammered in his chest and he knew that if he spoke he'd hear an unmistakable shaking in his voice. Even worse, they'd hear it too.

"Of course, I don't have no problems with signing you up as a prospect," Wombat said. As he spoke, the bikers were widening their circle, coming around Ollie from either side. "I wouldn't even make you do all the crazy shit most of the other guys would, out of respect for the badge and all. But, you'd have to watch out for Orange." At the mention of his name, the bald one sneered at Ollie with black eyes that glittered like onyx. "He just hates pigs," Wombat said.

"Look," Ollie said, falling back on his small-town, aw shucks, I'm everybody's friend routine. He smiled wide, hoping they didn't see him lay his right hand across the top of his gun, ready to snatch it out of the holster. "Why don't we step outside and talk this over. I'm sure it's just some kind of misunderstanding."

"Is there a misunderstanding?" Wombat said, looking sideways at the owner. "No, I'm pretty sure everyone is crystal clear."

The owner stared at Ollie, pleading with him to do something.

"All right, enough," Ollie said. "I've been real polite to you guys so far, but I'm not letting you come around here and harass people."

"I think you misunderstand the situation, friend," Wombat said. "What's happened is, so far, we've been real polite with you."

There were five of them, Ollie thought. All of them with bulges under their vests that could be anything from knives to guns to tire irons. How was this happening? He pictured himself drawing his revolver and firing, knocking down the biker closest to him. With only six bullets, that didn't leave any room for error. They'd be firing back, he thought. Or rushing forward. How the hell did I spend two years in Vietnam and come home without a scratch just to get in a goddamn gunfight in my own hometown?

They kept moving forward and Ollie reached down to unsnap his holster, feeling the inevitability of it all. An unseen tide pulling him out into the deep waters. He wrapped his hand around the revolver's handle and they reached inside their vests in unison, when the bells on the glass door behind him clanged again, making everyone freeze in place.

Ben Rein shuffled into the store, hands thrust down inside his army jacket, his head low. He walked past Ollie without speaking and passed in front of the bikers without bothering to acknowledge them. He moved toward Wombat, who grinned at him in confusion, and kept going, making his way toward the back of the store.

"Who is this guy?" Wombat said, turning to peer down the aisle. "You know him? Hello? Sir? We're kind of in the middle of something here."

Ben came back up the same aisle, carrying a case of beer. He went past Wombat, turning close enough in front of him to brush the biker with his army jacket, and planted the case on the register counter. When no one moved, he turned and looked at the owner. The owner's mouth trembled, but nothing came out.

"Oh, right," Ben said, scratching the side of his face. "Listen, I'm real sorry about what happened the other day. Can I buy this beer now? I have money."

"Hey, idiot," Wombat called out from behind him. His right hand snaked inside his vest, reaching for the weapon dangling under his armpit.

"Tell him, Ollie," Ben said, glancing at his brother. Ben's hands were starting to shake. "Tell him I'm sorry and we came here to get beer, like you said."

"Shut up, Ben," Ollie said through clenched teeth, his grip tight around the revolver's wooden grip.

"You two seem real familiar with one another," Wombat said. He looked Ben Rein up and down, taking in the man's coat and tattered appearance. "How about you, friend? You go overseas too? Were you a secretary like ol' Ollie here?"

"Leave him out of this," Ollie snarled.

Ben looked back at the man standing behind him, seeing his long, braided beard. Reading the man's patches and symbols, through his squinting eyes.

"No, you weren't no secretary," Wombat whispered. "Boys, look at this beautiful son of a bitch. Look at his eyes. Man, don't you know what you're seeing, standing right in front of you? Your own kind." Wombat threw his arms out. "You belong with us, Ben. We can help you. We understand you. You think some fucking secretary who sucked every dick he could find to keep from going into the field knows what you went through and who you really are?" Wombat's eyes were glazed over, a shabby mystic preaching to his flock. "I knew we were brought here for a reason, didn't I say I felt called to this place?" he asked, looking at his men. "We came to find you, Ben."

"Take it," the owner urged. "Go! All of you, just take it and go." He waved them all forward, shepherding them toward the door like a frenzied sheepdog.

Ben lifted the beer from the counter, heading toward the entrance. Wombat followed close behind, not wanting to let go of his new find. The others fell in line behind their president, and

Ollie stepped backward without looking, feeling the cold glass against his back, and pressed the door open to let them all walk past.

Ben carried the case of beer to the police car and set it down on the hood. Sweat covered his face and he wiped it with the sleeve of his jacket. He looked pale and withered by the overhead sun. Inside the store, the owner threw the lock on the door and disappeared from the windows.

"You see that?" Wombat called out, arms resting on the handlebars of his motorcycle. "That's how people respond to warriors, Ben. With fear. Warriors are what we are, and that's what you are. Come with us. We don't answer to anyone but each other. We're a unit. The same as it was over there, except this time, we aren't taking orders from any suits, safe at home in their beds. We are free, in a way you can't imagine." He extended his hand toward Ben. "What do you say?"

Ollie watched in disbelief as Ben left the beer on the hood of the police car and headed toward the bikers. "What are you doing?" Ollie hissed.

"Let us take you home," Wombat urged. "We're your brothers."

Ben stopped just short of Wombat's outstretched hand, his eyes fixed on the patches decorating the biker's vest. The US Army patch, the *C,* and the *20th.* "You were all Charlie Company," Ben said.

"That's right," Wombat said, his mouth curving into a wolfish grin. "Not too many are proud to say that anymore, but those pussies in Washington can't take that away from us."

"Were any of you on Task Force Barker during the Tet Offensive?"

"Every single goddamn one of us!" Wombat whooped, clapping his hands together. "Oh shit, were you there too?"

It was Ben's turn to smile, his eyes bright and clear. He scanned each of their faces, studying them one by one. He stopped at the bald one, squinting, then kept going. Ben turned back to Wombat and said, "And you were all somewhere else too. I've seen your photographs before."

Wombat's laugh died in his throat and he cleared it away. "That right? And where's that?"

"Five hundred civilians at My Lai, including women and children. All those babies. Oh yeah, I've seen your pictures," Ben said. "All of you."

"How about you stop talking about things you don't want to know about, Ben," Wombat said.

"I know about Phillip White," Ben replied. "He did the most depraved of the raping. He died in a hotel room fire in Saigon a few weeks later. I know about Ernesto Palmer. He was seen tossing babies up in the air and catching them on his bayonet. He committed suicide the day he was supposed to go back to the States. I know a few more, if you want to hear about them. They're all dead too."

Wombat leaned back against his bike's handlebars, away from Ben. He glanced at the bald-headed one. "What was the name of your squad leader? The Mexican. It was Ernie, wasn't it?"

"Ernesto," Orange said, staring at Ben.

"He shot himself in the shower, from what I recall," Wombat said. "Left a note for his wife and everything."

"It was a nice letter," Ben said. "From the heart."

Wombat's right eye twitched, and he squeezed it shut for a moment to control it, rubbing it like he had something in it. "So you know us?" he said. "We were all there. You know any of our names, Ben?"

"No," Ben said. "If I knew your names, we wouldn't be here having this conversation."

None of them spoke as Ben turned to go back to the police car. He hoisted the case of beer off the hood and got into the passenger side, dropping into the seat. Ollie stood for a minute, unsure of what to do, then followed his brother into the police car and started the engine.

Ollie watched the bikers mount their motorcycles and rev their engines. He backed up his police car, giving them a wide berth as they peeled out of the parking lot, laying down smoke and the stink of scorched rubber.

"Holy shit," Ollie said, wiping his face with the flat of his hand. It was soaked in sweat.

Ben tore the cardboard open on the case of beer and tugged one of the cans out. He cracked it open, pressed it to his mouth, and drained it until the aluminum crumpled in his hand. He tossed it on the car's floor, pulled out another, cracked it open, and drained it too. He pulled out a third, cracked it open, and as he pressed it to his lips, Ollie said, "Hey!"

Ben looked at him, beer foam covering his lips.

"Give me that," Ollie said, taking the beer out of Ben's hand and chugging hard.

CHAPTER 13

A Liston Borough police car was waiting in the parking lot when Ollie returned to the station. The driver tipped his wide-brimmed cowboy hat and took a long drag from his cigarette as Ollie pulled up alongside him. Walt Auburn blew the smoke out, sending it into Ollie's window and said, "Good to see you."

"Walt," Ollie said. "What brings you into town?"

"Just passing through. Figured I'd check in on you. See how the other half lives and all." Walt Auburn was a skinny, wiry man, with a long neck and an Adam's apple the size of a Ping-Pong ball. It looked like a tumor trying to get away from the rest of him. His starched shirt collar was buttoned tight and pinned with a polyester clip-on tie, making him look like a plant that had only one long stem with a bulbous growth at the end of it, which, in this case, was wearing a gray Stetson. His eyes were hidden behind mirrored sunglasses, and when he looked at Ollie, all Ollie could see was his own reflection.

"How's your boy?" Ollie said. "Stevie, right?"

"Doing well. Getting big. How about you, making any time with the ladies around here?"

"No," Ollie said. "Never can seem to get off work long enough to go anywhere."

"You just don't know how to play it, that's all," Walt said. He took another drag and blew out a long trail of smoke. "Time passes, don't it?"

"That it does."

Ollie watched him stub out his cigarette in the car's ashtray and flick the stub between their cars into the driveway. "I heard you ran into some friends of mine," Walt said, looking out into the driveway.

"Who's that?"

"The motorcycle boys. Wombat, or whatever the fuck he calls himself, and his crew. You giving them a hard time?"

Walt was looking at him directly now, and Ollie could see a reflection of himself in each eye, giving him a firsthand view of the stupid look on his own face. "They're friends of yours?"

"Well, it's not like they come over for dinner or anything, but they're good folk. Decorated military veterans. Those boys all saw some serious shit over in 'Nam. Now, sure, they aren't exactly the Sunday school type, and they like to kick things up now and again, but I've been dealing with them a long time, and they never gave me one lick of trouble. In fact," Walt said, "they're actually good for the community."

"Is that right?" Ollie asked. "How's that work, exactly?"

"You go ahead and scoff, but it's true," Walt said. "Having them around tends to keep out the riffraff. Especially if people know you and them are sympatico." Walt touched his fingers together when he said the word, giving Ollie a visual aid. He drew another cigarette from the pack and stuck it in his mouth and lit it. "Let me talk real plain to you, Ollie. You work alone. You've got a better chance of seeing a colored president than seeing this place let you hire another police officer. Am I right?"

"I've never asked them to hire anyone, so I'm not sure," Ollie said.

"Point is, friends like these are good friends to have. I'm not saying they'll be raping and pillaging and you'll be standing here watching the town burn down around you. I'm just saying, be polite to them, and they'll be real, real good to you. They know how to return a favor, believe me. Do you believe me?"

Ollie watched Walt extend his hand through the window, offering it to him.

"I believe you," Ollie said, taking it and squeezing. Walt's hand stunk like tobacco.

"Good," Walt said, shifting his car into drive. "You know, some-day soon, these bozos are gonna wake up and realize it's stupid to have two different police departments and fire companies and public works departments, and so on, in such a small area. They're gonna combine things, and when they do, it's important we stick together. I'll make sure you're taken care of, Ollie. Get you a lieutenant's spot. No, a captain's. What do you say?"

"Sounds great," Ollie said.

Walt tipped his hat before he drove away, leaving Ollie in his own parking lot, facing the wrong direction.

On any other day, time passed slowly in school, but that day it passed quickly. Whenever J.D. looked at the clock, it kept leaping forward like a horse unbridled. It went faster as the day drew to a close. Miss Sanderson, who always droned in a flat monotone, seemed to fly through explanations about fractions and long division, and by the way, J.D., as soon as you leave this building, Fred Eubanks is going to stomp on your little balls until they pop like grapes. You're going to cry in front of everyone. You're going to *die*.

"J.D.?" Miss Sanderson said.

His head snapped away from the window overlooking the playground. When she saw she had his attention, the teacher turned back to the blackboard and continued talking. J.D. looked at the clock. Only a few minutes were left. Just a few rows above his, Adam was already sliding his pencil into his pencil case and zippering his schoolbag. Adam squinted at the clock from behind his thick glasses, seeing the time, and drew out his inhaler to take a long, rattling dose.

The bell rang, with Miss Sanderson still giving their homework assignments. J.D. didn't bother writing them down. He didn't figure he'd live long enough to hand them in. He hoisted his schoolbag and waited for Adam at the door. Neither of them spoke as they joined the other students heading for the exit.

J.D. looked at the floor as he walked. He didn't want to hold his face up and risk anyone seeing how terrified he was. He felt like he was floating through the air, disconnected from himself. He didn't look back up until Adam whacked him on the arm and pointed at the end of the hall, saying, "Look."

J.D. peered through the crowd of kids, a sea of knit hats with fuzzy balls at the top, and saw Hope. She was standing outside the hallway door, waving at them through the window. She was smiling, a smile as wide and big as the sky, and the curls of her red hair came down against her pale skin. J.D. had read books where women were described as having alabaster skin, and he didn't know exactly what it meant. He thought an alabaster sounded more like a fish, or some sort of railing inside a mansion. Writers loved to use the same old descriptions when it came to girls. Golden hair. Chestnut hair. Ruby red lips. Hourglass figures. Alabaster skin.

He looked at Hope and decided that must have been what they were going for. Whatever it meant. However they meant it. For him, it would always be her face, framed by that red, red hair.

She waited for them on the landing, holding the door open to let the others pass through it faster. It was like pulling the plug on the bathtub drain. J.D. realized he was being carried forward faster than he wanted, closing in on the entrance, and about to be spat out into the courtyard. Hope was waving him on, though, and there was no way to turn around.

"Come on," she said. "It's fine." She pointed at the far end of the parking lot where the school buses were idling, and the empty corner where none of their tormentors stood. No Fred Eubanks. No Little Ritchie. No crowd of their friends. She leapt down the steps, landing on her feet, and spread her arms wide. "See? We stood up to them and they ran off."

Neither J.D. nor Adam moved from the landing, though they were bombarded by schoolbags as the rest of their classmates rushed past. "Maybe they're hiding," Adam said, taking his glasses off and wiping the lenses with his gloved fingers.

"Where?" Hope said, exasperated. "It's not like they're waiting for us on the buses. Stop being babies."

J.D. looked at their bus, measuring the distance from the landing to its open doors. "All right," he whispered.

"Do you guys want to walk home together?" Hope said.

"Are you out of your blasted mind?" Adam replied.

J.D. punched him in the arm. "I told you to stop saying that. Nobody says blasted. You sound like a dork."

Adam cried out, rubbing his arm. J.D. turned back to Hope. "We aren't walking home, that's for sure. We all live too far away from one another. Why don't you get on our bus, we'll make sure Adam gets home, and then you and me can get off at my stop, and walk to your house."

She said okay, but her eyes were on Adam. "You all right?" she asked.

"I'm fine," he said, storming down the steps past J.D. and her, his face flush with embarrassment.

"What did you hit him for?" Hope asked, as they fell in behind him.

"He says comic book words that nobody says in real life," J.D. told her. "It makes both of us sound dumb."

She didn't respond, and in her disappointed expression it was like some kind of light flickered throughout the universe on the verge of going out. "I'm sorry I hit him, okay?" J.D. said.

"Are you sorry you did it, or sorry I saw it?" she asked.

J.D. walked ahead and tugged on Adam's sleeve. "Hey, I'm sorry I hit you. I'm really blasted sorry."

They got onto the bus and hurried down the aisle to find an open seat. The three of them pressed in together, holding their schoolbags on their laps. The bus hissed and began to move.

As Adam went down the bus's steps, J.D.'s face was pressed to the window, checking for signs of movement. Adam bolted for his front door, inhaler tight in his hand and his schoolbag swinging wildly from side to side. Adam was only halfway up the driveway when the bus started moving again. J.D. shouted, "Wait!"

Everyone lurched forward as the driver stomped on the brake, glaring at J.D. through the wide rearview mirror that let her watch all of the kids seated behind her at one glance. "What's the matter?" she barked.

Every head on the bus was turned toward him. He turned and looked over his shoulder through the window, seeing Adam race up his front steps to safety. "Nothing," J.D. said as he slid back down into his seat. "Sorry."

The bus came to its last stop, and the remaining children filed down the steps. Hope followed J.D. down the steps and stood with him on the side of the road, watching the rest of the kids run off to their homes.

"Which one's your house?" Hope asked, looking at the homes scattered along the street.

He dug his sneaker into the gravel road, pretending that he didn't hear her.

"If you're not going to talk to me, I could have just taken my own bus home instead of riding with you," she said.

J.D. pointed at the last one at the far end. The worst-looking one, with grass that hadn't been cut, and shutters hanging lopsided. It hadn't occurred to him how awful it looked compared to all the other houses until she saw it and said, "Oh."

She asked him if he had to go home first, and he told her that he didn't.

"If you don't want to walk all the way back to my house, I can just call my dad to come get me," she continued.

"I said I don't want to go there," J.D. snapped. "I wanted you to ride with me so I could make sure nothing happened to you or Adam, okay? There, that's my stupid house. You saw it. Now can we get going?"

"All right, fine," she said, reslinging her schoolbag over her shoulder and starting to walk. "I was just trying to be polite. You ever heard of that? It's a thing where you don't punch your friends and you don't yell at them when they're just asking a simple question."

He walked alongside her without speaking, hands stuffed in his pockets. "Here," he said, reaching for her. "Give me that."

"Give you what?"

"That," he said. He lowered her schoolbag down from her arm and free of her hand. "I'll carry it."

She watched him hoist her schoolbag onto his free shoulder, now carrying hers on one and his own on the other. "I didn't need you to do that."

"It's a long walk," he said. "You'll get tired along the way and start complaining, I bet, so let me carry it."

"Why, because I'm a girl?"

He was about to answer yes, but the look on her face made him pause. "Because I'm being polite," he said instead.

Hope smirked and rolled her eyes. "I bet you don't know the first thing about girls."

"Yes, I do."

"Name three."

"I know you like flowers," he said. "And stuffed animals."

"And?"

He remembered what he could of his mother. Trying to recall what she liked or the things she'd done that no one else in the house had. Only one thing came to mind, and he blurted it out without thinking. "You all sit down to pee."

Hope laughed at that, loud and hard, a high-pitched sound that filled J.D. from the pit of his stomach to the top of his head with boiling embarrassment. "Well, you asked," he muttered.

"You're blasted right, I did," she said, flashing a smile, and they both laughed. "Since I'm asking stuff, how come they call you J.D.? Don't you like your real name?"

"My dad says it's a dumb name and my mother forced it on him, so when she died, he started calling me by my initials."

Hope looked at him, sliding a dangling curl back behind her ear. "What's your name?"

"It's stupid," he said.

"I bet it isn't."

He found himself upended by her eyes, like a man strapped to a carnival wheel at the wrists and ankles, spinning endlessly, with no sense of what was up or down. "Jacob," he said.

"Jacob Rein," she said. "I like that. I'm going to call you Jacob from now on."

"Don't. It sounds like it's from the Bible or something."

"Well, J.D. Rein makes you sound like a redneck race car driver," she said.

The sun was cresting over the tops of the trees, leaving the street partially in shadow. They stayed in the shadows to keep from having to shield their eyes. "Was your mom sick or something?" Hope asked.

"Yeah, she had cancer."

"I'm sorry," Hope said. "That must have been awful."

"I don't remember it. She died when I was still real young."

"So it's just been you and your dad?"

"Yeah. Well, except for my uncle Ollie. He moved out here a few years ago and we spend a lot of time together."

"I talked to my mom about you," she said.

"You did?" J.D. said, not knowing if that was good or bad.

"She asked if you were related to the chief of police, but said she'd never heard of anyone else in your family."

"My dad doesn't go out much," J.D. said. "We moved here when I was little. My dad said it was cheap enough and far enough away from everything that he wouldn't have to see anyone. I guess he got his wish."

"Can I ask you a question?" she said. "Do you not like your dad very much?"

He frowned. It was something he'd never considered. His father was just something in his life that had always been and felt like it would always be. It was pointless to fret over. His father was as constant and inescapable as the sun or the moon or the air itself.

"I'm sorry," Hope said. "That's a dumb question. I was just wondering why you never want to go home."

"It's hard to explain. Sometimes he has these dreams, even

when he's awake. He forgets where he is, and he gets crazy. I'm kind of used to it, but it scares other people when they see it."

"When my dad drinks beer, he falls asleep on the couch and snores like a grizzly bear," Hope said, making a few loud snorts to imitate the sound.

"I like it when my dad drinks," J.D. said.

"You do?"

"He's happier and nicer to me."

"What happens when he doesn't drink?" she asked.

"He's not."

They reached Hope's front door by five o'clock. The sun had already retreated from the sky, leaving nothing but strings of clouds beyond the crimson horizon. Neither of her parents was home. Hope stopped at her front steps, looking up at the house. "I'm probably not allowed to have a boy in the house without them here," she said.

J.D. unslung her schoolbag and handed it to her. She carried it up the steps, then stopped and looked back at him. "I'll see you tomorrow?"

"Of course," he said, waving good-bye to her. She vanished inside the front door and J.D. stood there, heart pounding in his chest for no reason. He stretched out his aching shoulder, glad to be free of the weight of the second schoolbag, and started home. He went around Hope's house, toward the backyard. He decided he'd take the long way and go through the woods. It wasn't completely dark yet, and he needed to wait before he went home.

If he got back too early, his dad might still be sober. Sometimes, Ben didn't wake up until the late afternoon, depending what kind of night he'd had. Then he'd have to find a way into town and get beer or liquor, depending on what he could afford, and whether or not he had any in the house. There normally wasn't anything left in the house. That could take hours. Plenty of times J.D. made it back from school before Ben got home, and he'd have to stay in his room, keeping clear, until Ben got enough drink in him to mellow out.

It was best for J.D. to stay away as long as he could and not take chances. Ben never asked where he'd been or what he'd been doing. He didn't seem to notice when the boy wasn't there. If anything, it was the opposite. When J.D. was around, everything about the boy seemed to infuriate his father. Simple things, like the way J.D. spoke to him, or looked at him, or didn't look at him when being spoken to. Everything was some kind of challenge to Ben's authority, intentional or not, when Ben wasn't drinking.

In school, some of the kids referred to their dads as nasty drunks. For J.D. it was the opposite. His dad was a miserable sober. J.D. understood why, though. No one had ever explained it to him, or given him any kind of reasoning behind it, it was something he just knew. For Ben, drinking was like medicine. A magic potion that kept him from turning into Mr. Hyde. When he didn't get it, the monster got loose, and good luck to the villagers who got in his way.

The only exception was when his father had an episode. Drunk or sober, it didn't matter. At times Ben Rein was possessed by some demonic spirit filled with gunfire and explosions and screaming at people to get out of the way.

In fifth grade, J.D. and Adam had become obsessed with Greek myths, and read everything they could about the adventures of the earliest heroes. They filled their days pretending to be Perseus and Hercules, fighting three-headed serpents and armies of skeleton warriors. It ended the day J.D. found a book containing the tales of Euripides.

In it, Hercules is confused by the goddess Hera and thinks his wife and children are enemies attacking him. He kills all of them with his arrows, and then, once the curse is lifted, he is left kneeling in a pool of blood surrounded by their dead bodies.

J.D. had seen his father emerge from those kinds of curses, sometimes kneeling in the backyard clutching a shotgun, sometimes running through the house screaming, "I'll fucking kill every one of you!" He'd seen his father standing in the doorway to his bedroom clutching a knife, covered in sweat, with his eyes so wide there was white on all sides of each iris.

When J.D. was younger, he'd slept under his bed, or in his closet, whenever it got bad. Now, he just pulled his dresser in front of his door to block it.

He made his way into Hope's backyard, able to see the clearing where her blanket lay. He could make out the lopsided brick chimney through the trees and realized there was a pair of eyes looking back at him from behind it.

J.D. froze in place, clutching the strap of his schoolbag.

He looked again, seeing nothing but shadows beyond the stones, and still did not move. "Hello?" he called out, hearing his own voice echo in the woods beyond.

A branch snapped and several birds fluttered from the trees overhead. "Who's there?" he said.

He turned and looked back at Hope's house, able to see through the back windows into the kitchen and washroom. Was someone spying on her and her family, he wondered. Some kind of Peeping Tom creep? He'd heard his uncle talk about them before. Maybe a burglar, or worse, trying to see if Hope was home alone. His fist tightened around the strap on his schoolbag and he felt lit with red-hot anger. He raced into the woods, growling like an animal, and took a running leap over the green army blanket spread out on the ground. He landed in the mud past the chimney, but nothing was there.

J.D. scanned the woods, listening over the sound of his own rapid breathing, searching the dark woods for signs of an intruder. He couldn't see past the first row of trees. He stood there, looking, until he heard someone behind him.

Hope leapt out at him from behind one of the trees, laughing at how he jumped backward. "What are you yelling about back here?"

"I thought I saw someone," he said. The amused look on her face made all of the anger spool out of him, leaving him feeling cold and foolish.

"You were going to protect me?" she said, stepping closer to him.

"If I had to, I guess," he said, swallowing.

She touched his face. Her fingers were warm against his cold cheek. "Have you ever kissed anyone?"

"Sure," he said. "Plenty of times."

"Are you telling me the truth right now?" she said, raising an eyebrow.

"No," he whispered, inching back from her. His knees were quivering.

She came closer to him, the steam of her breath touching his face. The fronts of their coats were crushed together. "Me neither," she said. "It's an important thing, I think. A first kiss."

She wrapped her hands around his arms and raised her mouth to his. Their lips touched. J.D. was about to pull back, but he felt her mouth open against his, and the warmth of her tongue twirling against his own.

They kissed like that, for how long he would never know. It was dark out by the time they came apart. His lips hurt. His jaw ached. It didn't matter. He would have kissed her again and again, a thousand times, if the lights hadn't come on in the back of her house and her father hadn't opened the rear door and called out, "Hope? Are you out here?"

They ducked down, out of sight. "I have to go," she whispered.

"Okay," he said, and she kissed him again.

"I have to eat and do my homework," she said, then kissed him once more.

"All right," he said, laughing.

"But after that, I can come outside for a little while."

He smiled at her, at the idea of seeing her again so soon. "I'll be here," he said.

She pushed away from him, then ran back, slammed into him and kissed him again.

"Hope! It's dinnertime," her father shouted.

"I have to go."

"Go," he said.

She kissed him again. "I'll be back. Meet me here in two hours, Jacob Rein."

"All right," he said. They kissed a final time. Soft. Precious. A kiss that would sit in his memory longer than he could ever have imagined then.

After that, she left. He watched her go, kneeling on the blanket, waving to her each time she looked back and waved at him. He watched her disappear inside the back door and stood up, looping his arms through his schoolbag, about to head home, when he spun suddenly to face the dark woods. Something, he felt, had been staring at him just then. Something close enough to touch him. J.D. waited, listening, but heard nothing. He told himself it was just his imagination. The scent of Hope was still on him, and he found himself wanting to relive their intimate closeness instead of standing alone in the woods staring at shadows.

He headed into the woods, leaving the clearing behind, lost in his own thoughts. If anything was lying in wait in the shadows, he didn't look for it, or think about it, because all he could think of was Hope, and how much he wanted to see her again.

Ollie's police car was parked in front of the house when J.D. arrived home, and the front door was already opening by the time he went up the first few steps. His uncle appeared at the screen door, looking down at him. "You're home late."

"I was at a friend's house," J.D. said, coming through the door.

The sound of heavy snoring filled the living room. Ben Rein was passed out on the couch, his head draped backward over the armrest, mouth wide open. Each breath released a nauseous gas from his stomach full of beer. Crumpled cans littered the living room, surrounding his father in a pile.

"Do you have any homework?" Ollie asked.

"Just a few things."

"All right. Bring your schoolbag with you."

"Where are we going?" J.D. asked.

"Out to get something to eat. I've been waiting here for you all afternoon."

"I was going to eat here tonight," J.D. mumbled.

"Eat what? The fridge is empty. Come on."

"But I can't."

"Why not?" Ollie said. He looked at his brother, then back at the kid, and sighed. "Listen, I realize he's your dad and you want to look out for him, but reality is, he's not doing a good job of taking care of you. That means I have to help out. Now come on, we're going to get some food. We can eat anywhere you want."

"I don't want to go out to eat!" J.D. shouted. "I want to stay home!"

Ollie's face hardened. "Well, I'm not giving you that option, young man. Let's go."

J.D. slammed the door open as he left the house, smacked his schoolbag against the porch railing and kicked the police car's tire as he passed it. From the porch, Ollie watched him as he closed and locked the front door. Ollie unhooked his car keys from his police belt as he made his way down the steps. "What the hell's gotten into you tonight? I thought you liked spending time with me."

"I do," J.D. said, folding his arms across his chest in a huff. "It's not that, okay? I just had something to do."

They both got into the car. Ollie started it and backed up, rolling the wheel to turn toward the street. "Something here at home?" Ollie asked.

"No," J.D. muttered. "Not here. Back at my friend's house after dinner."

"That Adam kid with the glasses?"

"No."

"Another friend? I didn't know you hung out with anyone else. What's his name?"

When J.D. didn't answer, Ollie watched him from the corner of his eye. A smile widened across his face, and he poked the boy in the side. "Holy shit, a girl?"

J.D. laughed despite himself and smacked Ollie's hand away. "Stop, it's nothing."

"What's her name, you big stud?"

"Hope."

"Hope?" Ollie said. "That is a beautiful name. I *hope* you treat her like a lady, that's what I *hope*. And her parents were okay with you coming back over so late?"

"Sure," J.D. said, trying to sound confident. "Yep."

"I've been a cop long enough to know when somebody is full of it, and kid, that was the most full of it response I've ever heard. Okay, listen, because this is important. Never, ever get found inside another man's house when he doesn't know you're there, especially when you're with one of his daughters. And most definitely with his wife."

"Why would I hang out with Mrs. Pugh?" J.D. said.

"Disregard that last part," Ollie said. "But seriously, if you want to spend time with this girl, be a man about it, and don't go sneaking around, okay? Sit down with their family and have dinner and act like a gentleman, so they know you're not some scumbag."

"All right," J.D. said. He was crushed that he wouldn't get to see Hope again that night, but it all made sense the way Ollie was explaining it. He could see himself going over to her house, shaking hands with her father, even laying a napkin across his lap when they ate. He'd tell her what happened at school the next day, and it would all make sense to her then.

"So tonight, we go out and get some food. Then maybe we'll pick out a special date night outfit for you. Something you can wear over to her house, or when you take her to the movie or arcade or something. How's that sound?"

"That sounds great," J.D. said, smiling, because it did. He couldn't wait to see Hope the next day.

Except he wouldn't. As J.D. sat with his uncle, eating pizza, laughing and joking with one another, talking about Hope, she was being raped in the clearing behind her parent's house. She'd gone out to meet him, as she said she would. She'd been eager to see him again too. She brought her stuffed bear with her, intending on giving it to him. She was going to tell him it was his for nights when he was having trouble with his father, just in case. Childish, she knew, but it was her favorite thing, and she thought he might appreciate it. In fact, when she heard someone coming up behind her, from around the chimney, she'd thought it was him, and laughed because of how much he'd scared her. In the time it took her to realize who it was, she was already being thrown onto her back on the thin army blanket.

She died struggling, clutching her bear, suffocated by the gloved hand keeping her from screaming, tears running down the sides of her face. Unable to fight. Unable to move at all, except to scrape her feet against the blanket. A little girl, gasping for breath, as her innocence was stolen. Not innocence in the physical, sexual way. Innocence in the idea that the world is fair, and good will win. That God, or her parents, would protect her. That her first true love would rescue her, believing he would come until her eyes fluttered shut and her heart stopped and all the light and life drained out of her into the infinite nothingness.

III

LOCKED DOORS

CHAPTER 14

*E*verything happens in shit weather. In November, there's nice days, when the sky is clear and it might be cool, but a sweatshirt and jeans will suffice. Nothing happens on those days. It waits to hit until there's a freezing rain. Steve Auburn lifted the wooly collar of his patrol jacket to cover the back of his neck. His cowboy hat was like a shingle, pooling stinging cold water in its brim until he lowered his head to spill it out.

The sloped mountainside was slippery enough to send a man tumbling down the steep incline. He could picture himself rolling ass over tin cups all the way down, until he smacked into a tree thick enough to smash his brains out. He gripped the roots sticking up through the ground above him, taking it slow. He was a hundred feet above where the bones of the little girl's foot had been found, searching for the place they'd slid down from. They were searching in sectors, each man taking a small piece of each area. Ahead of him, he could see Officer Paul waving his hands in the air. "I got something, Chief! Over here!" Paul cried. "Come on!"

"I see you, for God's sake. Stop hollering," Auburn shouted back, gripping a handful of tree roots and making his way toward the next. "You see me coming right toward you, don't you?"

"I know, but," Paul huffed, clutching his chest like he was afraid his heart might burst through it, "I got something."

Auburn came up alongside him and looked down at a small

pile of what looked like black dirt covered by wet leaves. There was a scrape of mud going through the center of it, etched with the pattern of department-issued police boots. At the slash's center was a narrow bone, brown with age, the length of a child's forearm.

"I stepped on something, and it rolled my ankle," Paul said.

Auburn pulled out his phone to take a quick photograph of the bone and the mudslide. He could see what looked like more bones sticking out of the debris pile. It was easy to tell what had happened. The body had lain there for decades until it grew brittle enough that the rain eventually washed pieces of it down the hillside. Whatever they couldn't find here, they'd find somewhere below, Auburn thought.

He pulled out his police radio and pressed it close to his mouth. "Chief Auburn to all search units. I think we found it." He gave them his location and said, "Everybody meet me up here. Somebody bring all the crime scene stuff from the back of my car, and don't forget the camera and tape. Somebody get ahold of that girl detective from the county. She's gonna want to know about this."

By the time Carrie arrived, they'd recovered most of the skeleton, laying it out on a large blue tarp spread across the flattest part of the incline they could find. The majority of Hope Pugh's bones were intact. It looked like only the extremities had come apart. Only a few fingerbones and pieces of the right leg were missing. The men were spread out across the hill, combing through the dirt with their gloved hands, looking for them.

Steve Auburn came up beside her and looked down at the remains. He was holding a sealed coffee can in his hands, the large kind they sold in bulk stores. He set it down on the tarp by the skeleton's feet, and stood, taking off his cowboy hat to wipe his forearm through his sweaty hair, so he didn't touch himself with his rubber glove. "I guess that's that," he said. "Probably for the best. I never was a fan of mysteries."

Carrie slid on a pair of gloves and bent over the skull, peering at it from every angle. No cracks. No bullet holes. No chunks missing. She looked over the rest of the skeleton. No visible signs of damage to any of the bones.

"It's funny, I remember my parents talking about this case when it happened," Auburn said. "My mother said she probably ran off and was hitchhiking on the highway. She said the girl's father was probably doing things he shouldn't have been doing, because that's the only reason a little girl would run off like that. My dad said it was more likely she was playing up in the mountains and she slipped and fell and broke her neck. Either that or a bear got her." He smirked and said, "Can you believe that? The old man was right."

Carrie looked up at him. "What do you mean?"

"She's exactly where he said she'd be. Poor kid. I hope it wasn't a bear."

"You see any teeth marks on any of these bones?" Carrie asked. "There's not a single scratch. She didn't fall and break her neck, either. There's a thousand scavengers in these woods, and they'd have torn a rotting body to pieces. She'd be scattered all over the place. She had to be buried right after she was killed. She decomposed in the ground and got washed out of her grave over time. It's the only explanation."

"I'm sorry, I didn't realize you were some kind of expert in exhuming bodies, Miss Santero. Is that something they teach you at first-year county detective school?" Auburn hiked up his gun belt. "What, you thought I wasn't gonna ask around about you? They might have sent you out here to keep you out of their hair for a little while, but don't you think for one second I'm gonna let you turn this into some kind of freak show."

"Look, I'm not trying to make this a freak show. I'm just trying to figure out what happened to her."

"We figured out what happened to her! She came out here, got dead, and now forty years later I'm stuck dealing with the cleanup. You're dismissed."

Carrie watched him walk away, planting his ridiculous cowboy hat on his head as he headed back up the incline. She heard hol-

lering from up the hill. One of the searchers had found a finger
bone. She waited for Auburn to get far enough up the hill that
she lost sight of him in the trees and bent down to the coffee can
and popped the lid off. It was filled with the tattered remains of
sopping wet cloth. Most of it had turned black, but as she spread
it out and unfolded it, she could see small indications of colorful
patterns. Underwear, with balloons on it, Carrie realized. She
found another clump of cloth at the bottom of the can and
dumped it onto the tarp. It was thick and fuzzy, and as she peeled
it apart, she saw the faint traces of its light blue fabric. The match-
ing sock to the one back in her hotel room.

None of it was any good for recovering trace evidence, she
thought. Too wet, too damaged, too exposed to the elements. In
books, crime scene experts can compare grains of sand to imaginary databases that list distinguishable grains from all the beaches
in the world, and all sorts of other fantastical bullshit. That's not reality. She'd found entire strands of hair at crime scenes and been
told they were useless, because they didn't have the root attached.

In the real world, putting a big case together is a pain in the
ass, and the people you rely on for help don't want to do jack shit.
Nobody cares. The labs don't care. The courts don't care. You
were lucky if the victim cared, six to eight months down the road
when it finally went to court and they had to keep taking off work
and coming back to testify. That was the reality of police work
they don't tell you in the police academy, she thought. No wonder Auburn wanted to put this case to bed as quickly as possible.
Missing person. Found body. No cause determined. Parents noti-
fied. Case closed.

Go home, she thought. They don't want you here. Tell that
dickhead Harv Bender you helped out, didn't cause a fuss, and
most certainly didn't hook up a bug zapper in a hotel room to
base the entirety of your investigative suspicion on. Because nobody else cares, and neither should you.

She looked at the skeleton of the little girl spread out on the tarp.
The caverns in her skull where her eyes had been. The crooked
teeth in the jawbone, not yet fitted for braces. The tiny bones of her

ribs, and narrow bones of her hips. Some asshole had ground down on top of those same hips, doing the unthinkable, and then he killed her.

"Fuck that," Carrie said aloud.

She looked to make sure no one was watching, then slid her cell phone out of her pocket and took a quick photograph of the clothing items all together. She picked up the sock in her gloved hand, hiding it there, and took it all the way back to her car, needing a bag to put it in.

CHAPTER 15

*T*he only person working at the front desk of the Vieira County district attorney's office was Miss Mabel, the staff secretary. Mabel was seated behind the glass window at the entrance, doing a crossword puzzle. Past her, Carrie could see everyone else in the office had crowded at the rear of the main room, back where the county detectives worked. Some of them were standing on chairs to look over the heads of their colleagues.

"What's going on back there?" Carrie asked.

"They caught that police impersonator who went after that poor girl," Mabel said.

"You're kidding me."

"Chief Bender has him in the interrogation room now," Mabel replied, filling in one of the words.

"He getting a confession in there, or what?" Carrie asked.

"So far all I heard was him screaming and yelling. There might have been some tears, but knowing Harv Bender, that was him too."

Carrie stifled a laugh. "Do you have access to the old records room?"

"Why? Don't you have a key?"

"I can't get into any of the records rooms or supply closets," Carrie said.

Mabel opened her desk drawer and searched through a pile of keys. "They trust you detectives with guns, but they're afraid you're going to run off with all the paper towels and toilet paper."

"That's because they know how little they pay us," Carrie said.

Mabel handed her the keys. "Now you be careful in there. Everything's a mess, and there're boxes stacked all the way to the ceiling that look ready to come down any second. Last time someone was in there, they saw a rat and screamed so loud everybody came running."

Carrie took the ring of keys and tapped the gun against her hip. "I'm ready for any rats, trust me."

"Just try not to accidentally shoot anybody through the walls," Mabel said, then leaned forward to whisper, "not unless it's somebody I don't like."

"I'll do my best, Miss Mabel," Carrie said, walking down the hall. "If you hear me scream, make sure you duck."

She worked the key into the door to the records room and pushed it open, groaning at the sight of towering columns of cardboard boxes stuffed full of loose papers. The lower boxes had buckled, crushed beneath each tower's weight, but all of the stacks leaned together at the top, somehow supporting each other enough to stay upright.

Rusted filing cabinets lined the walls, with a few scattered throughout the middle of the room. Boxes were stacked on top of them, too. Carrie stared at this strange interconnected labyrinth of columns and boxes and cabinets. The danger wasn't rodents. The danger was bumping into a load-bearing tower and having it collapse on top of you.

"God damn, I hate Jenga," she muttered, sidestepping her way inside the room. She clipped one of the oddly angled boxes with her shoulder and cringed when it swayed, but it didn't fall.

Many of the boxes were covered in ancient water stains and split open along the seams. They were held together with duct tape, bursting with papers that had been stuffed inside. Everywhere she stepped was littered with containers that had fallen apart and vomited their contents across the floor.

Case numbers were printed on yellowed labels that peeled away from their box's surface, or had been scrawled across the front of the folder in Magic Marker. Each tower seemed to be stacked by year, and as she reached the back of the room, they grew shorter.

She reached the last tower and realized they only covered until the midnineties. All the years beyond that were stored in the filing cabinets.

She found the cabinet for the 1981 cases. Everything was organized by blue index cards, going by type of incident, and the date. She searched for the February cases and had to bend down to the lowest drawer. She pulled it, but it was stuck. "Oh, shit," she whispered, looking up at the towering stack of case files piled on top of it.

Carrie covered her head with her hand and yanked. The files above her swayed back and forth, but held. She gently pulled the drawer the rest of the way out. Toward the back, she found a file marked *Hope Pugh, Missing Juvenile*. She pulled it free, disappointed at how thin a case file it was. Most of it had nothing to do with Hope at all. Someone had collected articles related to Oliver Rein's suicide and Walt Auburn's heroic last stand as well as correspondence from that time.

Someone, Carrie thought. It had to be Jacob Rein.

She sat down on the floor and leaned back against one of the filing cabinets. She spread the file across her lap and picked up the first page. It was a letter from Chief Walt Auburn, written to the county detectives on February 16, 1981. The same day Auburn died.

> *Dear District Attorney and Chief of County Detectives:*
> *It is my sad duty to report that Chief Oliver Rein has died as a result of suicide, and I am temporarily assuming command of the Patterson Borough Police Department's jurisdiction.*

Beneath the letter was a newspaper article showing a picture of Walt Auburn. The headline above his photo read, THE HERO OF LISTON.

> *Liston Police Chief Walter C. Auburn was killed last night as a result of his duties. Auburn was investigating a local motorcycle gang and had tracked the bandits to their hideout. In confronting the sus-*

pects, Auburn engaged them in a gunfight and killed all five by himself. In doing so, he received fatal wounds and succumbed to them at the scene.

The newspaper article showed two photographs of each motorcycle member. A military photo taken when they were younger and fresh out of boot camp, and mug shots taken years later for various crimes. Each one of them had aged hard, Carrie thought. Whether that was from the war, or drugs, or just bad living, she couldn't tell, but if she'd seen any of them in a dark alley, she'd have put her hand on her gun and been ready to pull it.

Next was a yellow piece of legal paper covered in handwritten notes. This is Jacob's handwriting, she realized, reading the page more carefully.

At the top of the page was the name Hope Pugh, with her date of birth and Social Security number written beside it.

On the left side of the page was a series of boxes, written as questions, and on the right were the answers, and they all said the same thing.

Driver's License Photo? No record found.

Credit History? No record found

Voter Registration? No record found.

Arrest Record? No record found.

Passport History? No passport issued.

Next to every remaining category on the list was a blank response. There had been no name changes. No activity on her Social Security number. No bank accounts had ever been opened by her. If Hope Pugh had survived into adulthood, there would be some record of her, somewhere.

Jacob Rein was looking for her, all those years later, still clinging to the idea that Hope might still be out there.

She wasn't.

Carrie could see Rein's handwriting weaken as the list went on, as if the strength to answer his own questions were being wrung out of him with each hard truth.

She pictured him sitting at his desk all those years ago, alone, searching for a person who could not be found. As alone as she felt in that moment, sitting on the dirty floor in the records room, and no closer to the truth.

Carrie turned down the corridor and headed toward the crowd of attorneys. They'd surrounded the interrogation room. Some had backed away from what they saw through the one-way glass, their faces pale and stiff. The ones who stayed looked on hungrily.

The wall shook with a loud crash, and the hulking form of Harv Bender pressed against the window, his forearm wedged under another man's chin and chest. Harv was close enough to him to fling spit at the other's man's face when he said, "You like to rape defenseless women? Yeah, scumbag? You like to dress up like a cop? Since you like rape so much, tell you what. I'm going to put you in a place where rape happens all the time. I don't think you'll like the way they do it, though. A nice little white boy like you. You're gonna be real, real popular in there."

Blood trickled down the suspect's nose, leaking onto Bender's white dress shirt, but he didn't mind. He was winding it up for his audience. Shouting loud enough to make sure everyone heard. Slamming the suspect into the wall must have gotten a big reaction for him to do it so soon again. The guy was a foot shorter than Bender, and gagging on the forearm wedged under his throat, squirming to get enough room to breathe. "I didn't rape anybody!" he gasped. "I told you, I was just trying to go around that lady because she was driving too slow."

Bender tossed him aside, scowling in disgust. He lifted his beefy arms to inspect them, seeing the bloodstains there, turning them to make sure everyone standing behind the window could see, too. "I'm going to give you time to think things over. When I come back, it's either going to get a lot better for you, or a lot worse. Worse than anything you can imagine. I've got guys with toilet plungers standing outside, and they are dying to come in here. You better tell me something I want to hear when I get back, or else."

Carrie watched the man rub his throat and sit on the floor, lowering his head into his hands. Bender came through the door, beaming at the crowd gathered there who'd been watching him perform. He held his finger to his lips, telling everyone to keep quiet as he pulled the door shut behind him with a soft click. "These walls are thin," he whispered. He pointed through the window. "See how he's sitting there with his head down? That's a classic give-up pose. He knows he's beat, so he's conserving his energy. When I go back in there, he'll crack like an egg."

Carrie could see the man's shoulders and back twitching as he sobbed into his arms. She'd heard of suspects laying their heads on the interrogation table as a sign of them giving up, but never tucking themselves into a ball in the corner of the room and crying like a baby. Give-up signs and the like were all part of the body language bullshit shysters got paid teaching seminars to gullible people like Harv Bender. That was one of the first things she'd learned from Jacob Rein.

Bender saw her staring through the window and tapped her arm, smiling wide. "See that? The old dog still has some tricks up his sleeve after all. How long did it take me to solve your fake-cop rapist case? A few days?"

"Yeah, nice job," Carrie said. "How'd you get him?"

He waved for her to follow him down the hall toward his office. Along the way, Bender stepped into the kitchenette to scrub his arms in the sink. He rinsed off the soap and checked his arms for blood. "Rod Turley, that's our guy," Bender said over his shoulder. "Mr. Turley tried pulling a woman over on a deserted road out past the water treatment plant this morning. Real isolated area. Unfortunately for him, she'd read something in the paper about your case. What's your victim's name? Monica Gere?"

"That's right," Carrie said.

Bender dried off his arms with a handful of paper towels, then tossed them away. "So this chick calls nine-one-one. Turley sees her on the phone and tries taking off, but the locals stopped him. My victim ID'd him at the scene. Now he's all mine."

Carrie followed Bender into his office. "Was he dressed like a cop?"

Several large paper bags lay open on Bender's desk. "No. No uniform, no badge. None that we found yet, anyway. No flashlight, either," Bender said, reaching into the largest bag. "But he did have this."

The chief pulled out a rectangular light box with four blue bulbs and a long cord with a cigarette lighter plug-in attachment. Underneath the box was a bracket where it had been mounted on a car's dashboard, and chunks of the dashboard were still stuck to it from where the cops had ripped it out. Bender held it up triumphantly, displaying his prize.

"A volunteer firefighter's blue light?" Carrie said.

"That's right," Bender said. "This is what he stopped my girl with. And we got it before he had time to ditch it. I've already got a phone call in to that Monica Gere gal, but from what I heard about her being a psycho, I don't expect to hear back."

"She told me it was definitely blue and red lights that pulled her over," Carrie said. "Kind of a difference, right?"

"Happens all the time," Bender said, dropping the blue light back into the evidence bag. "He probably read that article in the paper and knew it was time to change his MO. You of all people should know these mutts don't always fit the usual profile."

"Right," Carrie whispered. "Well, nice job, boss," she added.

"Now do you see why I was telling you to slow down? You never want to run with your choke out in these kinds of situations." He tapped his finger against the side of his head. "You always gotta use this, okay?"

"Okay, Chief," she said. "I'll remember that."

"Good. So talk to me. How'd it go out in Liston-Patterson?"

"They found the rest of the body, which is good, I guess," Carrie said. "But that chief out there, he's different."

"How do you mean?" Bender asked. "You know he called here,

checking up on you? I only talked to him for a few minutes. He seemed to feel like you were done with your assistance."

"I gotta be honest, I'm glad to be out of there. The guy kept saying shit about us. How we don't know our asses from holes in the ground. How you are just some political hack who blew enough people to finally get the chief's job. I had to tell him to shut his damn mouth a few times. I'm telling you, boss, if this guy worked for you, you wouldn't put him in charge of a school crossing."

Bender's brow twitched as she spoke. Carrie gave it a second, letting it all sink in before she went on. "I'm not surprised he wants the county out of his little kingdom. I don't think they know what the hell they're doing. He's terrified I'm going to see something and come back and report it to you, and you'll come down on them like holy hellfire." Carrie leaned against the doorway, staying casual, not looking at Bender's sweaty, inflamed face. "Anyway, that's what I think."

Bender ran his hand through his hair. "Tell you what. Give it a few more days down there. Lay low, stay quiet. I want you to report back to me on every single thing that little cocksucker does and says. Maybe I'll go have a little chat with him when this is all wrapped up and explain just who is who in this county."

"You sure?" Carrie asked. "I'd rather be up here, helping you with this rapist case."

"I've got this under control," Bender said, hiking his pants and belt up over the lower lid of his belly. "You just get back there and make sure those bozos don't miss anything important."

"Understood," Carrie said.

"Now excuse me," Bender said, moving past her to go back down the hall toward the interrogation room. "I have to go have another conversation with my new friend and see if he wants to play nice or receive the worst ass beating of his miserable life."

"Hey, boss?" Carrie called out after him. "I forgot to ask, *is* this guy Turley a volunteer firefighter?"

"He said he was a few years ago, but I haven't checked it out yet. Those guys are supposed to hand those blue lights back in once they stop being active members. Him still having it is what we call, in the detective world, Exhibit A."

Bender went back through the door, into the interrogation room. The people still gathered around the window pressed forward again. Carrie hurried by, wanting to be as far away as possible from whatever was about to happen inside that room. As she passed, Turley looked up from the table, as if he could see her through the mirror, his wet eyes pleading with her to stay.

Maybe he was the right guy, Carrie thought. Maybe he really did swap out his entire scheme as a cop, which was completely effective, just to try out something lame and nonsensical instead. A volunteer firefighter with a plug-in blue light. Of course, that wouldn't work, Carrie thought. The most people did was slow down to let blue-lighters go around them. Nobody ever pulled over and stopped. And if they did, they damn sure didn't provide their driver's license information to a volunteer firefighter or comply with their orders. Jesus Christ, they barely complied with cops. Rod Turley would have to be the biggest idiot in history for running that ruse, especially if he'd already found a good one that worked. And if there's one thing about bad guys that she knew, when they found something that worked, they didn't abandon it. They improved.

She looked back at the shriveled man through the window, even as Bender leaned toward him and seethed, "You going to tell me what I want to know or am I going to have to get unpleasant?"

Maybe Monica Gere was wrong, Carrie thought. Maybe she was lying. Maybe she was trying to make it sound bigger than it actually was, or justify why she hadn't fought back, or a million other possibilities that could somehow explain how Rod Turley was the right guy for the rape.

But not likely. The overeagerness to fit a suspect to a crime, instead of letting it evolve organically, is any criminal investigator's Achilles' heel. She knew that only amateurs and idiots took any oddly shaped puzzle piece and rammed it into the one opening they most desperately needed to fill. Forcing it to fit didn't make it true. Even if a jury came back with a guilty verdict, that didn't

make it true, either. When it was true, you could see it. Prove it. Examine it a thousand different ways and it still remained. It never had to be bent. The truth rings clear, like a bell, and even if it's crazy, it always makes sense.

Carrie tucked the Oliver Rein case folder tight under her arm, heading for the exit. Inside the interrogation room, Rod Turley was crying out for someone to help him, but Carrie let the door slam closed behind her and kept going.

CHAPTER 16

*O*n the morning of his preliminary hearing, Rod Turley shuffled into the district court lobby wearing the same orange jumpsuit he'd worn since being placed in County Prison. He was shackled across his hands and feet, and shuffled past his mother and father, too ashamed to look at them.

"Come on, this way," Dave Kenderdine said. He escorted Turley into the courtroom and sat him down at the nearest table next to the public defender. She was an unhappy-looking woman with long black hair and a purple blazer. Turley leaned in to ask her a question, and she told him not to speak.

Judge Jean Smythe entered the courtroom in a black, flowing robe. Everyone but Turley stood. The judge was in her late sixties but fresh faced and smiling. She looked like someone's grandmother. She even smiled at him and said good morning. Turley wiggled out of his chair and stood as well, as hard as it was with his limbs chained together.

"Please, be seated," Judge Smythe said.

"Your Honor?" Turley called out.

"Sit down," the public defender said, pulling on his arm.

"Your Honor, I didn't do anything! I'm innocent!" he said, talking over the sound of the judge slapping her gavel on the bench.

All the judge's grandmotherly goodness evaporated as she leveled a crooked finger at the public defender. "Advise your client not to say another word. That's the first and last warning he gets."

"Keep your mouth shut and let me do the talking," the public defender said through clenched teeth.

Turley looked around the courtroom. His mother and father were seated behind him. His father's arm was clenched tight around his mother, and she was weeping. Only a swinging wooden gate separated where they sat from where he was, but it seemed a thousand miles away. At the table to his left was the prosecution side.

The assistant district attorney looked like he wasn't old enough to shave. He wore thin, stylish glasses and his hair was slicked back with so much product it reflected the lights from the ceiling above. Seated next to him was the fat cop who'd beaten Turley up and thrown him in prison. Harv Bender, chief of county detectives, Turley had heard him say, over and over. Bender had called him a rapist and a scumbag. On the way to the jail, when they were alone, Bender had said he'd see to it that the guards beat Turley on a daily basis.

Now, Bender looked sweaty and agitated. Both his legs were bouncing up and down in his seat like he was running as fast as he could but not going anywhere.

"Your Honor," the assistant district attorney said, raising his hand to silence Bender, "before we begin, the commonwealth would like to request a continuance."

"On what grounds?" Judge Smythe said.

"Our victim could not be here today," the ADA replied.

The public defender shot to her feet. "Objection, Your Honor. Nothing in the paperwork indicates there has even been a positive ID on my client. I'd respectfully like to know if the victim is even cooperating at this point?"

"We're not prosecuting the case right now. You'll see our evidence when we are ready to proceed," the ADA said.

"Your Honor, I move for immediate dismissal," the public defender said. "My client has been held in prison for days based on nothing but Chief Bender's criminal complaint, which, with all due respect, is nearly incoherent."

Judge Smythe looked at the ADA, who looked about to protest, but had nothing to offer. Behind him, Harv Bender made a small choking sound.

The judge slid the criminal complaint across her desk and read through all of Turley's information and the list of charges. She licked her thumb and turned the page to the affidavit of probable cause, a long narrative that detailed all of the events in the case, written and signed by Bender. Judge Smythe's eyes narrowed before she finished the first paragraph.

She looked up from her desk. "Did the DA's office review this before it was filed?"

"No, Your Honor," the ADA said, moving slightly away from where Harv Bender sat.

"I can't accept this," the judge said. She smacked her gavel and said, "Dismissed. If and when the Commonwealth is ready to proceed, this court is ready to hear their case." She snapped her fingers and said, "Sergeant Kenderdine, release this man from custody, immediately."

Turley was too confused to realize what was happening when the sergeant took him by the arms and raised him out of the seat. "Just hold steady," Kenderdine said. "Raise your hands so I can get the key in."

"Yes, sir," Turley said, too numb to move. "What just happened?" He felt his mother and father come up behind him. His mother wrapped her arms around his back, embracing him.

Kenderdine unlocked the cuffs. He saw Harv Bender rise up from his chair, face purple with rage, and patted Turley on the shoulder. "You can go now. There was a problem with the paperwork. Listen, stay out of trouble and lay low for a while, all right?"

"It wasn't me. I told them that from the beginning. I hope you get whoever it is, I really do," Turley said.

"I'm sure we will," Kenderdine said, watching Bender slam the swinging gate open to pass through it. The man's hands were curled into tight fists.

Harv Bender shoved the courthouse door open so hard it smacked the wall behind the entryway. "Son of a bitch!" he shouted.

He bent forward and pounded his fists against his thighs. "Son of a freaking bitch!"

"Bad day at the office, Harv?" a voice called out to him.

A shabbily dressed man sat on a park bench nearby. His thick beard and threadbare clothing made him look like a homeless person killing time. No, not a homeless person, Bender realized. Something much worse.

"What are you doing here?" Bender said. He stood up and straightened his tie. "Get arrested again?"

"No, not lately," Jacob Rein said. "I came to talk to you about your case."

"My case?" Bender snorted. "Why would I possibly want to talk to you about my case?"

"Because you arrested the wrong man. I knew that before I came here, and now everyone in that courtroom knows it too. That word's going to spread, Harv."

"You," Bender seethed. "You . . . pompous, arrogant, convicted felon piece of shit! Who the hell are you to tell me anything about police work?"

"That's right, I forgot," Rein said, turning to look at the road alongside the courthouse as the cars raced past. "You're the *master detective* who caught the Omnikiller. Isn't that what the press release said? I read all about it in the papers. There's still reporters trying to talk to me, you know. I was hoping I could just let the story you gave them suffice." He glanced back at Bender. "I mean, really, what could I add?"

Bender looked back at the courthouse doors, making sure no one was coming who could overhear them. He moved closer to Rein and said, "What do you want?"

Rein stood up and walked toward Bender's unmarked police car, a brand-new SUV, all black, with tinted windows so dark they were like mirrors. "I told you, I want to talk about your case. Get in the car. I need you to drive me somewhere."

"Jesus H. Christ, am I a taxi service now?" Bender asked. He pulled out his keys and unlocked the doors, then tossed the useless evidence bag in the backseat. He slid into the driver's seat and started the car. "You're lucky I don't want to be seen in public talking to you, or else you'd be taking the shoe leather express. What do you want to tell me?"

Rein reached in his pocket for a small scrap of paper bearing an address on Fawn Drive, only a few miles from where they were. He passed it to Bender and said, "Over the past year, there's been six reports of suspicious vehicles following women or road rage incidents where a male was swerving in the lane all around them, possibly trying to get them to pull over. It's always at night, always on some back road."

"And how do you know that?" Harv asked.

"I filed freedom of information act requests at every police department in this part of the county," Rein said. "You'd be amazed what they hand over if you fill out the right forms."

"Turley's the guy," Bender said. "He had the emergency light in his car, for Christ's sake! He was in the right area, at the right time, trying to pull someone over."

"Monica Gere didn't say he had that kind of light," Rein said. "She said he had red and blue lights, like a police car."

Bender sneered. "Oh, you'd just love that, wouldn't you? You'd just about cream your jeans if this turns out to be a cop. Why, so someone can finally replace you as the most recent cop arrested in this county?"

"I never said this was a cop," Rein said. "Think about it. Six reports of women being followed, but none of them lead to an encounter. None of them are successful. Criminals evolve. They learn. So what does he do? He gets himself a light bar and a uniform. That works just fine. And now that he's got a method that works, it's only going to get worse."

Bender glanced at Rein as he talked. Still the same old smug asshole he'd been back in their county detective days. Except now, Rein had a beard that grew down to his chest and clothes so worn out they looked like rags. "What's your deal now?" Bender asked. "You some kind of homeless investigator? You riding the rails solving mysteries for the other hobos?"

"Can't I just want to help?" Rein said.

"Please," Bender said. "I know you, man. I know the real you. You don't do this shit because you want to help. You did it for the attention, and to prove everyone else wrong, and maybe now you do it out of guilt for what you did to that little girl you hit when you were drunk driving, but none of it, not any of it, is because you want to help."

"Maybe," Rein said. "Or maybe I just can't stand to sit back and watch someone like you do it so badly."

Harv Bender checked the address on the slip of paper and the numbers on the mailboxes as they drove along Fawn Drive. "This is the one, right here." He pulled up to the curb in front of the house and said, "Well, Rein, have a nice day. Feel free to drop dead and never bother me again, if that's all right with you."

Rein looked out the window at the house. A red Honda was parked in the driveway. "You're coming with me," he said. "Bring a notebook and a pen."

Bender leaned forward to look at the house. "What are you talking about? Who lives here?"

"Monica Gere, your victim," Rein said, letting himself out before Bender could stop him.

"Are you crazy?" Bender hissed, keeping his voice down. He hurried out of the car to get hold of Rein and drag him back. "This chick is nuts! She'll freak out if we show up like this. I called her five times. When she finally called me back she told me she'd sue me if I didn't stop harassing her!"

"Too late now," Rein said, raising his head toward the front windows of the house. A shadow passed behind the curtains, peeling one of their edges back just enough to peer through. Rein headed up the driveway, waving.

"This is bullshit, Rein. Even for you," Bender called out, not moving from the sidewalk. "I'm not getting sued for you. Forget it."

Rein pulled open the screen door and knocked. The curtains stopped moving, but the door stayed closed. "Monica?" Rein said, leaning in. He could see someone standing behind the door's frosted-glass windows. "I'm Jacob Rein, and I'm here with Chief Bender from the county detectives. Listen, I know you don't want to talk to the police, and I understand that. We're not here to force you to do anything. I just want you to give me a minute of your time. Hear me out, and then I'll go away if you want."

Monica Gere's voice, fragile and faint, came through the door. "I read that they arrested the man who did this."

"It was the wrong guy," Rein said. "The cops screwed up. They did it with good intentions, but to be honest, without your help, they went down the wrong path. The real bad guy's still out there. I was hoping you could help us with that."

"Are you a police officer?" she asked.

"Why, don't I look like one?" Rein asked. When she didn't answer, he smiled and said, "I'm kidding. No, ma'am, I'm not a police officer. I just know a lot about the kind of person who hurt you, and I wanted to tell you something about him."

He could hear the floorboards creak behind the door but it didn't open, and she didn't speak.

"You see, right now he's congratulating himself on picking someone he thinks is too weak to come forward," Rein said. "He's thinking he has all the power. He figures he made you afraid and you'll stay that way for the rest of your life. What he doesn't know is that you hold his entire future in your hands. You are the one who decides what happens to him. You want him to get away and do it to someone else? That's fine. Do nothing, and that's what will happen. But there's another path. A path where you help us find him, and we drag him in front of you in chains. Where you watch him weep and beg for mercy and collapse when the judge sentences him to prison for the rest of his life. It's up to you. Choose to live in fear, or fight back and teach him what it means to be afraid."

He waited, looking at the door. Behind him, Harv Bender was leaning against his SUV, shaking his head.

"Step away from the front door," he heard Monica say.

Rein stepped back and let the screen door close.

The deadbolt on the door clicked as it turned. The handle beneath it jiggled and the door came open to reveal a disheveled, stricken-looking Monica Gere. She looked past him at Harv Bender, seeing his badge, and then at Rein, taking in his disheveled appearance. She locked the screen door and stood behind it. "I'll talk to you like this, but you can't come in."

"That's fine," Rein said. He waved for Bender to come up, enjoying the way the man's chubby face tightened and turned red. "Miss Gere would like to speak with you," Rein said.

"Kiss my ass," Bender said under his breath as he made his way toward the front door.

"That's close enough," Monica said, halting Bender before he could come any closer. "Are you the man I talked to on the phone?"

"I'm Chief Bender of the county detectives," Bender said. He saw Rein roll his eyes. Bender tried again and said, "I'm Harv, ma'am. I'd like to help you with your case if you don't mind."

"What is it you want to know?"

"First, what makes you so positive this was a police officer?" Bender asked.

Rein held up his hand. "Hold that thought, Miss Gere. We don't know anything about the suspect. Let's start with the basics, okay?"

"All right," she said.

"Was he white, black, or something else?"

"White," she said.

"How do you know that?" Rein asked.

"I saw his arm when he reached into the car to grab me."

"Was he a tall guy, or short?"

"Average," she said.

"What's average? My height?"

"I'm not sure," she said. Her voice quickened and she seemed short of breath. "He was standing over me while I was in the car, and then he—then he—oh God."

"It's okay," Rein said gently. "Do you want to take a break?"

"I need to sit down," Monica said.

"That's fine," Rein said. "You take as long as you like. Me and Harv aren't doing anything except working on this case. We'll wait out here all day if you want, right, Harv?"

"Rein," Bender muttered.

Monica threw the lock open on the screen door and said, "This is stupid. Just come in."

"Yes, ma'am," Rein said as Monica retreated into the living room. He held up his bare wrist and looked at Bender. "What was that, five minutes?" Bender's eyes narrowed, and Rein added, "Maybe it was ten. I can't be sure. I might be slipping. Let's say it was ten."

"Excuse the mess," Monica said as they entered. She was curled up on a chair next to a dark fireplace, with her legs tucked beneath her. The living room table was littered with takeout food containers, all of them nearly still full. "I haven't left the house since I came home from the hospital," she said. "You're the first people I've spoken to."

Rein and Bender both sat down on the couch across from her. "Is there anyone we can call for you? A friend or family member?" Rein asked.

"I haven't told anyone," she whispered. "I just want it to go away."

"It doesn't go away," Rein said. "Not on its own."

"There's an agency in the county for victim assistance," Bender said. "Their number will be in the packet of information you got at the hospital. If you give them a call, they can help. They're real good."

"I'll think about it," Monica said. "So what else do you want to know about him?"

"Anything," Rein said. "Any little detail you can remember. A tattoo. A chipped tooth. Particular phrases he used when he spoke. Whatever you can think of."

"He was mean," she said. "He was strong." She gritted her teeth until her jaw quivered. "He was just so angry."

Bender wrote as she spoke, holding his pen on the page, waiting for her to continue. She didn't. He looked up at Rein, who frowned. "Okay, that's good. Is there anything about the way he looked that you can tell us?"

"It all happened too fast," she whispered. She covered her eyes with her hand. "All I can see is the bright lights flashing and him holding me down! Why did he do that? I was just trying to go home!"

Bender shook his head. This was a dead end. Rein hated to agree with him, but Monica had shut down. There was no point pushing her any farther.

"I'm going to leave you my card," Bender said. "It has my cell on it. You can call me day or night if you remember anything. I'm here to help. I mean that."

They stood up from the couch and Monica Gere shivered. Her hand stayed pressed against her face, shielding her from seeing them. Her voice was soft and weak when she said, "He was a smoker."

Rein and Bender stopped moving.

"He threw his cigarette away as he walked up to my car."

Harv Bender carried two full bags of trash down the driveway from Monica Gere's house. He'd gathered up all the takeout containers and whatever was stuffed inside her kitchen trash can. She'd told him he didn't have to. He did it anyway.

Rein was waiting for him at the car. "You mind giving me a lift out to where Monica was found?"

"Why, you going to pick up every cigarette butt you find along the side of the road?" Bender asked, wiping his hands on his pants.

"No, just the one where she saw him flick it," Rein said.

"Jesus Christ, you really are crazy," Bender said. "Come on, get in."

Once they were in, Harv started the car and pulled away from the curb. "The chances of us finding that cigarette butt are slim and none. The chances of it having any DNA on it after sitting out in the woods all this time are even less. What's the point?"

"Maybe he smokes a cigarette before he approaches each woman. If we can find it, we can identify the brand, and you can start pulling video from every gas station in the area to look for any white males of average height who purchase those kinds of cigarettes. After that, you see if one of them bought those particular cigarettes on any of the days marked on the calendar."

"What calendar?"

"This calendar," Rein said, pulling a folded sheet of paper out of his pocket. "I marked off all the days of the other incidents where women were being followed."

Bender unfolded the page as he steered, seeing Rein's handwriting scribbled all over it. "You have any idea how long it's going to take me to look for cigarette butts at all these places in the woods and then go through all that video?"

"Who are you kidding, Harv? You'll get one of your peons to do it for you."

"Yeah, but still. They'll be tied up doing this crap instead of other stuff I need them to do." He slid the page into his binder, tucking it away for later. "It must be hell for you, huh?"

"Seeing you as the chief of county detectives while I live in disgrace, Harv?" Rein asked. "I try not to think about it, to be honest."

"That's not what I meant," Bender said. "I meant, you know, owning a Ferrari and not being able to drive it."

Rein turned his head. "You'll have to walk me through this one. I'm not following."

Bender grimaced, struggling to form the concept in his head into the right words. "Okay, see, you're like a person who loves to race. You love nothing better than to get out there on the open road and put the pedal to the metal. It's what you live for. This case, it's like a long, clean stretch of track to you. And you've got a Ferrari, right? It's faster than anything else on the road. But instead of being out there racing, leaving everybody in the dust, your Ferrari just sits there. It's like you got locked out of your own race car and can't find the keys to get back in."

Rein stared through the window, watching the cars go past. "Yeah, it's something like that," he said.

CHAPTER 17

*T*here is family you are born with, and family you choose.

At Carrie Santero's age, her mother was already married. She had started a home, delivered a baby, and before that, she had toured the country with various bands. All of her mother's stories were about long nights of banjo music and becoming one with the universe and other fake-hippy bullshit. In just one more year, Carrie would be the same age her mother was when she left home and never came back.

Whenever Carrie's best friend, Molly, had offered to pierce her in some new body part, normally with nothing more than a safety pin heated by a lighter, she'd think of her mother when the pain hit. Whenever they'd mosh at basement clubs in distant cities, she'd think of her mother when it was time to jump up and kick the biggest asshole on the floor.

She and Molly would chug vodka from whatever bottle they'd stolen from the local stores. Sometimes they'd steal it from Penny, Molly's mom, and refill it with water. Molly was a goofy drunk, prone to collapsing in fits of laughter and passing out. Carrie never minded. She'd go outside and sit, looking up at the sky, and picture her mother. She imagined her dancing in some distant field, surrounded by dandelions, barefoot in the mud, surrounded by a drum circle or jam band or whatever lame-ass local musicians she'd attached herself to, oh so at one with the fucking universe, and Carrie would raise both her middle fingers and bare her teeth in rage.

It was the same feeling she had the night she graduated the police academy. The same one she felt when she got sworn in as the first female patrol officer in Coyote Township. It was the same internal fuck you that kept her going now.

She didn't hate her mother for leaving. She didn't now, and she hadn't then. She was angry, sure, but did not hate the woman. Not for that. Her mother's entire life, from what Carrie knew of it, was spent running toward some imaginary land that did not exist. An illusion of what life was like before modern technology and suburbs and cell phones. A place filled with rainbows where peace and love reigned and all the happy little white girls in dreadlocks ran naked through the forest.

People like her mother hitchhiked, or picked up hitchhikers. They wound up raped, or dead, but at least they hadn't compromised their commitment to peace and love. People like her mother believed in crystals and past lives and that all you needed was some organic carrot juice and fresh cilantro to cure cancer. They had a fiercely determined, self-centered devotion to illusion.

And that was what Carrie hated. Idiots and their illusions. Harv Bender's illusions of power. Steve Auburn's illusions of legacy and small-town bullshit. Mrs. Pugh's illusion that her daughter was on some farm, grown up and waiting to come home. Her own mother's illusions of happiness through music and peace and free love. Carrie knew different. Carrie knew it took strength, overwhelming strength, to look into the endless expanse of chaos that formed the universe, where destruction is constant, and stand up against it.

Reality was blood and steel. Fire. Reality was bad people doing bad things and good people burying their heads while it happened. No, Carrie told herself. The ones burying their heads weren't the good people at all.

Good people have scars. Good people are weary of the fight. Good people know they'll eventually get fed into the threshing machine, but goddamn it, they aren't backing down. Most of the good people died a long time ago, leaving the rest of us on our own. We're just the ones who got left behind, compelled to go on as long and hard as we can, until the abyss takes us, too.

Carrie stood at the front door and knocked, leaning her forehead against the glass and cupping her hands to see inside. Only shadows could be seen behind the small windows built into the front door. She knocked again and called out, "Hello? You guys home?"

A thick, clotted cough came from deep inside the house. Carrie could see the form of a small woman shuffling toward the door. "Hang on," and then, another cough.

Carrie stepped back, holding the screen open as the knob twisted. An older woman appeared from behind the door, her brown, tanning-bed-enriched skin looking like the underside of a wrinkled brown paper bag. Penny looked a hundred years older than the day her daughter, Molly, died. No, Carrie thought. Older than that. An unlit cigarette dangled from Penny's lips, leaving bright red lipstick stains on its white filter. "I thought you were away."

"I just got back," Carrie said, moving past her into the house.

"How many times do I have to tell you to use your key?"

"How many times do I have to tell you to use the deadbolt and chain?"

Penny rolled her eyes, then jerked her head back in surprise as Carrie's hand flicked forward, snatching the cigarette out of her mouth. Carrie held it up, between them both. "You promised you'd quit."

Penny snatched it back, breaking it at the center. She tucked it back between her lips. "I did quit. It's not lit, is it?"

Carrie's eyes narrowed. "That's not going to help you."

"I don't do it because I like cigarettes," Penny said, tapping Carrie on the arm and whispering, "I got one of them oral fixations."

Carrie cringed, unable to stop herself from laughing. "You're a dirty old woman, you know that?"

"You'll get there, kid. You hungry?"

"Starving."

Penny retreated into the kitchen, saying, "Well, go on up then. We both know I'm not who you came for, anyway."

"That's not true," Carrie said, peering around the corner. "I came to see you, too. Because I figured you'd be cooking." She flashed a smile and turned, making her way up the stairs, slow and deliberate, using just the ledge of each step to keep it from squeaking. She could hear a little girl singing from inside the first bedroom. The door was shut just enough to let Carrie come up the steps past it and lean along the wall, looking in. Nubs was brushing the long blond hair of one of her dolls and singing to it. Beside her was a long line of other dolls, ones Carrie had bought over the past year, all of them with neatly, newly brushed hair.

The bedroom was filled with toys, stuffed animals, and so many books they had to be stacked alongside the bookshelves that were too full to hold anything else. It was a little girl's room, full of hearts and rainbows, and it made Carrie laugh to think of how differently it looked now.

As a young teenager, when she'd first met Molly, the room was covered in posters for punk bands and cut-out pictures from magazines of all the famous people Molly thought were hot. She'd loved candles and painted skulls and tarot cards and anything she could find that looked Goth. The only normal thing Molly had was a bright blue vase she kept on her desk that was never filled with flowers. It was where she hid her pot.

By the time Carrie moved in with Molly and Penny, the room hadn't changed much. The only new additions were a few 45-rpm records they'd bought at True Vinyl, the store they both worked at after school. They'd pinned the records to the wall to display them, and even now, Carrie could see the faded outlines where they'd hung. The records were long gone. She'd have given almost anything to have them back. Songs she and Molly would listen to for hours and feel so deeply. Even when they weren't high.

When Molly got pregnant, the two of them had stripped the room down to the bed frame and bare walls. They had cleaned it on their hands and knees and built Nubs's crib together in the center of the empty room.

After Molly died, Carrie had stripped the room down once more. She'd done it alone, sending Penny and Nubs out for the day, while she'd cleaned, and cried, and boxed up every reminder of her beloved friend. She kept some T-shirts for herself. She saved the rest for when Nubs was old enough to wear them. By the time they came back, Carrie presented Nubs with her brand-new, private personal bedroom. The only reminder was a framed photograph of Molly holding Nubs, hanging in the center of the wall.

Penny had stood on the porch hugging Carrie that night for half an hour, sobbing into Carrie's shoulder, and Carrie cried with her.

She knocked softly on the door. Nubs stopped singing and looked up from her doll, the smile wide and brilliant across her face. "I like your song," Carrie said, coming into the room. She sat down on the floor across from the little girl, picked up one of the dolls, and felt its hair. "You did a great job on these. They look beautiful."

"Do you want me to brush yours?" Nubs asked, holding up her plastic brush.

"Of course!" Carrie said, then paused. "Hang on," she said, reaching for the sides of Nubs's face. "Do I see a new missing tooth in there?"

Nubs opened her mouth and pointed to an empty space in her gum. "It came out yesterday."

Carrie's eyes widened. "Did you lose it in a fight?"

Nubs stifled a laugh. "No, it just came out, the same as the others."

"Are you sure? I don't think you're supposed to lose that many baby teeth so soon. You must be growing up super fast or something. Here, stand up and let me look at you." Carrie gasped as Nubs stood up. "I think you are twice as big as before. You must be going to bed on time and eating all your vegetables. That's the only explanation."

"Except brussels sprouts," Nubs said, making a face.

"Well, duh," Carrie said, wrapping her arms around Nubs and

pulling her in for a long embrace. "Nobody likes them until they turn into an old person."

"Do you like them?"

Carrie sighed and said, "God help me, I'm starting to."

By evening, empty plates and bowls were scattered across the table. Penny's thick, homemade sauce was smeared across their rims and stained on the napkins stuffed inside the empty drinking glasses. Penny sipped the last of her wine, her left hand outstretched, stroking Carrie's hair the way she'd done it over the years whenever there had been trouble. They didn't talk about it. There was never a need to.

Nubs was nestled against Carrie's side, the little girl's head resting on the curve of her breast. She was scratching Nubs's back with her nails, making the child giggle whenever she went too high, up onto the delicate skin of her neck. The TV was on. Something Nubs wanted to watch. Carrie's feet were up on the table, resting. It was good. And it was safe. She fell asleep.

IV

WHERE WERE YOU?

CHAPTER 18

J.D. looked for Hope in the halls, and he waited for her at her locker, but she never came. At the last bell, he hurried to the exit, standing off to the side. He pressed himself up on the tips of his toes, trying to see over the heads of the first wave of kids rushing toward the exit. She wasn't there. He waited.

Within seconds, the hallway was filled. Everyone was running and pushing to get through the doors. They raced down the steps toward their buses, and it was all J.D. could do to keep from being dragged down the steps with them. He felt a tug on his arm and spun around, his face broadening into a smile that froze when realized it wasn't her. Adam pressed his inhaler between his lips and took a deep breath, holding it in his chest before releasing it slowly. "What are you standing around for? The bus is getting ready to leave."

"Not yet," J.D. said.

Adam peered through the door, searching for Fred Eubanks or the rest of his group. "There's nobody out there. We're safe."

"I can't leave yet. Go on without me if you want."

Adam leaned against the wall next to him, folding his arms across his chest. "What are we waiting for?"

"Did you see Hope today?"

"Not that I remember. Was she here?"

"She should have been."

"What's the big deal?" Adam asked. "Maybe she stayed home

sick, or her parents picked her up, or something." He pushed the door open. "Come on, we have to get going or we won't be able to sit together."

They fell in behind the rest of the stragglers running for the buses. Some of the drivers were already closing their doors, ignoring the kids shouting at them and waving their arms. Adam sucked wind as he ran, trying to catch a decent breath. J.D. was lagging behind, running with his head turned, looking back at the exit.

"Come on!" Adam wheezed, smacking J.D. on the arm. "Your girlfriend's fine. We have to go!"

"Yeah," J.D. said. "Probably right."

Adam jerked his thumb at the bus. "Race you."

J.D. flew past his friend, making it up the steps to the bus and blocking the doors before they could close. Adam's glasses were cockeyed and his lungs sounded like a clogged drain by the time he reached the bus. J.D. pulled him up the steps and out of the way as the doors hissed closed. Adam bent over, hands on his knees, gasping for air. "I almost got you that time," he said, pulling his inhaler out of his pocket and sticking it in his mouth. "You're just lucky I went easy on you."

They found an empty seat toward the back. J.D. slid in first, his eyes staying on the school, wanting to see Hope come busting through the exit. He could see her so clearly in his mind that he wanted to jump up and cry, "Wait!" If the bus driver tried to keep going, he saw himself grabbing the wheel and wresting it out of the man's hands, or leaping through the doors as it sped off, doing whatever it took to let her know he'd waited for her. Instead, the school's doors stayed closed. The bus rumbled and hissed and drove off.

Adam unzipped his schoolbag and pulled out a dog-eared copy of *Starlog Magazine* with a Klingon on the cover. "Do you want this? It's from last month, but I'm done with it."

"I already read it at your house," J.D. said, still looking at the school.

Adam pulled out a copy of *Mad Magazine*, shaking his head at the drawing of Alfred E. Neuman as Yoda on the cover. "Did you read this one yet? They do Empire Strikes Back. It's kind of funny."

"Yeah, it was okay."

Adam flipped open the *Mad Magazine* and looked through the pages. "I have so many Star Wars proof of purchases saved, they better do another mail-in offer when they do the next movie. Do you think they'll do the third movie soon?"

"I guess," J.D. said.

"I know they will," Adam said. "I can feel it in my bones. Do you know how many proof of purchases it cost to get Boba Fett?"

"Four," J.D. said.

"Just four measly proof of purchases!" Adam cried, shaking his fists in frustration. "I had so many more than that, and my stupid mom threw them all out before I could send them in! I had enough to get one for both of us."

The proofs of purchase were medallions printed on the cardboard backing of each Star Wars figure, at the bottom. J.D. had seen Adam's stack of the cardboard backings with the medallions. They were wrapped together with a rubber band, hidden under his dresser.

"I wonder what the new figure will be. Maybe another bounty hunter. Or maybe even a ship, if you send in enough. Or maybe," Adam said, eyes glittering, "The new Jedi."

"Maybe," J.D. said. He should have figured out Hope wasn't at school earlier. That way he could have gone to her teachers and asked for her homework for that night. He could have gone to her house and handed it to her mom or dad, and made a good impression on them, even if she was too sick to come downstairs. She'd know he'd been the one to bring it. Maybe she'd come to her bedroom window and wave to him as he walked away from her house. He could picture her in that window, framed by the afternoon fading light, smiling down at him.

"I bet it's Luke's brother. That has to be who Yoda meant," Adam continued. "A secret brother. Or uncle. At first I thought it might be Obi-Wan's son, but then it wouldn't make sense for

Yoda to tell him there is another, right? Because Obi-Wan would already—" Adam had to pause, stuffing his hand into his pocket and pulling out his inhaler to take another stiff dose. He waited, forcing himself to slow down, then said, "Obi-Wan would already know he had a son. Do you think the new Jedi will be more powerful than Luke? What color lightsaber do you think he will have?"

J.D. shrugged, no longer listening. Something was eating at his insides. A feeling he recognized but was not experienced with enough yet to understand. He'd felt it before. Around his father, mainly. Those were the times he'd locked himself in his room and slid his dresser in front of the door, before the screaming and crashing began. He'd sensed it the way a dog senses a storm before any rain clouds form on the horizon. They can smell ozone in the air. The feeling was always strong but it was not always true.

In the years to come, when his wife came home late and didn't call, or when he dropped his son off at school, or heard news about some mysterious illness that left people disfigured or changed irrevocably, the feeling was there. A sense of impending doom. That the cruel hand of fate was hovering over you all the time, ready to snatch away whatever you held dear.

As an adult, he'd tell himself it was just fear, born of so many years of delivering death notifications to unsuspecting families, or investigating violent crimes, or seeing the things he'd seen and could never unsee. He'd tell himself it was no different for surgeons, who cut people open for a living. Who could look at a human being and visualize exactly what innards and organs were jumbled together just below the surface.

Many years later, after he'd spent a lifetime looking below the surface of existence itself and seen what was writhing there, any other way of viewing the world would be stolen from him. He'd learn to live in never-ending dread. But back then, as a boy of twelve, watching the houses and fields and familiar trees along his bus route home, on a pleasant day of calm weather and bright sun, he found himself deep in the throes of that sickening feeling. It was still new enough that he listened to it.

J.D. hopped down from the bus at his stop and hoisted his schoolbag over both shoulders, securing it in place. He'd be able to move faster without it, and his house was just at the end of the street. But as he turned and looked down the road, he decided it would take too long and started to run.

He was sweating through his jacket and huffing for breath by the time he reached Hope's street. He bent forward, trying to catch his breath, wondering if this was how Adam felt every time he reached for his inhaler. J.D. stood up, smearing a sheet of sweat from his forehead onto his coat sleeve. He'd made it in half the usual time. The sun was still shining. As he stood up, attempting to make himself presentable, he stopped at the sight of something both familiar and horrifying. His uncle's police cruiser, with the light bar on top and the faded Patterson Police insignia on the side, was parked in the Pughs' driveway.

Ollie Rein came out of their front door as J.D. raced up the sidewalk. It took the chief a second to realize who was shouting at him. "Uncle Ollie! What's happening! Is everything all right?"

Ollie hurried down the steps, catching the boy before he could run into the house. "Hang on a second, just wait. What are you doing here?"

J.D. gulped for breath. "Hope wasn't in school today. I came to see what was going on. What's wrong? Is she okay?"

Ollie looked up at the house and his face darkened. He turned back to J.D. and lowered his voice. "Is Hope the girl you were telling me about last night?"

"Yeah," J.D. said.

"The one you wanted to go see?"

When J.D. nodded, Ollie snatched him by the shirt collar and dragged the boy down the driveway, taking him away from the front of the house and out of earshot. J.D. grimaced in fear as his uncle lowered his face toward his, growling, "You'd better tell me every goddamn thing, right now. What do you know about this?"

"About what?" J.D. cried.

"She's been missing since last night! So help me God, if you know where she is or what happened to her, you'd better tell me right now. This is not playtime, J.D.!" Ollie wrenched him forward, shouting, "Where is she?!"

"I don't know!" J.D. shouted back, tears spilling down his face. He clawed at his uncle's fingers and kicked him in the shins through his thin police pants, shouting, "Get off me! I have to go look for her! Let go!"

"Look at me," Ollie said, shaking him. "I'm not kidding, you better look at me. Did you leave my house last night?"

"No," J.D. said, swallowing hard and wiping his eyes.

"I swear to you I will know if you're lying. Did you leave my house last night?"

"No. I didn't leave your house last night, Uncle Ollie."

"All right," Ollie said, letting go. The boy's shirt collar was stretched out of shape and hung loose around his neck, revealing the red marks where it had been twisted around his skin. Ollie laid both his hands on J.D.'s shoulders. "Listen, I just had to be sure."

"Sure about what?" J.D. said, pushing Ollie's hands away.

"Sure you don't know anything about this. What do you think her parents would say? They'd think you had something to do with it, J.D. And here you go showing up the next day. Anybody who didn't know you would think you were coming here trying to see how the investigation was going. That's what bad guys do, J.D. They show up and say they want to help, but really, they just want to enjoy all the panic and turmoil they caused."

"Well I'm not," J.D. said, glaring at his uncle. "I just came here to see Hope." He reached up and touched his neck, where it was raw. "You didn't have to grab me and yell at me like that."

"Okay, all right?" Ollie said. "You want to help me?"

"Help you how?"

Ollie ran his hand through his hair, brushing it out of his face. "I'll take anything at this point. The parents don't know squat. They said Hope had dinner with them, then went into her room to do her homework. They haven't seen her since." He looked at J.D. "Where were you supposed to meet up with her?"

"Around back," J.D. said. "There's a clearing in the woods where she goes."

"Show me," Ollie said, heading back toward the house until he realized J.D. wasn't following him. "Hey, I thought you wanted to help."

J.D. was too ashamed to lift his eyes from the ground. "Why did you think I had something to do with it? Do you think I'd ever do something like that?"

Ollie went back and knelt to look the boy in the face. "No, not in my heart. I could never think that, kiddo. You're my nephew, my blood, and I love you. But look at me." He raised J.D.'s chin. "Hey. Look at me. With a case like this, I have to shut all that out and do whatever it takes to find this little girl. Do you understand?"

They walked around the back of the house, through the Pughs' backyard toward the woods. Every so often, Ollie turned his head to look at the back of the house, judging how far away it was, and how dark it would be at night. "These woods go all the way up into the mountains," Ollie said. "If she decided to go walking, she could have gotten lost. Do you think she tried going to your house?"

"No," J.D. said. "She knows I don't want her coming there. It's not a good place."

Ollie followed him into the woods. It was getting dark, with the lowering sun trapped in the canopy of trees. If he squinted, he could make out the profile of a small brick chimney through the cluster of trees. J.D. waved him on, but Ollie held the boy back. "Hang on a second. I want to get a look at this before we go trampling around."

They inched forward until Ollie could see the green army blanket spread out across the ground in front of the chimney. He walked around the blanket's edge, with J.D. following close behind. Sticks and leaves were scattered across the blanket and the mud was dug up all along the sides of it, but that could have been from anything. There weren't any discernable footprints in the mud, not even from animals. It was probably too cold for the ground to be soft enough to show tracks, especially at night. Ollie pulled his flashlight from his belt and looked down at where they'd been walking. Nothing.

"Oh no, look!" J.D. said, thrusting his hand forward.

Ollie raised his flashlight to where the boy pointed, seeing a small, curled-up sock, and beside it, a stuffed animal. J.D. raced to grab the bear, but Ollie snatched him by the schoolbag, holding him back. "Hang on," Ollie said, pulling J.D. away from the blanket.

"But that's her favorite thing," J.D. said, panicking. "She'd have never left it out here. Never!"

"All right, just calm down," Ollie said, scratching his chin as he looked the items over. "If something did happen, we don't want to mess up any evidence. You stay put right here." Ollie shined his flashlight over the rest of the blanket and area surrounding it, making one wide circle around the area, until he was almost back to where J.D. was standing, when he saw something on the ground. It was hidden by leaves, but its metal mirrored surface flickered in the fading light. He covered it with his boot to keep it hidden, standing awkwardly as he tried not to push it into the ground.

J.D. stared at Ollie in confusion as he tried to balance himself.

"What?" Ollie asked, folding his arms across his chest.

"Nothing," J.D. said, looking back at the blanket. "I'm telling you, Uncle Ollie, she wouldn't have left that bear out here. Something happened to her. Something horrible."

"Now, don't go leaping to conclusions," Ollie said. "A lot of things could have happened, but it won't do us any good to lose our heads." He fished in his pocket for his car keys and tossed them to J.D. "Go to my police car and get me my camera, a big paper bag, and a few plastic ones. They're in the trunk. Can you do that?"

J.D. repeated the items back to his uncle. Ollie nodded, saying, "Hustle up, now. We're losing light."

He waited for the boy to vanish into the woods before lifting his boot. He bent down on his knees and looked up, making sure no one was watching, and turned his flashlight on. There, half embedded in the mud, was a switchblade knife with a cheap black handle, its blade still extended.

Ollie reached into his back pocket and pulled on one of his wool winter gloves to pry the knife out. He held it under his light. It hadn't been outside long. No rust or wear showed on any of the parts. He turned back toward the blanket, wiggling the knife between his gloved fingers, looking at the bear and little girl's sock and the wide expanse of woods behind this secluded place so near to her home and yet so far, and he muttered, "Aw fuck."

CHAPTER 19

*O*llie opened his eyes into the harsh glare of the emergent sun, which blinded him, spreading light and heat across his face. He turned away, scowling, waiting for the spots behind his eyelids to dissolve so he could get his bearings. He was parked on a trail that ran along the mountainside. It was flat enough to drive, so he'd driven it all night long, high beams on, alley lights from the sides of his light bar on, using the powerful spotlight mounted to his window frame. He'd seen deer and possum and foxes, but no sign of any little girls. He'd meant to pull over for only a little while. Half an hour, tops. Long enough to keep from crashing the police car into a tree or rolling it down a ravine.

Someone was walking toward the police car. A weathered old man dressed in a hunter's coat and thick plaid hat. It was the farmer Franklin Hayes, and from the bemused look on his face, he'd been watching Ollie sleep. When Hayes realized he'd been spotted, he came toward Ollie's car with such a pronounced limp he almost fell over.

Ollie wiped his face and rolled down his window, smiling with embarrassment. "How you doing this morning, Mr. Hayes?"

"I'm good, young fella. What you doing all the way out here asleep in your police car? You get kicked out by your woman?"

"No, sir," Ollie said. "I was out all night looking for the Pugh girl. She went missing yesterday. I guess I fell asleep. You didn't see any kids wandering around by any chance, did you?"

Hayes's jaws clapped together, wrinkling the flabby sides of his cheeks, like he was chewing the question there. "No," he said. "Weren't no children out. I did see something that caught my eye, though."

"You did?" Ollie asked, laying it on. "What'd you see?"

Hayes eyed him, turning his head sideways, muttering as he ground his toothless gums together. "Well, I don't reckon I ought to tell you."

"Why's that?"

"I don't truck much with no law ever since you all shot me."

"Well, that makes sense," Ollie said. "I'd be mad too. But you understand, they didn't shoot you on purpose. That was an accident."

"Careless, is what it was," Hayes said.

"I'm not saying otherwise," Ollie said.

"I still got a limp, you know," Hayes said, pointing at his leg. "Can't hardly walk on it to this day."

"I can see that. I'm astonished you made it all the way up here without falling down." Ollie scratched his chin and looked at himself in the mirror. It had been days since he'd shaved and his face was starting to itch. The old man hadn't moved away yet. Ollie took that as a good sign. "Hey, I heard you kept that bullet. That true?"

"I got it right here," Hayes said, patting himself on the chest.

"Can I see it?"

Hayes dug into his shirt and pulled out the long strand of leather he wore tied around his neck. Dangling from the center of the necklace was a small clump of misshapen lead. He pointed at the center of the wad and said, "I told the doctor to save it for me, then I drilled a hole through it after I got home from the hospital."

Ollie whistled in admiration. "I'll tell you what, I've seen bullets smaller than that cut people in half. You must have been some kind of badass back in the day. Bet you had legs the size of tree trunks from working the farm all those years. Must have been what saved you."

Hayes grinned. "Clean living. That's what it was. A hard day's work and good food. Real food, not like the poison people eat nowadays. Back then, we'd just kill it and eat it."

"Those were the days," Ollie said. "Well, I sure do appreciate you showing me that bullet." He stepped on the brake and dropped the transmission into drive. "You ever change your mind about what caught your eye, you let me know."

Hayes pulled back from the car, turning his head to each side, to see if anyone was coming. He leaned down toward Ollie, nearly sticking his head through the car's window. "You don't tell anybody I told you this, all right?"

"All right."

"I saw them bicycle riders coming and going all over town, you know which ones I mean? With the loud engines?"

"Motorcycles."

"That's what I said," Hayes said. "I kept hearing their damn engines after dark, somewhere back behind my property. I went out there this morning to make sure none of those bicycles is tearing up my land."

"Were they?" Ollie asked.

"No, and it's lucky for them too. I had my shotgun."

"What did you see?"

"I seen their hideout," Hayes said. "Some kind of cabin they built way out in the back of the woods where nobody could see what they was up to. And that's not all," Hayes said. He lowered his voice. "They were carrying something into it."

"Could you see what it was?"

"Some kind of trunk. Heavy enough that it took two of them to carry."

"How big?" Ollie asked.

"About yea big," Hayes said, holding his arms out wide. "Big enough to hold that little girl, now that I think on it."

Ollie took the long way down the mountain trail, winding around the Hayes farm and parking in the state game lands just beyond it. Franklin Hayes had stapled DO NOT TRESPASS and NO HUNTING signs on every tree at the border. Knowing Hayes and his shotgun, he was sure anybody who violated that border would feel the hot wind of bird shot sailing over their heads.

It would have been easier to park on the Hayes property and walk down, but Ollie didn't trust the old farmer. Besides being trigger-happy, he was a gossip, and forgetful. If you wanted to spy on an enemy encampment, the fewer people who knew about it, the better. Ollie couldn't risk the Disgraced finding out he knew where they were if they had Hope Pugh. They'd move her in the dead of night and he'd lose her forever.

He walked for an hour, until sweat was seeping down his back and cooling the sides of his face. The sun was high but it was cold in the shadows beneath the trees. He walked quietly in the woods, careful to avoid branches and dry leaves, out of a habit taught from an early age. Don't disturb the animals around you, because if you kick up a flock of birds, the enemy will know you're coming. His father had taught him and Ben that as kids. Move silent, so the Nazi bastards can't hear you, their old man always said. Everybody was a Nazi to him. The mechanic who wanted to charge too much money to fix their car was a Nazi. The tax man was a Nazi. The factory foreman who caught the old man drinking in the locker room and fired him was the biggest Nazi of all.

Christ, he was always so drunk he probably saw Nazis everywhere he looked, Ollie thought.

Ben had taken the brunt of the old man's rage, always holding him off so Ollie could escape. They practically lived in the woods as kids, trying to stay away.

He came to the edge of a creek that ran through the game lands and wound down through the Hayes farm. It separated Liston and Patterson Boroughs, and no bridges spanned it for miles. Where he stood no slope went down into the creek. Just a steep drop-off into cold, rushing water, five feet below. The creek ran deeper in some places and shallower in others. He knew because he'd fished it. In some pockets the bass would run fishing line so far down he thought he might reach the end of his spool. Others were shallow enough to walk across and barely get the bottom of your pants wet.

Jumping off the edge into the water, he decided, was too risky.

It would be stupid to break his ankles on any rocks hidden beneath the surface. Even stupider to jump down and sink into one of those bass holes, bogged down by the weight of his clothes and gun belt, and drown.

He spied a gravel bed on the other side of the creek. If he could get down there, he could walk along that until he found somewhere to lower himself into the water. Ollie walked along the ledge, until he ran out of it, surrounded by thick bramble bushes with thorns the size of snake fangs. A tall tree loomed overhead, its stout branches draped in thick vines. Ollie wound several of them around both his hands, pulling to see if they'd hold. They seemed like they would.

"Here's goes nothing," he said.

He stood with his boots dangling over the earthen edge, clutching the vines, and took his first step down, digging his toes into the roots and dirt wall hanging above the water. He took his time lowering his other foot down, now suspended over the creek with nothing but the vines wrapped around his hands. They were straining and cutting his flesh, but they held.

Ollie took another step down, and his foot slipped on the slick mud, sending him skidding. The vines helped control his fall, keeping him upright, but he landed in a tremendous splash, knee deep in freezing-cold water. He unwrapped his hands and slogged through the creek, making his way toward the other side.

His boots squirted water through their sides every time he took a step. "Waterproof, my ass," Ollie muttered, lifting them up one by one to inspect their soles. After an hour walking along the embankment, they were caked in mud and small rocks were wedged in their rubber treads. His pants were soaked. The bottom of his holster was soaked. His feet ached from the cold and the wet. He could feel sand between his toes and grinding against the sore, shriveled flesh of the soles of each foot. And, of course, the moment he came up from the creek, the wind kicked up, cutting through his clothes like they were tissue paper.

Ollie leaned back against the nearest tree, collecting himself.

Using a small stick, he scraped the bottom of his boots clean and pried out the rocks. He untied their laces and took them off, shaking out as much water and dirt as he could. He pulled off his socks, shivering on the cold mud, and wrung them out. When he slid them back on and got his feet back inside the boots they were still wet, but he told himself it wasn't as bad as before, and somehow, it wasn't.

He smelled the place before he saw it. Burning logs inside a woodstove. He followed the unmistakable scent through rows of dense trees, bent low, moving from tree to tree, using them for cover as he leaned his head out just enough to peer around.

A truck was parked a hundred yards ahead of him, and an old, beat-up station wagon sat next to it. Both had New York state license plates, but he was too far away to make out their numbers. He saw a small shed near the truck and lowered himself to the ground, creeping toward it.

As he worked around the trees, he found the cabin Franklin Hayes had spoken of. It had a narrow column of smoke coming out of its chimney. On the grass in front of the cabin's entrance were five motorcycles.

The cabin was poorly assembled, with rotting walls and a dilapidated roof. The windows along the front and sides were obscured by what looked like old bath towels hung up behind them, probably just nailed into the window frames or even the walls themselves. There were two cables strung to the roof that vanished into the trees. A hunting lodge this far out with electricity and telephone service, Ollie thought. Now that's damn peculiar.

The door burst open and the bald biker they called Orange emerged. He spun back toward the entrance and yelled, "I heard you the first five fucking times, Wombat. We'll drive like little old ladies going to church."

Ollie dove for the back of the shed and pressed himself against it. He could hear footsteps coming toward him. Orange's voice again, saying, "Hang on, it's a long way to New York. I gotta hit the head."

The shed's door creaked open and shut again, and Ollie could hear someone on the opposite side of the wall unbuckling his pants. He held his breath to keep from making a sound.

"That's a good idea. I better go too," a second biker said.

"You gonna be waiting a long-ass time," Orange said. "Them grits I had at Ruby's are tearing my guts up inside. Swear that old bitch put something in them."

Ollie was close enough to hear what was happening inside the shed and cringed as the smell hit him. He lowered his face into his fist, trying to use his fingers as a makeshift filter.

"Hurry up, man, I gotta take a piss," the other biker said.

"You dumb motherfucker, go piss in the woods and leave me alone. Bad enough I gotta shit in this cold-ass outhouse."

The other biker was coming around the shed right toward him. Ollie scooted around the side as fast as he could behind the wall and braced himself against it, listening. The other biker had stopped walking. Probably wondering what the hell is hiding behind the shed, Ollie thought. He wrapped his hand around the handle of his pistol.

A stream of piss hit the ground right next to him, steaming in the cold air, splashing off the ground at his boots. Ollie grimaced and raised his face away as much as he could, telling himself he was going to shoot someone if any piss hit him on his bare skin.

"What time are we going to be back?"

"Couple hours, each way, give or take," Orange called out.

The stream of urine trickled to a stop. "What if we hurry?"

"Why you in such a rush?"

"Man, I didn't get to try any of that girl yet. The rest of you got some, but Wombat told me I had to wait."

Orange chuckled from inside the shed. "That's because he knows how crazy your ass get."

"Well, I expect to get some the second we get back. You really think they're not in there partying while we're out doing this shit?"

The shed door opened and Orange emerged, saying, "Just get in the goddamn truck. We got a long drive and I'm not listening to you bitch about wanting some white girl the entire time. Faster we get back, faster you get your taste."

The truck's engine started. Ollie leaned out, watching it turn around on the soft grass and glide down the woodland path until it vanished between the trees. Ollie's teeth clenched together and his eyes flickered with anger. He looked at the cabin's front door, at the motorcycles parked in front of it, and the covered-up windows hiding whatever was happening to little Hope Pugh inside.

CHAPTER 20

*O*llie held the bottle of whisky in his hand and waved it as he spoke, knowing his brother's eyes would follow it. Ben watched the bottle like a serpent following a snake charmer's flute. Ollie had bought a small bottle, on purpose. Ben sat on his living room couch with his head leaned back against stained pillows, dressed in a filthy tank top and boxer shorts. His hair was matted and greasy.

"I need your help," Ollie said, putting the bottle down on the table, close enough to snatch back if Ben tried grabbing it.

"Let's open the bottle," Ben said.

"I need your help finding a little girl," Ollie said. "I think I know where she is."

"So go get her. After we open the bottle."

"It's not that easy," Ollie said. "I think she's been taken. Abducted by those bikers we saw at the beer store. I got a tip they had a hideout out in the game lands, past the Hayes farm. Sure enough, I found it. That's where they're keeping her."

Ben looked up from the bottle at his brother. His eyes were red and bleary and he kept clenching them together. "Don't you have other people you can call? Call the Liston cops."

"I don't trust the Liston cops," Ollie said. "Walt Auburn came to see me that afternoon and told me to try to get along with those biker scumbags. He said there might even be some money in it for me."

Ben licked his lips, leaning forward like he might make a grab for the whisky. "How about the State Police? You could call them."

"See, that's the thing," Ollie said, laying his hand down over the bottle's cap. "Where the bikers have her isn't in my jurisdiction. It's in Walt Auburn's territory. If I go there, it's not exactly on the official side of doing business, if you catch my drift. State Police won't touch that with a ten-foot pole. They'll notify Auburn, and as soon as he finds out, first thing he'll do is call those Disgraced assholes."

The veins in Ben's eyes were so thick it looked like they were bleeding. "Then call somebody else," he said. "What the fuck do I know? This is your shit, Ollie. Just open the bottle."

"Don't you think I tried getting help?" Ollie asked. "I called the FBI and county detectives. Both told me to send an official letter requesting their assistance and they'd see what they could do. I'm not holding my breath waiting for a response."

Ben's hands shivered and he didn't bother hiding it. He was getting the shakes and the sweats. "What do a bunch of bikers want with some little kid, Ollie?"

"I heard them talking about it. I went down there and heard one of them saying they were all getting a piece of her, and how he couldn't wait to get back to get some for himself. You heard about what those maniacs did in My Lai. Hell, they probably got a taste for raping children and now they've got another one. I swear, it was all I could do not to kick the door in right there and start shooting."

"So why didn't you?"

Ollie pressed his hands together, leaning them against his forehead. "Because I was afraid if I went in there shooting they'd start shooting and she'd get hurt."

Ben stared at him, his eyes dark and vacant. "Is that why?"

"Yeah, that's why. What else would it be?"

"Nothing," Ben said. "Tell you what. Open that bottle and I'll tell you what I think we should do."

Ollie sighed and twisted the cap to break the seal. He looked at the sink full of dirty dishes and said, "You got any clean glasses around here?"

Instead of answering, Ben grabbed the bottle from the table and raised it straight to his lips, chugging hard. His Adam's apple bobbed as he swallowed.

"Hey, come on," Ollie said, reaching for the bottle. Ben smacked his brother's hand away, still drinking as he rocked back on the couch, raising his feet to kick if Ollie was dumb enough to make a second attempt. He drank until the bottle was empty, even wiping up any that spilled down from his lips with his finger and sucking the liquor off that too. He slammed the empty bottle on the coffee table and gasped for air, then sneered at the horrified look on Ollie's face.

"It's your fault for bringing such a small bottle."

Ollie was too exhausted to argue. "Look, you had your drink. Now, pay attention. The best way is to come up through the game lands on the Liston side," he said, drawing a circle for the house and a line for the road on the table with his finger. "We can park close enough to bring whatever gear we need. There's mountains on that side that look right down over the cabin. We can take up positions and surveil the place for as long as we want."

Ben wiped his mouth again, then wiped his hand on his boxer shorts. "Let me get this straight. You think this biker gang took a little girl, and now they're holding her as their sex slave. You think the local cops are somehow in on it. Now, you want to go there and try to free her, and you want me to come with you as your backup."

"That's right," Ollie said. "So are you in?"

Ben laughed. "Hell no, I'm not in. And people say I'm the crazy one?"

Ollie pushed himself up from the chair to leave.

"Hang on," Ben said. "You asked me for my help, so here it is. You ready? Forget the entire thing and go get us another bottle of booze."

Ollie stared at him. "Are you serious?"

"Hell yes, I'm serious. Do you have any idea who these Disgraced assholes are?"

"I'm not afraid of them!" Ollie shouted.

"Well you should be," Ben shouted back. "They're straight killers, Ollie. Every man in that company was knee deep in the shit, the real shit, not like some fucking secretary. They probably have five hundred kills between them, if not more. You go anywhere near that place and they'll gut you like a fish."

"I don't give a shit who they were in 'Nam. Over here they're just another group of outlaw assholes," Ollie said, jabbing his finger at the badge on his chest. "And I'm not no secretary anymore. I'm the goddamn chief of police and those cocksuckers took a little girl from my town. I won't stand here and let them just have her. Now are you with me? I'm asking you as your only brother, will you come with me and have my back?"

Ollie stretched his hand out across the table toward Ben. There was eager pleading in the younger man's eyes. "What's this little girl to you? You don't know her, or her family," Ben said.

"I took an oath to protect her, just like everyone else who lives here. You going to take my hand or not?"

"Listen to me, Ollie. Call the State Police and tell them everything you just told me. Let them handle it. If they call this Walt Auburn asshole, that's not on you."

"I can't do that," Ollie said.

"Just let it go."

"I can't do that!" Ollie repeated himself. His hand was still outstretched, hovering in the air between them. "Me and you, big brother. The Rein boys. Kicking bad guys in the ass. I need you. What do you say, soldier?"

Ben looked at the hand, and then up at Ollie. "I'm not a soldier anymore, little brother. I'm just a man who drinks and tries to forget. I say no."

Ollie pulled his hand back without another word and turned to the door, pushed it open, and left the house. Ben pushed himself up from the couch and came after him, calling out, "Ollie! Hey, wait. Come on, man. Don't go doing anything stupid. Ollie!"

Ollie was already down the steps and pulling the door of his police car open. He looked back at Ben and said, "How old's your son?"

Ben's face contorted. "What?"

"How old is he?" Ollie asked. "What grade is he in?" When Ben didn't answer, Ollie pounded his fist on the car's roof. "You only had to take one look at those biker assholes to remember exactly who they were. You knew the names of the people they served under. You know every single detail about the war, but can't remember to feed your own kid. I used to think the war fucked you up, Ben, but that's not true. It just revealed who you really are."

"Hey, Ollie?" Ben said, holding up his middle finger. "Do me a favor and go get yourself killed, you moron."

"Fuck you."

"Fuck you right back."

Ollie slammed the police car door shut and sped off, kicking up a plume of dirt and gravel behind it. Ben stood there, watching the disappearing car, then staring at the empty road, not moving for a long time.

CHAPTER 21

*O*llie looked at the woods through his windshield. With his head leaned back against the headrest, he listened to the birds and insects through the open car windows on either side. It was a good sound.

At Long Binh, he'd spend the evenings outside, looking at the tops of the trees through the barbed wire strung along the outer perimeter. Normally, the only sounds he heard were helicopters and gunfire. Explosions in the distance would light up the night sky like fireworks. But sometimes, when it was quiet, which it wasn't often, but sometimes when it was he could hear the birds and the lizards.

The only lizard in that part of Vietnam was the tokay gecko, a small spotted creature with large eyes. The birds were Blue-eared Barbets. They were beautiful, with bright green bodies and multi-colored heads. The tokay gecko and Blue-eared Barbet each made distinct sounds, often trading calls with one another, until their voices echoed through the jungle.

One night, Ollie was sitting on the roof of his barracks watching the explosions on the far horizon, listening to the animals, finishing a six-pack left behind after one of the command staff dinners. The window underneath where he was sitting opened and one of the cooks, a black southern soldier on the last month of his tour, poked his head out. "What are you doing sitting out here?" he said, looking up at Ollie.

"Enjoying the peace and quiet," Ollie said, holding out a beer.

The cook climbed up onto the roof and sat next to him, cracking his beer open and taking a long sip. He wiped his mouth, then cocked one ear toward the jungle and scowled. "Oh, man, how can you stand listening to fuck you and the re-ups?"

Ollie could only hear the birds and lizards, going back and forth, in full chorus. "What are you talking about?"

"Them birds, the green things, don't you hear what they're saying? They're saying, 'Re-up! Re-up!' And the lizards keep saying, 'Fuck you.' But they ain't saying fuck you back to the birds. They saying it to us. They working together, Rein, listen. 'Re-up. Fuck you! Fuck you. Re-up!' Goddamn jungle working to convince us all to stay *in* this motherfucker. Get us all kilt. My last day, I'm gonna catch me a dozen of them bastards and fry them up real good to eat on the plane home."

Ollie handed him another beer and the cook slid back down through the window, leaving him alone on the roof. Ollie cracked open another beer and realized it was true. They really were saying, "Re-up" and "Fuck you." He finished his beer and went back inside.

He couldn't remember the cook's name. They'd played cards together and talked about all the things they'd do when they got home. The women they'd go see. The food they'd eat. How good it would be to get out of the army. They'd exchanged addresses and promised to stay in touch, but they never did. It was like that. People always made a big deal about old soldiers writing each other postcards and finding one another after years apart. Ollie had found that when he got home, he didn't want to look back, and no one seemed to want to look back at him, either.

It wasn't like he was haunted by the war or suffered the same kind of nightmares as his brother, or many of the men he'd known over there. He'd never seen any combat, let alone killed anyone. It was something Ben could see in him as sure as look at him. Something he was lacking. The Disgraced could see it too, Ollie knew. They'd immediately embraced Ben as one of their own, because kind is attracted to kind. They'd treated Ollie like a buffoon for much the same reason. And now, he was going into their lair, facing a den of trained killers, all alone.

He closed the police car door, opened the trunk, and grabbed the items he'd stacked on top of the spare tire. A small pry bar, a pair of binoculars, and the long camouflage scabbard he'd brought from home. He dropped the pry bar into the rear pocket of his uniform pants, draped the binoculars around his neck, and unzipped the scabbard to pull out his twelve-gauge Remington pump shotgun.

He'd driven up through the game lands on the Liston side this time. There wouldn't be any delay getting to the cabin. He'd parked the police car in the woods as close as he could, knowing that once he had what he was looking for, he might have to get the hell out of there in a hurry.

Ollie slung the shotgun over his shoulder and looked at the dense column of trees, trying to decide which path to take. Instead, he opened the police car door again and leaned in to grab the microphone. He stayed standing, leaning against the car's frame, keeping his eyes on the woods as he pressed the TALK button. "Hey, you there, Pretty Lady?" he asked.

"Of course I'm here, handsome," she replied. "Didn't think I was going to hear from you today. You avoiding me?"

"No, just been busy, that's all," he said. "I'll be on a follow-up, off-radio for a bit, and just wanted to let you know."

He could hear her typing into her computer. "What's the address?"

Ollie looked out at the woods and said, "I'll be on foot in the game lands, looking for that missing girl. I'll let you know when I get back."

"Sounds good. Be careful out there, handsome. Good luck, and I hope you find her," she said.

"Me too," he said, about to hang up the microphone, but he raised it again and said, "Hey, what are you making for dinner tonight?"

"Why, you coming over?"

"If it's any good, I might."

"Roasted chicken and mashed potatoes. The real kind. Made from scratch. You want me to save you some?"

Ollie stopped himself from saying one of his typical responses. Only if you wear that blue dress you once told me about, or something like that. Playful banter. Instead, he found himself looking at the woods and trying to picture what she looked like. He'd wondered about it a thousand times. He clicked the TALK button. "You know, I'm going to be out near your work sometime next week."

"Is that right?" she said.

He shifted the shotgun strap around his shoulder to redistribute the weight. It was getting heavy, just standing there holding it. Ollie clicked the TALK button and said, "I was thinking about getting lunch while I'm out there. How about we meet up, just so I don't accidentally pick a place that likes to spit in cops' food?"

"That depends," she replied. "You mind if my husband comes along?"

Ollie cursed under his breath. He clicked the TALK button and said, "Hey, never you mind me. I was just fooling around."

She giggled, as light and soft as the dandelion wishes floating across the tops of the tall grass. "I'm just messing with you. I got divorced two years ago. Man, you should have heard your voice."

Ollie laughed then, and said, "You got me pretty good."

"You come out here next week and I'll make it up to you, handsome," she said.

"It's a date, Pretty Lady," he said, then hung up the microphone and closed his police car door.

"Enjoy your walk in the woods," she replied, but by then, he was gone.

He reached the cabin before dark, with the horizon washed in red and gold fire beyond the trees. It was so cold he shivered, leaning against the trunk of a thick oak tree, peering around the corner. He could hardly move, and his teeth wanted to chatter so he let them, just for a second to get it out of his system. Except it wasn't that cold, no more than it had been, and he knew it.

Smoke wafted from the top of the chimney pipe on the cabin's roof, but now the car and truck were both gone. The motorcycles remained parked outside of the front door, but they were covered over with bright blue tarps. Ollie looked at the empty driveway, thinking it over. Motorcycles were loud and drew attention. It made sense they'd leave the bikes behind sometimes.

Plus, they'd need extra space if they had a little girl tied up in the trunk, he thought. The thought of it pumped blood through his muscles and helped him get moving again. They'd left the woodstove burning inside the cabin. Only two reasons to do that. Either they were coming back soon, or there was someone inside they didn't want freezing to death.

If it was the girl, it made sense that they'd leave someone behind to keep an eye on her. That was what the Remington was for, he thought, tucking its walnut stock deep in his right armpit. He crept across the grass toward the cabin's nearest window and stooped to listen. Nothing. He poked his head up, trying to see between the spaces where the towel was draped behind the glass. Darkness. As he looked, he saw the window's cold glass fog from the heat of his breath.

He bent back down and went around the back of the cabin, stopping at each window to listen, and look, and at each one there was nothing. He went around the entire cabin that way until he came around the opposite side, facing the driveway once more. It was time to go in. Enough stalling.

He hurried toward the front door, keeping under the windows and out of sight, while pulling the pry bar out of his back pocket. He slid the pry bar's flat surface into the narrow wedge between the door and frame, gave it a quick strike with the palm of his hand, and cranked it. The wood frame split apart, loud, and by then it was too late to hesitate. Ollie reached for the shotgun, clutching it with both hands as he leaned back and kicked the door dead center. "Police!" he shouted, barging in with the shotgun raised. "Nobody move!"

The room was bare except for a filthy couch and several plastic lawn chairs and a large wooden trunk in the far corner. Ollie ignored the trunk, racing around the rest of the cabin as fast as he could, making sure no one was hiding inside. He found another door and kicked that one open too. It was just a small bedroom with nothing but a mattress on the floor and an empty closet on the opposite wall. He hurried back out, checking the small kitchen and closet, making sure they were empty as well.

Sure enough, there was a phone mounted to the wall next to the refrigerator. There were two phone numbers written in pencil on the wall next to it. The first one said *New York*. The one just beneath it said *Walt Auburn*.

Ollie looked back at the trunk, feeling the hairs stand up on the back of his neck.

If the little girl was with them, they were on their way to sell her, or relocate her, and he'd lost her forever. If she was inside the trunk, something far worse had happened. "Hope?" he called out, willing himself forward. "Are you in there?"

He wrapped his fingers on the underside of the trunk's lid and tried to lift, but it was sealed shut. He knocked on its hard, wooden surface. "Hope, if you're in there and can't talk, just give a knock or kick or something. Anything, kiddo. It's going to be all right. I'm here now. Nobody is going to hurt you anymore."

Ollie laid his shotgun down on the couch and picked up the pry bar from the floor, went across the room with it, and drove it under the trunk's lid. It was an old trunk, with a steel lock hidden behind a metal latch, and wouldn't give. He rammed the pry bar in even farther and kicked it, crinkling the wood surface but not opening it. He beat on it, sliding the pry bar in and out like he was stabbing it to death, sending shards of wood flying, and filling the room with sharp, echoing cracks. He was out of breath by the time the front wall of the trunk snapped off. The lid never did open, but he was able to jam the pry bar into the cracks along the sides and stomp on it until he could tear the front panel up and away from the rest of it. He heaved the lid, still locked to the front panel, up and over the back in a heap of thick, splintered wood and looked down at what had been hidden so carefully within.

He was out of breath. Sweat trickled down the tip of his nose and off the slope of his chin, dropping onto the shining plastic surface of multiple bundled packages of what could only be pure cocaine.

The packages were packed like bricks, wide and flat, with tape around their edges. The trunk was so heavy it would take two men to lift it.

Ollie stepped back, then bent forward with his hands on his knees, groaning in disbelief. He never heard the car come down the driveway. He never saw it cut its lights off when the occupants realized the front door was busted open. He never noticed them creeping into the living room behind him, watching him tearing apart their trunk with their million dollars' worth of coke. He stood there, bent over, huffing, until he heard a familiar voice say, "I took you for a coward, Ollie, but I didn't take you for no thief."

Ollie spun around with his hand on his pistol but stopped short of drawing it. All five of the Disgraced were standing in the shadows, each of them with a pistol in hand, pointed at him. It was too dark to see their faces except for Wombat's. He was bathed in the last remaining light pouring in through the window. It shimmered on the nickel-plated revolver in his hand. It showed the strands of white in his narrow, pointed beard. He wagged the gun at Ollie, telling him to get his hands up.

"I don't care about the drugs," Ollie said, raising his hands. "I'm just looking for the girl."

The other bikers cocked their heads at him. The smallest, most nervous-looking one of them dropped the hammer on his pistol and said, "Let's smoke this idiot now."

"Hang on," Wombat said. "What girl are you talking about?"

"You know goddamn well what girl!" Ollie shouted. "The little girl. Hope Pugh."

"Never heard of her," Wombat said.

"You rapist fucks took her! I was up here earlier and I heard everything. The two men you sent to New York. I heard them talking all about it."

Wombat closed his eyes and shook his head, chuckling. "Oh, you mean the *white* girl."

Ollie would have leapt forward and clawed the man's eyes out if every hammer on each of the guns pointed at him wouldn't have dropped back the second he moved. "Don't you stand there and make jokes about her," Ollie warned him. "I just want her brought back to her family. I don't care what you do with me."

Wombat laughed and wiped his eyes. "This is unbelievable," he said, looking at the men standing next to him. "Ain't this unbelievable?" They nodded that it was. "Listen, genius. We didn't take no kid. We're businessmen. The *girl* you heard them talking about, well you found it." He tipped his gun toward the destroyed trunk behind Ollie and said, "The finest Colombian powder money can buy."

"No, that's not what he meant. He was talking about Hope," Ollie said, his voice trailing off. He looked back at the trunk, seeing the packages of cocaine stacked one on top of the other.

Man, I didn't get to try any of that girl yet. The rest of you got some, but Wombat told me I had to wait, the one biker had said before leaving for New York.

The hairless one had told him, *That's because he knows how crazy your ass get.*

"Goddamn, we tried to get you to play ball, you asshole," Wombat said and grimaced. "All you had to do was tell us you were looking for a little kid, we'd have torn this town apart to find her. And if we got our hands on the fucker that took her, well, let's just say you'd have never had to worry about him touching another kid again. But you had to be a big shot, didn't you? You didn't want to be associated with us, and now look where it's gotten you."

"Listen," Ollie said, lowering his hands, "we can talk about this."

Wombat's gun jerked forward, eyes widening. "No, there's no talking about this! See, I know how this conversation goes, Ollie. You tell me something like, I'll just walk away and pretend I never saw anything. And you know what happens? Later on, you start running it all back through your mind over and over again, till it starts to eat at you. You decide to make it right, and come after us, because you just can't live with the fact that you looked the other way. Sooner or later, you'd convince your friends in the State Police and FBI that we need to be taken down. Then, a whole lot of people have to die, Ollie. From both sides. Instead, I could just kill you right now and be done with it."

"It doesn't have to be this way," Ollie said. His mind was racing to find anything that might buy him some time to either draw his gun or get them to let him leave. There had to be something. Think, Ollie, think, he thought. Say whatever it takes and fight however you have to. For J.D. That kid needs you. For Pretty Lady and that lunch date next week. Hell, even for Ben.

"You know what the shame of it is?" Wombat said. "I kind of like you."

"Wait a second, guys," Ollie said, forcing himself to smile. "Obviously I misread what you all were into, and I really screwed up today. I admit that. How about we just take a second to figure out how to handle this to everyone's best interest?" When no one else spoke, he tried again, sounding desperate and knowing it. Hating himself for it but talking until the moment he was going to draw his gun and start shooting. He talked and talked, trying to stall, trying to decide when to go for his gun, but he did not beg and he did not blubber. Deep down, he was proud of that.

The light had retreated from the window and Wombat's face was draped in shadow as he pulled the trigger. Ollie saw the bright burst of flame erupt from the barrel, a brilliant, blinding display in the dark room. At the center of the flame, moving in slow motion, Ollie swore he could see the tiny chunk of metal spat out of the barrel, spinning in midair, coming right at him.

It was adrenaline. He knew that from something he'd read. Everything slows down except the mind. Microseconds stretch wide, leaving your mind room to whirl, and your body not even time to flinch. Leaving him time to think these thoughts even as the bullet split the distance between him and the flames from which it sprung. It hit him in the forehead so hard he felt his head snap back on impact. There was no pain. Just the shock of being struck, and then it was like all the lights went out. Like someone unplugged the TV set. Whatever story was in the middle of being shown, it all just vanished.

You are an uncle, and a brother, and a human being full of life and aspirations and hopes and needs and plans and a place in this world. You go from being all that, and one instant later, you are nothing at all.

CHAPTER 22

*T*he knock on the front door came early the next morning, in the dim hours before sunrise. J.D. was awake already, lying in bed waiting for his alarm clock to go off, thinking about Hope. He'd seen her in his dreams each night since she'd vanished. Each time, they were together in school and she was sitting at the desk next to him, confused about why he'd thought she went missing. She'd been visiting her grandmother, she said, or on a family trip, or hadn't been missing at all. Her going missing had been the real dream and now she was back. But she never was.

In the last dream, he'd looked up from his desk and seen her sitting there next to him, working on a complicated math equation. She wrinkled her nose the way she did when she was concentrating, making all the freckles bunch up, and swept a long strand of dangling red hair back over her ear. She caught him staring and said, "What are you looking at, Jacob?"

"Where are you?" he asked her.

She looked confused. "I'm right here. You see me, don't you?"

He reached out and took her hand, squeezing it, feeling it as if it were real. The rest of the seats were empty. It was just them in the classroom. "Hope, just tell me where you are, and I'll come find you. No matter what."

She opened her mouth to say, "I'm near the—" but choked on her words. She grabbed her throat, eyes wide and straining, and something wriggled at the bottom of her nostril, black and slimy.

J.D. watched in horror as a thick, reticulated worm slithered out of her nose and spilled down onto her shirt. Another fell out after it, and then another, until they were pouring out of her nose and open mouth. They splashed J.D.'s hand and he tried to pull away, but Hope wouldn't let go. The worms slithered up his arm toward his neck. He gasped, trying to shake himself free. Hope sat in her seat, pinning his hand to the desk, staring at him while the worms fell out of her.

J.D. woke then and hadn't been back to sleep. He lay in his bed, haunted by his dream, listening to his father snore down the hall. When the knock came at the front door, his entire body stiffened. The second knock was louder, and someone called out, "Ben Rein? It's Chief Auburn from Liston Police. Anybody home?" The knocking grew more insistent. "I need you to open up the door and talk to me. It's important, Ben."

J.D. slid his bedroom dresser out of the way and opened his door, then peeked around the corner. Downstairs, the living room was dark and there was no light flickering from the TV. That meant his dad had gone to bed that night instead of passing out on the couch. He'd probably run out of liquor. J.D. counted the days in his head and that made sense. It was the sixteenth. Two weeks since Ben's last disability check from the government. He'd drunk all that money away long ago. The knocks kept coming, with the man on the porch saying, "Hello? Somebody home? Open the door."

He stared down the hall at his father's bedroom. The door was closed. J.D. swallowed, realizing his father's bedroom had gone silent. The door at the far end of the hall creaked open and Ben Rein stood in the darkness, naked and covered in sweat. He crept down the hall on his toes, moving silently. J.D. backed up, staying out of sight.

Ben slid down the steps and bent so low he was nearly on his knees as he crossed the room toward the farthest window from the door. He tilted his head to peer through the curtains. Lights were coming on from the front porches of the houses around the street.

"Ben Rein?" the man outside called. "It's Chief Walter Auburn. I need to speak with you. Are you in there? It's about your brother."

J.D. crawled to the top of the steps and saw his father emerge from the shadows to stand behind the door. Bathed in the moonlight, the muscles of Ben's legs and back were drawn tight. Scars of all shapes slashed across his flesh. A ruined patch ran down his right side from the small of his back to his upper thigh from where he'd been struck with white phosphorus. He pulled the door open to reveal Walt Auburn standing on the porch, holding his police hat in his hands.

Walt's eyes were lowered already, and the first thing he saw was Ben Rein's dangling privates, framed in the doorway's narrow opening. He jerked backward, using his hat to cover the sight of Ben's crotch. "I'm sorry to bother you," Walt said, "but I'm afraid it couldn't wait. Do you want to go put some clothes on?"

Ben's voice was flat. "What about my brother?"

"Well, it's just, you see, there's been a terrible tragedy." He looked up, waiting for Ben to say something, but the man's eyes were like hard black stones, shining in the darkness. The eyes of madness. "I hate to have to tell you this, but we found Ollie about an hour ago. It appears he took his own life."

Ben's jaw tightened, but he did not move. "How?" he said.

"Sorry?"

"How did he take his own life?"

Walt cleared his throat and cocked his head to one side like he was trying to shake water out of his ear. "Well, it looks like he put his gun up to his forehead and pulled the trigger. He was sitting against a tree out in the game lands. Somebody heard the gunshot and called it in. I went out there looking for him and I'm the one who found him. Now listen, I don't want you to think less of him because of this. Sad to say, but it's common in law enforcement. People go through suffering others can't even imagine, even if they never talk about it. I seen it a lot over the years." Walt's voice petered out. Ben Rein still hadn't moved or shown any sign of comprehension of what he was saying. "So, I just

wanted to let you know how sorry I am. You and your boy going to
be okay?"

"Where is he?" Ben asked. "His body. Where did you take it?"

"I called Claus Schumacher, the funeral director. He's a friend
of mine and didn't mind coming out. I'm pretty sure I can convince the borough to pay for the funeral, so as not to put a bur-
den on your family."

"I'll be dressed in five minutes. Take me there."

"Come again?"

Ben closed the door in his face. He turned around, seeing J.D.
looking down at him from the top of the steps. "Get dressed," he
said.

"Is it true?" the boy sputtered. "Is Uncle Ollie dead?"

Ben was already coming up the steps. "I said get dressed."

J.D. cried behind his cupped hands the entire ride, while Walt
Auburn looked at his passengers through his rearview mirror.
Ben Rein sat in the backseat next to his son, motionless, his hands
folded in his lap, never once reaching to comfort the boy.

Walt reached into his glove box and fiddled around with the
contents while he drove, until he felt a few napkins stuffed in the
back. He passed them back to J.D. "Here you go, son. It's going to
be all right."

J.D. took them and wiped his eyes and blew his nose, but the
crying continued. "I've got a son about your age," Walt said.
"Maybe a few years younger. His name's Steve. You two probably
seen each other in the hall at school and didn't know it." He kept
driving. The sun was coming up. "You like school?"

The boy never answered. His eyes were red, but they'd stopped
spilling. Now the car was quiet, and Walt liked that just fine.

They arrived at Schumacher Funeral Home at the far end of
town. It was a small, squat home that had been converted. The
bodies were processed in the basement. The living room and
kitchen had been renovated to form a viewing parlor, complete
with a dozen metal folding chairs. It was decorated in somber col-

ors with framed photographs of flowers and uplifting spiritual sayings.

Claus Schumacher greeted them at the front door, dressed in a dark suit. A crown of thick white hair surrounded the bottom half of his head and a bald dome shined on top. His liver-spotted hands shook as he held the screen door open to let them in. He smiled with closed lips at Ben as he walked up and lowered his head as Ben walked past him. "My condolences. I'm sorry for your loss." He lifted his head again to J.D., repeating the same words and movements.

"Where is Ollie?" Ben said.

The old man looked at Ben in confusion, then turned to Chief Auburn. "I'm sorry, but I don't understand. I thought you all were coming to make funeral arrangements."

Ben's hands tightened into fists. "Where is his body?"

Schumacher flapped his hand in the air as though he were trying to swat the entire discussion away. "I'm sorry, but no one is allowed into the processing area," he said. "We have safety precautions. You have to be licensed and bonded, that sort of thing."

Ben's face reddened and Walt stepped in, calm and slick, saying, "I know it's not usual, Claus, but I'd like you to make an exception just this one time. Ben here just wants to see his brother and say a prayer over him, given the circumstances of how he passed. I'll go down with you and make sure there's no trouble."

The old man's lips trembled, like he couldn't get them working right at first. He coughed into his hand and said, "Well, all right. But just a minute or two. Long enough to say a prayer. This is highly irregular, Chief Auburn."

"I know," Walt said, standing aside as Schumacher headed for the basement stairs. He winked at Ben, who ignored him. Walt pointed at J.D. "You sit down. We'll just be a minute. Don't get into anything, all right?"

"I won't," J.D. said, taking a seat on the nearest metal chair. The basement door closed behind the chief, and he could hear the men going down the steps. The funeral director was saying, "Just so you're prepared, he's still the same as when he was brought in. I haven't had the chance to attend to him yet, if you understand my meaning. Are you certain you wish to see him?"

Ben kept walking. J.D. held the cool metal underside of his chair, swinging his legs back and forth.

"Here he is under the tarp. Now, I must warn you, he is in bad shape. If you start feeling sick, turn away and let it out on the floor by the drain next to you," Schumacher said.

J.D. could hear the whisper of plastic cloth crackling below, and then Chief Walt's voice, gentle. "We'll give you a minute to yourself, Ben."

Silence sucked the sound out of everything around him. Even the sound of his own heart seemed to cease. J.D. seemed to be floating. He was an astronaut detached from his ship and floating through the vacuum of space, soundless and weightless, without any chance of going home.

A sound erupted beneath him. Inhuman and terrifying, making him clench the chair with his legs and hands. An animal sound rising up through the floor, echoing throughout the house and throughout his being. A sound loud enough to crack the foundation of his existence and give way to the howling winds of the void. It could never be unheard. That roar of ultimate suffering and rage, cast from his own father's mouth, would reverberate through the boy forever.

CHAPTER 23

*B*en Rein came up the steps from the Schumacher Funeral Home's basement and shoved his way through the door, went down the front steps before the screen door banged shut. J.D. stood up, watching Ben head down the street, unsure of what to do.

Walt Auburn came up the steps next and stopped, laying his hand on the boy's shoulder. "Your dad's going to be okay, son. Just give him some time. You want me to give you a ride home?"

J.D. said no thank you and ran after Ben, calling for him to wait up.

Ben didn't notice. His face looked made of stone and he stared straight forward as he walked up the side of the road, never stopping for traffic when he crossed or looking to see if cars were coming. A few drivers honked at him when they had to slam on the brakes to avoid crashing into him. J.D. hung back, holding up his hands, waving for the people to go around.

The old steel mill's cooling tanks and smokestacks rose over the tops of the trees ahead and J.D. realized where they were going. Ben made a left down Ollie's street and vaulted up the front steps of his house, moving faster than J.D. had ever seen him do. Ben thrust his hand down into the soil of a potted plant at the far corner of the porch, digging through it until he came up with a key. He stuck the key in the lock and twisted. J.D. thought it was lucky the door opened, otherwise he was sure his father would have kicked it down.

Ben went straight into the kitchen and ripped open the cabinet doors under the sink. He tossed soap boxes and cleaning sprays over his shoulder onto the linoleum floor but stopped when he saw a bottle of drain cleaner, shaking it to make sure it was full. He put that on the counter and kept looking. "There we go," he said, pulling out a large container of bleach, then a large container of ammonia, and setting them on the counter as well.

With nothing left in the cabinets, he whirled around the rest of the kitchen, in search of things that made sense only to him. He pulled open each of the counter drawers until he found the junk one, and scooped out handfuls of whatever was inside it and tossed it on the floor. He stopped when he found a box of matches and a bone-handled pocketknife and dropped them into his back pocket.

J.D. didn't talk or move from his place in the living room. He saw his father turn toward Ollie's bedroom and nearly cried out in protest, but he kept his jaw clenched shut. The shoebox of money was inside the closet in Ollie's bedroom. One look at that, and every penny would go straight to the man at the liquor store, J.D. knew. He dug his fingernails into the palms of his hands to keep from saying anything. Ben stopped at the bedroom doorway, seeing something that interested him more. Ollie's liquor cabinet. He grabbed the first bottle he saw, a large bottle of vodka, nearly empty. "Go put this on the counter," he said, passing it to J.D.

J.D. did as he was told. When he looked back, Ben was twisting the cap off a half-empty bottle of whisky. Of course you are, J.D. thought. The second we got here, I knew you'd be stealing your dead brother's liquor. He watched in astonishment as Ben set the bottle down, opened another bottle instead, and poured the contents of the half-empty one into it. He passed the empty one to J.D. and said, "Take this."

Soon, the counter was littered with empty bottles. Ben counted them. He twisted the cap off the vodka bottle and poured the contents down the sink, then put the cap on and set it back. He stepped back, looking from one bottle to the next, muttering like he was doing calculations in his mind. Whatever answer he came up with, it wasn't enough.

Ben went for the door at the rear of the kitchen and made quick work of the rusted sliding bolt keeping it shut. He went down the back steps, hurrying past Ollie's truck and riding mower. Reaching a shed at the edge of the property, Ben pulled its doors open and grabbed the first thing he saw, a large Styrofoam cooler that was cracked down one side. It was useless to hold anything, but Ben lifted it and admired it, then set it on the grass. He pulled out several gas cans and placed them next to the cooler, then disappeared inside the shed. J.D. heard metal clanging against the shed's concrete floor. Tools were flung out onto the grass to get them out of the way. J.D. heard the sound of a thousand iron nails spilling. After that, Ben emerged holding a large metal bucket, a length of rubber tubing, and a pair of thick work gloves.

J.D. came outside and stood in front of the items, waiting to be instructed. "The cooler and the bucket," Ben said. "Put everything else inside of them and bring it all out and set it in the back of Ollie's truck. Find Ollie's keys. They should be hanging on a hook by the front door."

The boy ran back into the house and filled up the cooler with the empty liquor bottles. He put the bleach and ammonia and drain cleaner inside the bucket. The ammonia bottle's warning label was facing him, and he read it: *Do not use or mix with bleach, drain cleaners, or other household chemicals. To do so will cause the release of toxic gases that can be fatal.*

When J.D. came out of the rear door, his father had stuffed one end of the rubber tubing into the gas tank of Ollie's lawn mower and put his mouth around the other, sucking hard until he gagged and spat out a mouthful of gas. He stuffed the end of the tubing into one of the empty gas cans and filled it halfway.

Ben grabbed the gas can and tubing and hurried around the side of the house, stopping at the curb and turning his head to look up and down the street. He squinted at the house nearby, making sure no one was looking, then walked over to the first car he saw parked in front of it. He bent down, popped open the gas tank lid, and stuck the rubber tubing down inside, repeating the same process as before, the gagging and spitting, and filled up his gas can the rest of the way, then capped it off. He dragged the tubing out of the car, still spilling gas, and ran back to Ollie's house.

J.D. was already sitting in the truck's passenger seat with the engine running. Ben tossed the tubing aside, dropped the gas can on the ground and ran back inside the house once more, then came out a few seconds later with one full bottle of whisky. He set the gas cans in the back of the truck next to the cooler and bucket, filled exactly the way he'd instructed J.D. to do. He opened the driver's-side door, stuffed the full bottle under the seat, and hopped in. Sweat dripped down his forehead. He wiped it away, letting out a quick breath before shifting the gears and backing out of the driveway and gunning it. Soon, Ollie's house was behind them.

J.D. turned and looked at the items rattling around in the truck bed, then back at his father. Ben kept his eyes on the road ahead.

"There's ways to tell when a man's been shot at close range," Ben said. "He'll have powder marks all over his skin. It looks like little black dots tattooed around the bullet's entry wound. If someone were to shoot themselves, say, by putting the gun up to their forehead, you'd see that clear as day." He grabbed the window lever and cranked it down, filling his face with cool air. "Ollie didn't shoot himself. That cop was lying. You know what doesn't lie? A dead body. Never. Not if you know what you're looking at."

J.D. listened to his father, absorbing what he was being told. He watched the trees whip past, as his father's long, greasy hair flapped away from his face. "You're going after those men, aren't you?"

Ben didn't answer.

"I want to come with you. Let me help."

Ben looked at his son, considering it. The mechanisms of his mind were working again. He'd been fighting it all for so long. So many years. Tried burying it down in the basement of his soul, doing all he could not to let it escape. But now it was out and running free, and Christ, it felt good. He looked at his hands. They were steady as could be.

He could use the boy. There were a thousand ways he could help accomplish the mission. Ben had used children for ruses multiple times in-country. Hiring village kids to deliver messages or scout a location or identify a target in a crowded place. They could get in and out easier because they were small and fast, and people had a natural aversion to killing them if they grew suspicious. Most of the time, anyway.

J.D. looked willing and eager. A small soldier wanting to serve. He'd make a good asset, Ben thought. Yes, the old brain was working once more and the voices were fading to a faint whisper, replaced by one clarifying voice that was back in control.

"What grade are you in?" Ben asked. "Fourth, right?"

When the boy didn't respond, Ben looked back at the road. "I'm just messing with you. I know you're not in fourth grade." He pointed at the glove box and said, "Take a look in there for me."

J.D. pulled the lever to lower the panel and looked at the pile of papers and napkins there. "What for?"

"Ollie's binoculars. Hopefully, he's got a pair in there."

J.D. moved a stack of mail out of the way and reached in, feeling the smooth, curved glass of a binoculars lens. He handed them to Ben, who set them on the seat between them and said, "At least he learned that much. You know how many times a good pair of binoculars saved my life? Plenty. Just taking that extra second to stop and look before you go rushing in somewhere. Essential field equipment for any and all operations. Never forget."

The boy picked them up and pressed them to his face, peering out through the truck's windshield. He turned the dials back and forth until the image tightened into one large, clear circle.

Ben muttered numbers to himself and held up his fingers, counting on them, messing up and restarting, correcting himself, and finally got it right. "You're twelve years old, and you're in *sixth* grade." He reached for the binoculars and put them back down on the seat. "Anyway, you're not going with me. You're going home."

CHAPTER 24

*B*en found ruts in the earth where a car had recently parked and bent down to inspect them. No footprints in the stiff mud, but he knew plenty of other ways to follow his brother's trail. Look at this mess, Ollie, you goddamn secretary, Ben thought. Somebody deaf, dumb, and blind could cut this sign.

In the old days, when they were kids, the white-haired hunters talked about cutting sign. Looking for animal tracks and scat that would lead them toward whatever they wanted to shoot. Those old hunters would bend down and pick up little turd nuggets and squish them between their fingers to feel how fresh they were, and how close the animal was. After that they'd just wipe their hands on their pants and keep going.

"You remember them cranky old bastards, Ollie?" Ben whispered as he crouched behind a tree and raised the binoculars to his eyes. He could see the hideout's roof from there, and the narrow trail of smoke rising up from the chimney. "That one sicced his dog on us for cutting through his property and it chased us right into a skunk. Mom made us take a bath together in tomato juice when we got home."

He could hear music playing inside the cabin. Psychedelic rock, just like the good old days. A beat-up truck and a station wagon with wood paneling sat parked in the driveway leading up to the cabin, near the outhouse. Purposeful, nondescript vehicles, perfect for transporting various supplies, both with New York plates.

There was another car behind them that didn't fit in. A bright blue hatchback with beads and feathers hanging from the rearview mirror. Stickers spread across the back window sported silly slogans.

The front door opened, and a woman in high heels and a black leather miniskirt came out. Through his binoculars, Ben could see another woman inside the cabin, sitting on Wombat's lap. They were laughing at someone doing something near the wall, out of Ben's view. The room was filled with a smoky haze, and the girl on Wombat's lap was smoking out of an ornate pipe.

Ben watched the girl in the skirt go to the hatchback, get something out of it, and go back inside. The door shut behind her and the music grew quieter again. He walked back to Ollie's truck to get the things he would need.

He sat on a tree stump on a hill above the bikers' cabin, looking down on it. No other buildings were visible for miles around. No other columns of smoke rose above the trees, even as the wind turned cold and the temperature fell. The road leading up to the cabin was just a dirt path, kept flat by cars going back and forth. A set of wires connected the house to a pole down the road. It was the only sign of a more civilized world out in those vast woods.

The sun was fading, but he still had a good vantage point over the building and the vehicles. He watched one of the bikers lead a girl out of the house by her elbow, both of them so drunk they staggered, and take her around the back of the outhouse. He bent her over in the grass and pulled his jeans down to his ankles, laughing as he lost his balance and collapsed on the ground next to her.

There was no child in that building, Ben thought. Ollie had been wrong. And if he wasn't wrong, she was gone already. Or dead. Maybe the bikers had disposed of her somewhere in the woods. It didn't matter, he decided. She wasn't inside the building and he didn't have to factor her into his plan.

He snapped off a chunk of Styrofoam from the cooler and dropped it into the bucket, stirring it into the gasoline until it dissolved. There wasn't much left of the cooler, and the gasoline was becoming like a soft paste. He poured more gas in and added the rest of the Styrofoam, continuing to stir.

The United States Army spent tens of millions of dollars paying factories to manufacture napalm during the war, Ben thought. And here I am mixing it up in a bucket.

He picked up the bucket and moved it away from the stump, then stopped and inspected himself to make sure none of it had spilled on his clothes or boots. When he was certain he was clean, he set each of the five empty glass liquor bottles on the stump, making sure they wouldn't topple over. This was the part he needed to be careful with. He unscrewed the caps and set them down on the stump beside each empty bottle.

First, the bleach. He filled each of the bottles a third of the way. That was the easy part. He slid on Ollie's work gloves and picked up the bottle of drain cleaner, then poured some of it into the first bottle, making sure he saved enough to fill the remaining ones, and capped it. The chemicals inside the bottle bubbled, foaming against the glass walls and rising up. Ben picked up the bottle of ammonia. He took the deepest breath he could manage and held it while he opened the bottle. He quickly unscrewed the cap on the glass bottle containing the mixture, filled it the rest of the way with ammonia, and replaced the cap as fast as he could. His eyes felt on fire as he stepped back, gasping for breath. The stink of it filled the air.

He did it again, and again, until he could no longer force his tortured lungs to breathe. The trees swam before him, their lush green leaves melting and blurring as he braced himself against the stump, determined not to vomit, determined not to die.

Come on, you weak piece of shit. These cocksuckers think they know war. Let's show them war. There's just two more bottles to go.

The last song ended inside the cabin and no one started the music back up again. The night was clear and cool and quiet now. Ben took a deep breath and let it out, relieved he wasn't coughing anymore. From his position, he could see the entire cabin and the driveway leading up to it, and the woods all around. The front door opened. Two women stumbled outside, heading for the blue car. They were carrying their shoes and purses in one hand and pulling down the hems of their miniskirts with the other.

Someone appeared at the front door before it closed. The bald, black biker called Orange, Ben saw. No doubt, the hair all over his body had been burned off by too much exposure to defoliant chemicals dripping down from the trees overhead while he patrolled the jungle. He was bare-chested, his round black belly shining in the moonlight, as he unzipped his jeans and let out a stream of piss onto the grass. The room was dark behind him, but Ben could make out a few of the other bikers lying on the floor and couch. They were in various states of undress. One in his underwear. Another completely naked. Ben spotted Wombat, sitting on the couch with his shirt open. He was wearing sunglasses in the darkened room, head tilted back and mouth open, snoring.

Orange waved to the girls while he pissed and said, "Good night, ladies."

Ben watched the car drive off, and the cabin door shut once more. All around him, the woods fell quiet. Ben picked up the bucket and carried it down the hill first. The Styrofoam and gasoline mixture had formed into jelly. He set the bucket down behind the outhouse and climbed back up the hill to gather the five bottles of bubbling liquid. He set them behind the outhouse as well and withdrew, going far back into the woods until he was deep in the shadows between the trees. "There's a story I never told you, Ollie," Ben whispered, easing himself onto the cool ground.

He pulled out the bone-handled pocketknife and clicked it open. Digging the tip of the blade into the bark of the nearest tree, he picked at it while he spoke.

"Happened when we were just kids. I used to go down into the basement and root through Dad's stuff. I knew he'd whoop me if he found out, but I couldn't help it. He had that helmet with that big dent, remember? Said a shell had rolled off the back of a truck and coldcocked him. That helmet saved his life, he always said. One night, I'm going through his trunk where he kept his uniforms, and at the very bottom I find this different uniform. It was the wrong color. Wrong army, even. It had lightning bolt insignias on the patches and the cap had a skull pin. I knew right away what I was looking at. A goddamn Nazi uniform. I couldn't believe it. And not just any old Nazi, either. One of those SS bastards. The nasty ones. And worse than that, folded in the clothes were pictures of Dad as a young man wearing that same uniform.

"Well, I didn't know whether to shit or go blind.

"I remember I went upstairs and picked up the phone in the kitchen and called the operator. 'I need to call the FBI,' I said. 'Now just what do you need to bother the FBI for, sweetie,' the operator said. I told her, 'Ma'am, I think my dad's a Nazi spy.' She gets real angry at me, yelling there's no Nazis, don't you dare prank call the operator with such nonsense, and all that. So I hung up the phone and ran back downstairs, because I realize I'm going to need proof. I go back to the trunk and just as I'm about to grab the uniform and photographs, I hear him coming down the steps behind me.

"There he was, staring at me in the dim light, holding his bottle of whisky.

"Man, I thought I was dead, right there. I thought he was going to kill me and stuff my body behind the water heater or something, just to keep things quiet. He asked me what I was doing, and I figured, I'm dead anyway, so I might as well say my piece. 'I know you're a Nazi, you son of a bitch,' I said.

"He looked at me and said, 'What did you just say, boy?'

"I grabbed one of the photographs and held it up, shouting, 'You fucking Nazi!'

"And he slaps me across the face, real hard, with his whole hand. He had those roofer hands, all calloused and filthy, remember, and I thought he knocked my teeth loose. So I'm laying there, crying, and he goes over to the photograph, picks it up, and closes the trunk. He sits down on it and tells me to get up and sit down next to him. When he sees me rubbing my jaw, he says, 'I hit you for going through my stuff. I should hit you again for calling me a goddamn Nazi.' He showed me the photograph again, pointing out the trees in the background, and said, 'That's called the Ardennes forest. We had some terrible fights there. Killed a lot of Germans and a lot of Americans died, too. One day, we get in a shoot-out with some SS troopers and the ones we don't kill run off. I chased after the commanding officer and captured him single-handedly. Truth is, he surrendered pretty easily. As soon as he saw me coming with my rifle ready to fire, he threw up his hands and got down on his knees, begging for mercy. My lieutenant let me keep the man's uniform as a trophy. I put it on and started dancing around in it, just to make everyone laugh.'

"I'm sitting there rubbing my face, and I can feel my cheeks go hot with embarrassment. I felt like the world's biggest asshole. 'They must have given you a medal for that,' I said.

"He laid the picture facedown on the trunk and said, 'No, no medals. That night, the fucker got free and killed two of our boys by bashing their heads in with a rock.' He took a long drink of whisky and said, 'One of them was a good friend of mine. We hunted that Kraut bastard all night. He killed another one of us before it was over with, and by the time we finally caught him, he was laughing. He saw me and he was calling out to me, telling me it was my fault. Well, he wasn't laughing soon after that.'

"That's when I learned the truth about war. You don't take prisoners. You don't spare the ones who plead for mercy. In war, you kill every fucking one of them."

Ben stood up and stretched his back and his legs. He walked back to grab the bucket and carried it down the driveway toward the truck. He went back, gathered up the five bottles of liquid, and cradled them in his arms as he carried them to the motorcycles. He placed one bottle upright behind the front tire of each bike, hidden from view.

He scooped up some of the gasoline jelly with his gloved hands and smeared it across the lengths of the two sturdiest branches he could find, then unscrewed the gas caps on the truck and car in the driveway and stuck the branches halfway in.

He carried the bucket over to the motorcycles, grabbed another handful of jelly, and smeared it across the leather seats and gas tanks. He covered the front and rear tires of all the bikes, then took a handful of the jelly and squished it, squirting drops of it onto the ground all around the bikes. He used the remainder on each of the glass bottles, making sure their caps were good and gooey.

The gloves were still coated in jelly. He tossed them into the bucket and held his hands up in the moonlight to make sure there wasn't anything on them. He reached for the box of matches stuck in his back pocket and struck one, watching its tiny curling flame dance in the darkness. He waved the match first under the branch sticking out of the truck's gas tank, and it instantly ignited, engulfing the entire stick. He hurried over to the car and ignited that branch next. The sides of both vehicles were on fire, swallowed by a wall of flame and black smoke by the time he reached the motorcycles. He struck another match and flung it at the nearest bike, hitting it in the tire, and ran for the side of the cabin.

The truck's gas tank blew up, an explosion that echoed for miles, lifting the entire vehicle up in the air and sending it back down with a tremendous crash of glass and steel.

But the motorcycles were Ben's favorite part. Their tires caught fire so fast they melted, and the flames leapt from tire to seat, growing wider each time, until all of the bikes ignited.

The car's gas tank blew up next, an explosion as loud as ordnance on any battlefield. From inside the cabin, he heard someone shout, "What the hell was that?"

The curtains covering the windows were thrust aside. From around the corner, Ben could hear them cry out in horror at the sight of their burning motorcycles. Four of them screamed in outrage as they fought to get through the front door, running out wearing no shoes. Some were just in their underwear, dragging the towels from their windows with them.

They swatted at the flames, trying to beat them away, but it was no use. The towels did nothing but spread the burning jelly across the bikes. With all of the commotion, none of them noticed the bottles cracking open beneath them. They stomped around on the shattered glass and melted caps as the contents of the bottles released into the air, surrounding them in a cloud of invisible chlorine gas.

Wombat came running through the cabin door but stopped, crying out at the others to get away from the flames. He held his pistol, cocked, waving it in the air. The man knows napalm when he smells it, Ben thought.

The bikers wobbled and staggered around their bikes as they swung the towels, too dazed from the chlorine gas to realize their towels and clothing and skin were on fire as well.

Ben watched them sputter and choke, squeezing their throats with their hands as they collapsed against their motorcycles. Flames spread across their bare arms and torsos, and that was enough to wake them up from the chlorine haze, but it was too late.

Tears ran down Wombat's face as he watched, helpless. He screamed for them to get away, for them to roll into the grass. The bikers were thrashing into one another, overcome by the chlorine gas and black smoke in their lungs and the fire melting their flesh. Orange made an effort to escape, trying to run, only to be swallowed by flames. He screeched as the outer layers of his flesh peeled off, leaving raw white and red underlayers beneath that smoked.

Wombat covered his eyes, trying to prevent himself from seeing any more of it. The ones still on their feet didn't have the breath to scream. The ground around the bikes was on fire, and they danced in it, igniting their feet, vomiting from the gas through their fingers as they clutched their mouths.

Ben Rein crept up behind Wombat and slammed the length of his brother's pocketknife into the biker's right thigh, just above the knee. The blade was sharp and strong. It sank through denim and flesh and muscle, puncturing Wombat's femoral artery like an oil drill striking that first underground torrent of black gold.

Wombat cried out as the blood sprung from his leg. Ben took the gun from him, turning it over in the dim light, inspecting it as Wombat squirmed on the ground, trying to plug his leg before he bled out. The copper stench of blood and smoke and screams filled the deep woods again.

Ben closed his eyes and inhaled. It was good to be home.

CHAPTER 25

Wombat stirred and came to. Ben was standing in the kitchen over the stove, looking down at an iron pot filled with hot water. Bubbles were forming on the water's surface. Some of it spilled over the side of the pot and hissed on the red burner. He could hear Wombat's boots scrape against the wooden floor. The biker groaned, reaching down to feel where the length of bloody rope was cinched around his knee. Ben had used a steel rod and some rope he found inside the cabin to form the makeshift tourniquet, and he'd twisted so hard he thought the man's leg might sever, but at least it stopped the bleeding. It wasn't the best tourniquet, he knew. He hadn't even kept track of how long it had been on.

"Which one of you was the cook?" Ben asked, looking through the spices mounted on the stove and the boxes of spaghetti and noodles. Wombat writhed on the floor, clutching his leg, not hearing him. Ben didn't mind. The water was at a rolling boil now. "I have to say, I'm impressed you managed to run electricity and phone lines all the way out here. Must have cost quite a bit of money. I guess crime really does pay."

He didn't have to look out to know what Wombat was doing. The biker was scrambling around the floor, looking for some kind of weapon, anything to defend himself with. Maybe a knife or gun or even a screwdriver someone left hidden under the couch or tucked away in the clothing left scattered on the floor from their party. Good luck, Ben thought, because I already moved everything. He'd collected the knives and sets of brass knuckles scattered around the room. All the guns were already hidden in the closet in the rear bedroom of the cabin, too far for the injured biker to reach. The only other gun, Wombat's own pistol, was tucked in the back of Ben's waistband.

Wombat moaned and cried out, "Oh Christ, no! You sick fuck!" and Ben knew why. Wombat had found the charred bodies of his friends. Some of them were still smoking, despite all the water Ben had poured over their corpses before pulling them inside the cabin and sitting them propped up against the far wall. They looked like photos townsfolk would take in the Old West of dead bandits after a foiled bank robbery. Except these bandits had been set on fire. A few of their faces had burned away completely, revealing their blackened skulls.

Wombat, the hardened war veteran, the Disgraced's president, gaped in horrified disbelief at them. He turned and saw Ben, standing in the kitchen, next to the stove. "Listen to me," Wombat rasped, swallowing his disgust. He clawed at the floor to spin toward the kitchen, leaving a smear of blood as he turned. "I don't know what you think we did, but we didn't do it. We're businessmen. All we do is move a little coke around. We don't bother anybody!"

"Is that right?" Ben asked.

"I swear to God!"

Ben grabbed the handle of the pot and flung the boiling water at Wombat, who shrieked and covered his face. Water steamed off his clothes and skin. Ben stood there, waiting for him to stop whimpering.

"We both know I'm going to kill you," Ben said. "I won't insult you by pretending otherwise. How I do it, that's up to you."

Wombat grimaced, trying to sit upright. "What do you want?"

"It's real simple," Ben said. He grabbed the phone off the wall and held the receiver out toward Wombat. "You're going to call your friend Chief Auburn, and tell him to come here."

"He never comes here," Wombat said. "That won't work."

Ben cracked the biker on top of the head with the phone's

hard plastic receiver. He waited for Wombat to stop moaning before saying, "You'll make it work. Tell him there's a problem up here and he needs to get involved before it gets worse."

Wombat looked at the phone, but as he reached for it, Ben pulled it back and said, "I don't need to tell you what happens if you do anything to make him suspicious, do I?"

"No," Wombat muttered.

Ben dialed the number written on the wall and listened to it ring through the receiver in Wombat's hand.

Walt Auburn sat in his den, drinking his third whisky and soda that night. Not drunk. Just nice and warm. His feet were up as he reclined in his deep leather chair, watching the news. He swirled the remainder of his drink around the ice cubes at the bottom of his glass and took a sip. It had been a hell of a day, he thought. One for the ages.

He hadn't expected the phone call earlier that day from the Patterson Borough supervisors asking him to take over command of their police department. There were steps to take, official proceedings and all, but in this emergency circumstance they said they'd all sleep easier with a firm, steady hand at the wheel. They'd pay him, of course. It would almost double his annual salary.

He poured a new glass and held it in the air in front of his face. "Here's to you, Ollie, wherever the hell you may be."

Before he could drink it, the phone mounted on his wall rang, loud and shrill, making him start in his seat so hard he almost dropped his glass. "God damn it," he muttered, trying to work the lever of the chair to get himself upright. The phone kept ringing. He could hear his wife shouting from their bedroom, "Walt! The phone!"

"I know it's the damn phone!" Walt shouted back. He got out of the chair and snatched the receiver off the wall and pressed it to his ear. "Chief Auburn," he said.

"It's me," the voice on the other end of the line said. It was Wombat, that filthy biker fuck who liked to think he was some kind of criminal kingpin.

Walt closed his eyes and grimaced. He bent his head around the corner to make sure his bedroom door was still shut and his wife wasn't coming to see who was calling. She knew better. Calls that late at night could only mean trouble. Well, this call was trouble, too. Bad trouble. "What the hell are you doing calling my house?" he snarled.

"We've got a problem up here at the cabin."

"So? Handle it," Walt said.

"I need you to come here, right away," Wombat said. "You need to know about this before shit hits the fan."

"Know about what?" Walt asked, but the line went dead.

He cursed and slammed the phone back in the receiver, looking around the den for the pieces of his uniform he'd left scattered about. He grabbed his shirt and slid it on, made quick work of the buttons, and stuffed the tails into his waistband. He grabbed his gun belt and buckled it around his waist, adjusting it so his heavy revolver hung low on his right hip. He was fitting his cowboy hat onto his head when one of the bedroom doors opened, and his boy poked his head out. Steve's hair was matted and a crease ran along the side of his plump cheek from the pillow seam he'd been lying on. Barefoot in his pajamas, he looked at Walt sleepily and said, "I heard some kind of noise."

"It was just the phone," Walt said. "I have to go into work. Go back to sleep. I'll see you in the morning."

Steve yawned and said, "You going to get the bad guys?"

Walt tipped his hat at him. "That's what a lawman does, son."

He shut the front door behind him and headed for his police car. *If those idiots fucked something else up today, there is going to be holy hell to pay,* he thought. *Killing a man and making me clean up their mess wasn't bad enough? Bad-ass Vietnam vets. Bullshit. Just derelict drug-pushing fuckups on motorcycles, now.*

He stepped on the gas, flying down the back roads toward the game lands, eager to get to the clubhouse and handle whatever it was that needed to be handled.

Walt Auburn smelled the burning wreckage long before he arrived. It smelled like gasoline and charred rubber. As he came up the road he could see smoke rising off the truck's smoldering remains. It had been burned down to the frame, and as he slowed down he made out the clump of plastic and metal in front of it that had once been a car. "God damn," he said, driving wide around the vehicles, just in case the wind shifted and some burning ember leapt onto his police cruiser.

But that wasn't all, he realized. Holy Christ-loving shit, that wasn't all. Every single one of their motorcycles had gone up in flames as well.

Walt parked his police car and adjusted his hat. He stared in wonder at the pile of scorched chrome and steel, the twisted handlebars and melted engines of each motorcycle. "What in the fuck happened here?" he said aloud. It was hard not to laugh.

He walked through the front door of the cabin, keeping the wide brim of his cowboy hat low to keep them from seeing him smile. "I've heard of a cookout, but this takes the cake," he said. Before he could look up, he heard the mechanical click of a gun's hammer cocking back and felt cold steel touch the back of his neck.

Wombat was sprawled out on the floor in front of him, sitting in a puddle of his own blood. To Walt's left, the rest of the bikers, posed in ghostly silence, burnt to a crisp. The entire room stank like gasoline and charred meat. "You traitorous son of a bitch," Walt said, eyes glowering with hatred at the biker.

Behind him, Ben Rein kept the pistol pressed firm and tight to the police chief's neck while he reached around, unsnapped Walt's revolver from its holster, and pulled it free. He stepped to the side, coming between them both, aiming the police revolver at Wombat, and the biker's gun at Walt. Walt let out a muted cry in his throat, like a man choking at the dinner table.

Wombat was too far gone to notice. He was white as a sheet. Blood was seeping through the wound now.

"I caught the men who killed my brother, Chief," Ben said. He fired a shot through the side of Wombat's head with Auburn's gun, knocking the man's brains out and splattering them across the wall.

He turned with the gun, firing into the dead bodies of the

other bikers, one bullet each, making their bodies smoke, filling the cabin with such deafening noise and light that Auburn squirmed, looking away and trying to tuck his head down into his shoulders like a turtle.

The bodies flopped over on top of one another, their arms and legs akimbo, leaking whatever fluids remained inside them onto the floor.

Ben turned to face Walt, aiming the biker's gun at the center of Walt's forehead. "Now listen," Walt said, raising his hands. "I don't know what that piece of shit told you, but I didn't have anything to do with your brother's murder."

"Is that right?"

"You're goddamn right, that's right! They told me they found him out in the woods, and when I got there, it looked like exactly what they said. I guess those bastards staged it to look like a suicide. Now, maybe," Walt said, getting himself worked up, really pouring it on thick, "maybe I should have paid a little more attention. Maybe I was too overcome with emotions looking at your brother. He and I were friends, Ben! We knew each other for years. When he was laying there dead, I guess I just bought whatever they were selling." Walt even managed to work up some tears, letting them dribble down his face. "I swear on my little boy, I would never, ever, do anything to hurt you or your family. Now listen, here's what I'm willing to do to make up for it. I have a lot of power around here. More than you know. I can make things happen for you, Ben. First thing I'm gonna do is make all this go away. That's right. Neither one of us were ever here. Nobody is going to ever ask any questions! By the time someone realizes they're dead, I'll make sure it's all chalked up to some quarrel over drugs. Then, I'm going to get you a job with the borough. A good job, Ben. Something easy with good pay. I owe you that much. You and Ollie. What do you say?" Walt said. He took a chance and extended his right hand toward Ben, hoping he'd take it. "I can be a better friend to you than you can imagine."

Ben raised the biker's pistol and leveled it at the gold star on his hat, which said *Chief*.

"Now listen to me a goddamn fucking minute!" Walt said. "I am the chief of police! You can't point a gun at me like that! Put that weapon down right now, do you understand me, you drunk? You schizoid. You goddamn loser, you think you can just stand there pointing a gun at me? Put it down! I am the chief of police!"

"And here, I thought you said we were going to be friends," Ben said, and pulled the trigger.

The shot doubled Walt Auburn over backward like a gymnast trying to do a back handspring, except he fell straight and hard on the floor. His legs and arms shot out and retracted, scraping the wood. His mouth gaped wide, while blood filled the inside of his hat like a boat taking water.

Ben walked into the rear bedroom for the rest of the guns, collected them, and carried them into the main room. Walt Auburn was taking his time in dying. He'd managed to flop over on one side, slithering in his own filth like a worm. Ben cradled the guns in his left arm, several pistols and a shotgun. After selecting one of the pistols near the top of the pile, he fired it at Walt's back.

Walt cried out, jerking back and forth. Ben tossed the pistol into the lap of one of the burnt-up biker corpses. He grabbed the next one, shot Walt in the leg, and tossed it near the next biker. He took the next pistol and fired it at the wall and door where Walt had been standing, blowing holes through its surface. The pistol went empty and he tossed that one onto the pile of bodies as well. Walt was still moving, but not much. He'd flipped over on his back, moaning for Ben to stop.

Ben racked the shotgun slide, aimed the gun at the place on Walt's chest where his chief's badge was pinned, and fired. Walt's chest exploded in a volcanic eruption of red pulp, bringing a halt to the man's pleas.

Ben tossed the shotgun and positioned Walt's revolver so it was lying near him, then went outside to grab the bucket from around the corner. A few good scoops of napalm jelly remained at the bottom, along with the saturated gloves. He went back inside the cabin, stepped over Walt's ruined corpse, and used the gloves to smear the rest of the jelly on the walls and floor. Whatever towels remained on the windows, he made sure to get some on them too. Once the bucket was empty, Ben tossed it into the kitchen, threw one glove in there, and the other into the back bedroom. He stood at the doorway, looking at his handiwork.

Six human beings, who'd been alive and breathing just a short time ago, were now nothing more than clumps of waste. Ben struck a match and tossed it on the floor, where it set the smear of jelly alight. He threw the box of matches in after it and stepped back, watching the walls ignite. He watched until the glass windows shattered, the roof caught flame, and black smoke grew too thick to see through.

The cabin was cheaply made. It wasn't long before the walls buckled and the roof collapsed on one side. Soon, the bodies would be burned and buried beneath it, leaving nothing more than a smoldering pile of ash.

It was after midnight before J.D. saw the headlights of his uncle's truck coming up the street. He leapt to the door, threw it open, and waited. The truck swerved as Ben steered it toward the driveway, leaving it several feet from the curb. He stumbled out, clutching the half-empty whisky bottle he'd hidden under the front seat and started drinking along the way. He stood in the road, chugging, and J.D. realized he was covered in blood. It was smeared across his pants and shirt, even on his neck and face and in his hair.

Ben came up the stairs, barreled past his son through the door, and collapsed on the couch. He raised the bottle to his lips and drank again, not bothering to wipe away whatever dribbled down his face.

"What happened?" J.D. asked.

Ben laughed and took another drink.

"Dad? Are they all dead?"

Ben looked at him, eyes bleary, like he was trying to focus. A car turned down the street, coming toward them. Ben watched it, staring through his front window. It would be a police car, or a series of police cars, coming to kill him for what he'd done. Or maybe it would be other bikers. It could be anyone, really, and when they came, he would let them come.

The car turned into the driveway of one of the nearby houses instead, and the driver got out. One of the neighbors, back home late from work. It didn't matter. If not this time, the next, or the next after that. Ben took another swig. He waved his hand for the boy to sit down on the low table in front of him. J.D. did as he was told.

Ben could smell the blood on his clothes and skin, like rusted iron. It was sticky and dry, matted in the hair running along his arms. "Listen to me, J.D.," Ben said, and the boy leaned forward.

"You don't mean shit to me," Ben continued. "I don't want you. I never did. I kept you around because the government sends me extra money to take care of you, and because your uncle agreed to take you as much as he could, so I didn't cut your throat in the middle of the night. Do you understand?"

The boy's eyes filled with tears, but he didn't speak.

"Ollie truly cared about you, and maybe you should have been his son instead of mine, but too bad. Ollie is dead, and that's that. You're nothing to me, and I'm tired of looking at you. I don't want you anymore. Do you hear what I'm telling you? I don't want you. I'm throwing you away. You need to go, while you still can. I don't love you. Never have. Never will."

Ben took another drink, nearly emptying the bottle. When he finished, the boy was still sitting there, staring at him, eyes and face wet, lower lip quivering. Ben kicked the table under him, screaming, "Get out! Get out and don't ever come back!"

The boy jumped out of the way and ran up the stairs. Ben could hear him rummaging through his belongings. The bottle was empty with one last drink. Ben threw it across the room, smashing it to pieces. "You have thirty seconds!" Ben shouted.

J.D. came racing back down the stairs with his schoolbag slung over his shoulder. It was stuffed with clothes now. He grabbed his coat from his chair, looking back at his father one last time. It was all a bad dream. J.D. was about to plead with him to change his mind. Ben leapt up from the couch and lunged at the boy, who threw the front door open and ran down the steps, sneakers slapping the concrete as he fled.

Ben watched him go, then sat down in the doorway, looking past Ollie's truck, at the empty road. He rocked back and forth, saying, "Okay, you motherfuckers. Now come and get me. Let's get this over with."

The lights on the bus were turned down low so the passengers in the back could sleep, but one of the few sitting near the front had his overhead light on, using it to read. The driver looked at him through the wide rearview mirror over his head and said, "Must be a good book if you'd rather read it than go to sleep."

J.D. closed the book and covered the title with his arm, not wanting the driver to see the words *The Criminal Mind* printed on the cover. "It's okay," he said. He pulled a half-eaten candy bar out of his sweatshirt pocket, unwrapped it the rest of the way, and took a bite.

"You traveling alone?" the driver asked.

"Yes, sir," J.D. said.

"Shoot, when I was your age, my folks would never have let me go anywhere alone. They knew I'd get in a world of trouble."

"Mine don't mind," J.D. said. He slid the book back inside one of his three bags, on top of the other books he'd taken from Ollie's house. Buried under them, carefully hidden, were all of the thick bundles of cash that he didn't have stuffed in his pockets or hidden in his socks.

"It's a long way to where we're going," the driver said. When the boy didn't answer, he added, "Go a lot faster if we talked. You got a name?"

"My name?" The boy watched the driver through the mirror. The bus rocked as they drove. The highway was empty, with nothing but the lights of oncoming cars and the reflectors of mile markers set in the distance. He turned and looked back, seeing that all the rest of the passengers were asleep, and too far away to be disturbed by them talking.

Who was this man, and why was he so interested? Maybe he was on the lookout for runaways. Maybe the police posted bulletins of missing children like they did for wanted criminals. Or maybe there was another reason. Maybe this man was looking for children traveling by themselves for something else.

The driver's eyes flicked back and forth from the road to the mirror, both his hands wrapped firm around the bus's wide steering wheel. The boy knew he should be afraid, but he wasn't. He should blurt out that he'd left everything and everyone he knew behind and was vulnerable to the world and men like the bus driver, but he didn't. Something had changed. Down deep inside of him. Something that had peered through the crack in his childhood and seen into the shadows, and it wasn't afraid. It was angry. And it was hungry.

The driver had spoken true. Whatever was coming, and where they were going, was a long way away. There were ways to tell what was in a man's mind, even if he did not want you to know, and there was plenty of time to observe and find the right questions that would reveal it. The world, the boy now knew, was filled with real monsters. Not the imaginary kind he'd fantasized about all those times. Real monsters, who preyed on the innocent, and were disguised as ordinary people. He would find a way to uncover them.

And then, they would know how it felt to be hunted.

"My name is Jacob," he said.

V

SENECA FALLS

CHAPTER 26

A police car was parked in the chief's spot. Carrie parked in front of it, blocking it in. The station's cruddy yellow windows were even uglier in the morning light. Carrie juggled a box of donuts, a tray of coffees, and the Hope Pugh case file in one hand as she pulled the station door open with the other, not bothering to knock.

"Hi, Lou!" she called out, walking past the filing room.

"Who's that?" the clerk shouted from within. He poked his head out, magnified eyes squinting at her from behind his glasses.

Carrie passed him a coffee and flipped the donut box's lid open. "Is the chief in?"

Lou glanced at the office behind her, looking past the framed portrait of Walt Auburn. "I don't think so," Lou said, projecting his voice. He plucked a cream donut from inside the box and pointed toward the office, adding, "I haven't seen him around."

Carrie spun and headed for the office, using her shoulder to stop the door just as it was about to close. "Hey, Steve. Nice to see you."

Steve Auburn groaned and sat back down in the chair behind his desk. "What are you doing here?"

"I brought coffee and donuts. The universal peace offering among all law enforcement." She flipped the lid open, holding it out in front of him. "The ones on the left have jelly."

Auburn picked up one of the sugar-crusted jelly ones and said, "Great. Now you're not only ruining my day, you're wrecking my diet."

Carrie laid the case file open on the desk in front of him. "All I'm asking is you hear me out," she said. "If you listen to what I have to say, and you still don't want to pursue this, I'll leave and never bother you again."

Auburn swiped a smear of jelly from the corner of his mouth with his thumb and stuck it between his lips. "You'll leave?"

"That's right."

Auburn sat back in his chair, taking a sip from his coffee. "You've got yourself a deal. Lay it on me."

She held up the black-and-white photograph she'd found of the crime scene in one hand, and a report from the Pennsylvania State Police serology lab in the other. "This is a photograph taken by Chief Oliver Rein behind the Pughs' house. He believed this was the site Hope was abducted from on the night she went missing." Carrie showed him the blanket and sock in the photograph. "These items were inside that lockbox we found. I was able to get them tested."

Auburn took the State Police lab report from her as she passed it across the desk. He looked down at it, read it, and said, "Semen?"

"That's right," Carrie said.

"Did it match anyone in the system?"

"No," Carrie said. "But they have enough to do a match if we can find a suspect."

Auburn laid the report down. "How can we even prove it has anything to do with the Pugh girl?"

"This sock," Carrie said, tapping the picture once more. "It matches the one found on the remains in the woods."

Auburn half smiled as he opened the drawer next to his desk and pulled out a large case file, filled with 8 × 10 photographs. They were color images of Hope's skeleton. Auburn thumbed through them, finding the ones of her feet, and said, "Sorry to tell you this, but there was no sock. Thanks for the coffee. Have a safe trip home."

Carrie pulled another photograph out of her case file and laid it down on the desk. It was the one she'd taken with her phone, at the scene. "I'm sorry to tell *you* this, Chief, but there was. I removed it from her foot to have it analyzed."

Auburn's face flushed, and simmered with anger. "Lady, you got some balls waltzing in here telling me you tampered with one of my crime scenes. I should lock your ass up right now."

"First off, it was my crime scene too," Carrie said. "And not to pull rank on you, but I'm here as the representative of the district attorney, the highest-ranking law enforcement entity in this region. At that moment, you were in danger of wrecking the investigation because of a prematurely formed opinion that she went missing. I was protecting the integrity of the case." Carrie tapped the lab report. "As it turns out, I was right."

Auburn ran his hand over the top of his head, then folded his hands in front of his face, collecting himself.

"Steve, listen," Carrie said. "I don't want to fight. Let's work this together. Somebody did something bad to a little girl in this town and they got away with it. As a matter of fact," she said, "this would have been your father's last big case, right? When Ollie Rein died, your dad took over as chief, and that makes the Hope Pugh investigation his final responsibility. And we've let it sit all these years. What do you say we go close it for him?"

Auburn picked up the lab report again, biting his lower lip. "Semen. Son of a bitch. And we had that in the basement all this time. My God." He looked up at Carrie. "What do you propose we do?"

"We need to interview anyone who might have seen her on that last day. Any of her friends who might still live around here."

"I didn't know her," Auburn said. "We went to school together, but she was a couple years ahead of me. I have no idea who she hung out with."

"Did you know Jacob Rein? He was friends with her. Anyone he might have hung out with?"

"No, thank God. Him and his whole family have been nothing

but a disgrace to this town. I wouldn't piss on him if his guts were on fire." Auburn snapped his fingers and said, "We used to keep a collection of yearbooks, just in case we had to identify someone, before anyone had computers." Auburn held his hand to the side of his mouth and called, "Hey, Lou. We still have those copies of the yearbooks from back in the day?"

"Maybe," Lou called out from down the hall. "What year?"

Auburn counted on his fingers. "If she was in sixth grade in 1981, she'd have graduated in what, '87? We got 1987?"

"I guess we might," Lou said.

"Well, can you go get it then?" Auburn said. He picked up another cream donut. "We'll go through the names of people she should have graduated with and see if any still live around here," Auburn said. "It won't be easy. Most folks moved away to find work. The ones who stuck around are either drug addicts or dead. Who knows, maybe we'll get lucky."

"Sounds good," Carrie said. Auburn excused himself to go help look for the yearbooks. Carrie sat in the chair across from his desk. A framed photograph sat on the desk, black and white, with all the colors fading to gray. The man in the photograph wasn't smiling. He was stern beneath his cowboy hat with the star reading *Chief of Police* pinned to the front of it. Walt Auburn looked a lot less noble in photographs than he did in the framed painting hung on the wall outside.

The driveway leading up to the home was long and narrow, but at least it had been paved. The rest of the driveways were all gravel, and Carrie was sick of hearing stones great and small pinging off her car's undercarriage. She stopped at the wrong house first, with a large, dead tree in front of it that no one had bothered to cut down, and had to back out, nearly getting T-boned by a pickup truck spattered with political bumper stickers doing seventy miles an hour. Carrie was sick of pickup trucks spattered with political bumper stickers too. And the assholes who drove them.

She parked in front of the right house, a well-kept two-story that had been painted recently enough that it was fading but not chipping. The grass was freshly cut, and the smell lingered in the air. On one side of the shed, someone had stacked a pile of cut branches, and on the other, a stack of firewood, perfectly arranged.

Carrie got out, checking the door and windows for signs of movement. She made sure her badge was dangling in front of her shirt where it could be seen, and that her gun was hidden by her jacket. People reacted in surprising ways to armed strangers coming up to their front door. You could be wearing a badge as big as your chest and they'd never see it if they were focusing on the gun.

Carrie went up the porch's front steps and knocked on the glass door. She bladed herself off to the side, out of the way of the door, and waited. Beside her, a porch swing and a wicker chair looked out over the front yard and woods beyond. In the warmer evenings, Carrie imagined, someone would be sitting on the swing, sipping a cold drink, watching fireflies dance in the dark. Maybe it wasn't so bad out here, she thought.

"Hang on, I'm coming," a man called from inside.

A pair of filthy work boots sat near the door, damp and covered in fresh grass, left outside to dry. Carrie slid them aside with her boot just in case she had to back up, so that she wouldn't trip.

The door opened. Carrie held up her badge and said, "Mr. Kraussen?"

He had long gray hair, pulled back in a ponytail, and thick glasses. He was a slight man, with thin arms and shoulders that were hunched over a set of crutches and his right leg was in a cast. "Call me Adam, please. Can I help you?"

"I'm Detective Santero with the district attorney's office. I was wondering if I could ask you some questions."

"About what?" he said.

Carrie pulled out her notepad from her pocket and opened it. "Did you hear we found the Pugh girl's remains?"

"Hope, that poor kid," Adam said, grimacing. "Such a shame."

"You knew her, right?"

"We were in school together, and friends, to some extent."

"There aren't too many people left in the area who knew her. I could really use some help filling in the blanks here."

Adam pushed the glass door open and grunted, trying to maneuver himself outside. Carrie held the door open, almost stepping on the boots, and finding herself glad she had moved them. Adam lowered himself onto the porch swing, and held out his hand, offering her the wicker chair.

"How'd you break your leg?" Carrie asked.

"Remember that ice storm we had last month? I was carrying my groceries to the car and slipped in the parking lot. Went right down on my leg. It hurt like hell, let me tell you." Adam reached into his coat's pocket and pulled out an inhaler, then gave it a rough shake before pressing it between his lips and taking a deep breath.

Carrie waited for him to exhale and said, "I know it was a long time ago, but try to recall what you were doing on the night Hope went missing. I think it would have been February 13, 1981."

"My homework, probably, if it was a school night," Adam said. "Why do you ask?"

"I just have to cover all my bases, Mr. Kraussen."

"Are you asking me if I had anything to do with her going missing, Detective?"

"I'm trying to be nice about it, but yeah," she said. "Did you?"

Adam rattled his inhaler again and took a second blast, pursing his lips and holding it in until he shuddered and let it out. "Sorry about that. I have to use this more when I'm nervous," he said. "The last time I saw Hope was on the school bus. My stop was first, I got off and went into the house, and I never saw her again." He looked at her sideways. "I know for a fact she got home safely, because my best friend walked her there and saw her go in her house."

Carrie scribbled a few notes on her notepad, mumbling, "I don't mean to make you nervous, Mr. Kraussen," as she wrote. She felt the cool air on her face, carrying the scent of all that cut grass. "Who else lives here?"

"No one, not anymore," he said. "My parents both passed away a few years back. I live alone." He stuck his fingers into the top of his cast, scratching until he grimaced. "I can't wait to get this blasted thing off."

"And who's the best friend you mentioned? Is he around here too?" she asked. "Do you know how I can reach him?" As she spoke, she turned her head back to the boots lying near the front door. All that firewood, so neatly arranged. Those branches, stacked in a pile. The fresh cut grass. Those boots, still damp from recent work. There was a piece of duct tape wrapped around one of them, holding the sole and toe of the boot together. She had seen them before.

Carrie shot to her feet. She turned back toward Adam, who was rattling his inhaler again, looking at her with wide eyes. "Where is he?" she said.

"I don't know."

"Jacob!" Carrie shouted. She stepped back, cupping her hand to the side of her mouth toward the upper windows. "Jacob Rein, you come down here right this instant! How dare you let me sit out here making a fool out of myself, you ass!"

Adam took another blast from his inhaler and coughed. Carrie grabbed the handle of the glass door and pulled it open, looking back at him. "Is he inside?" she demanded.

"No," Adam said. "Go look if you want. He's not here."

"Damn him!" Carrie shouted, collapsing back in the wicker chair. "Where is he?"

"He didn't say where he was going. He's only been back a few days. Have you ever had a best friend, Detective Santero? I lost mine. For a long time. It's funny, but the second he came walking up to my door, it was like he'd never left. I guess he's changed a lot since we were kids, and he's sure been through hell, but having him here is like having part of myself come back. Does that make sense?"

"Yeah," Carrie said. "It certainly does."

"He talks about you, you know?" Adam said.

"Is that right?"

"He says you're good. Better than he's seen in a long time, even if you're still young. He told me you'd find me, and then you'd know what to do. And here you are. So, let me ask, do you know what to do?"

Carrie groaned in frustration, smacking her fist on the notepad. "Why does everything have to be a goddamn riddle? Why couldn't he just talk to me and tell me what the hell is going on so I'm not running around in circles trying to solve a cold case nobody else seems to give a shit about?"

"There's no riddle," Adam said. "J.D.—sorry—Jacob, said he can't get involved in the investigation."

"Why the hell not?"

"Because he didn't want to taint it. His family was neck deep in this case and all that came afterward. Plus, with all the trouble he's had over the past few years, I guess he figures it's better that he stays away. He's relying on you to get there on your own."

"I can see why you two get along," Carrie said, setting her notepad on her lap once more. "You're a cryptic pain in the ass, just like he is. All right. Let's get to it, then."

Adam grinned. "I always wanted to get interrogated by a beautiful lady detective. I wonder if there's any rough stuff involved."

"Don't get excited, pal," Carrie said, chuckling. "One old pain in the ass in my life is enough. So tell me, what don't I know about Hope Pugh?"

"There was an older boy," Adam said. "We had some trouble with him. He was pretty mean to us. Hope embarrassed him in front of the whole school, and after that, she went missing."

"An older boy," Carrie said, writing it down. "And after all these years, you never said anything about him to anyone?"

"No one ever asked," Adam said. "No one cared."

Carrie tapped her pen against the notepad and leaned her head back against the chair. "I've got no witnesses. Shitty forensics. Antique crime scene photographs. Pieces of a skeleton for a victim. And the only person you can think of who might be a suspect was the schoolyard bully? This case blows, man, it really does."

"Yeah," Adam said, folding his hands across his chest. "Jacob said to tell you that if it's too much for you, you can always call Harv Bender."

Carrie turned in the chair to look at him. "I'd deck you for saying that if I thought you knew what you were saying, cast or no cast."

Adam laughed. "He told me to duck right after I said that."

CHAPTER 27

*C*arrie sat in her car at the far back of the parking lot, tapping her fingernail against the window glass. She had the police radio turned down to a whisper, just in case anyone walked close. It was dark, and that was good. The vehicle they were looking for wasn't in the parking lot, and that was good, too. She wanted to see the man before she had to go inside. The speaker mounted under her dashboard hummed to life, and Steve Auburn said, "Target vehicle turning in now. You'll have the eye."

Carrie raised the binoculars sitting in her lap and watched the large silver Cadillac with tinted windows and chrome rims pull in. It headed toward the back of the lot, not far from her, and Carrie sunk down in her seat. When she popped her head back up, the Cadillac was parked on the line between two spots, taking them both up. Carrie muttered, "What a douche."

Fred Eubanks exited the vehicle and headed for the bar's rear door. Carrie clicked the microphone's button. "I've got eyes on target."

Steve Auburn's voice crackled through the speaker. "Copy that."

The disdain in Auburn's voice was mild, but present. It had been present ever since Carrie had pointed to Eubanks in the yearbook at the station and said, "That's our guy."

"Fred Eubanks," Auburn had said. "The insurance agent. Sponsor of the Little League team that won the regional championship two years ago. Jesus Christ, Carrie, he paid for the party when I got sworn in as chief. He's on the school board, the Rotary Club, everything. That's who you want to accuse of raping and murdering Hope Pugh? Why, because he was mean to a couple geeks when he was a kid?"

"So he grew up and became respectable," Carrie had said, looking at Eubanks's yearbook photo. "Doesn't mean he didn't do it."

Carrie looked at the clock on the dash. She wanted to give him time to get a drink or two down to loosen him up. She pulled down the visor and slid the mirror panel back, pressing her lips together to coat them bright red with the most expensive lipstick she could find at the local drugstore. She tore the mascara packaging open and did her eyelashes next, drawing them out thick and long. When she finished, she turned her head to look at herself in the mirror from either side. It wasn't an expert job, by any means, but it would do.

She picked up the radio again. "You're sure I'm good to go?"

"It's all taken care of," Auburn replied. "Just walk on in like you own the place."

The problem was her gun. She had no way to conceal it without keeping on her coat, and no way to keep on her coat and still accomplish the mission. She pulled it out of her holster and thought about trying to squeeze it into her purse or pocket, but that was a no-go. Glocks are good combat weapons because they can take a lot of abuse and still fire, but the damn things have no safety. The gun was more likely to go off accidentally than it was to be of use when she really needed it.

"Here I go, doing something stupid," she said aloud as she undid her belt and slid the holster off. She stuck the gun back inside the holster and dropped it into the car's glove box, along with her purse. "Rookie Female Detective Gets Taken Hostage by Suspected Child Murderer," she said, picturing it printed on a newspaper page hanging outside of Harv Bender's office. "That's gonna look great."

She picked up the microphone and clicked it, saying, "Going inside now. I'll be off radio."

"Roger that," Auburn said.

Carrie hung up the microphone and reached in for a pack of gum in the coffee holder. She stuck a piece in her mouth and slid the rest into her pocket and got out. It was time to go inside.

She opened the door to the bar and was hit by the stench of disinfectant and dirty water from a mop and bucket parked near the entrance. Dull rock music played on the jukebox in the corner. Midtempo garbage, but the people playing pool in the corner bobbed their heads to it anyway. She caught glances right away as the door closed behind her. Men and women alike, sizing her up. Carrie worked her way past the row of booths and around the pool table, getting a good look at where Fred Eubanks was sitting.

Eubanks leaned over his drink at the bar, stirring it with a small plastic sabre. He looked older than his driver's license photo, with thinning black hair and sagging jowls. He was bigger than she'd expected. Large hands, and thick, hairy wrists.

Carrie went behind the bar. She waved to the bartender and said, "Hey, I'm Carrie. Are you Paul?"

The bartender picked up a towel and wiped his hands. "You the new girl?"

"That's right. I'm supposed to hang out with you for an hour, see how things are done."

"What drinks do you know how to make?"

"Does rum and Coke count?" she asked. "Vodka and cran. Pretty much anything you just have to pour together."

"Just watch and learn," Paul said. He tapped the bar to get Eubanks's attention. "You want another drink, Fred?"

"I'm good, thanks. Need to get home a little early tonight," Eubanks said, not looking up. His drink was almost done.

"Give me a shout when you're ready to go," Paul said, heading down to the other end of the bar to check on the rest of the customers.

"How about a beer for the road?" Carrie asked. "Liquor before beer, never fear, isn't that what they say?"

Eubanks declined. "I'll cash out."

"Sure thing," Carrie said. "Let me go get your check."

She hurried across the bar to where Paul was filling two glasses of beer and pressed close to him. "Go in the back."

"What do you mean? I have customers," he whispered. "Steve said this wouldn't interfere with anything."

"Get your ass in the back and don't come out until I tell you to," she said, pulling the half-filled glasses out of his hands.

Paul tried to protest but Carrie grabbed him by the arm and shoved him through the double doors into the kitchen. She picked up the two half-filled glasses of beer and set them in front of the customers. "Something's wrong with the taps," she said. "These are on the house."

She returned to Eubanks and said, "It's going to be a few minutes. There's a problem in the back."

"It's always something in this place," Eubanks said. He peeled a twenty-dollar bill off a roll as thick as a tennis ball and tossed it on the bar. "Keep the change."

"Wait!" Carrie said, slapping her hand down on top of the bill. "You can't."

"Why not?" Eubanks scowled.

"I'm not allowed to accept money yet," she improvised. "They told me that when I started. Listen, just wait a few minutes for Paul to come back, okay? Hang out with me. I don't know anybody here."

"There's hardly anybody worth knowing in here," Eubanks said. He slid back into the bar stool and checked the time on his watch.

"I guess people in this town would rather play pool than drink," Carrie said. There were two people at the other end of the bar and a small group gathered around the pool tables. The only other person was sitting by himself in a booth, resting his head on the table, covering his face with the hood of his sweatshirt.

She picked up Eubanks's empty drink and realized she had no idea what to do with it. She dumped the ice cubes in the nearest trash can and dropped the glass in the sink, splattering herself with soapy water.

"Have you ever worked in a bar before?" Eubanks asked, watching her.

"It's that obvious?" Carrie said, wiping her hands on her pant legs.

"You're a pretty young girl. Even if you don't have any idea what you're doing, you'll still make more money in a single night than Paul does in a week. Especially if you wear something low cut."

"Well, I'd like to just make enough money to pay my student loans," she said.

"Tell me about it," Eubanks said. "My little girl's about to graduate next year. With the way my wife spends, we won't be able to afford community college."

"Hey," Carrie said, "as a special thank-you for being so patient, let me make you something."

"I don't like rum and Coke," Eubanks said.

"It's an old family recipe," Carrie said, grabbing two bottles off the shelf. "It's special, trust me. What were you drinking before?"

"Gin and tonic."

"Ugh," she said over her shoulder as she poured various liquors into a tall glass. "I drank gin once and thought I was going to be sick for a week. It tasted like the Great Depression." She grabbed a straw and stirred.

"What in the world is in that?" Eubanks said, eyeing the yellowish brown concoction in her hands.

"That's a secret," Carrie said, setting it in front of him. "Go ahead and try it. It'll put hair on your chest."

Eubanks pointed at his neck where thick tufts of hair sprouted and said, "I think I'll be okay on that end."

"Well, if you don't drink it, I'm going to have to tell everybody you were a sissy."

Eubanks snorted with laughter. "Good luck with that."

He picked up the drink and raised it to his lips, and Carrie cried out, "Hang on!" She dug in her pocket, fishing for the pack of gum. "I almost forgot the most important part." She held a stick of gum out and said, "You have to chew this first."

"Why?"

"The residual flavor. It's a big part of it. Come on, take it. Just chew it a few times and spit it out, then drink."

Eubanks leaned sideways to look past the double doors, checking for Paul. The bartender was nowhere to be found. "Oh, what the hell," he said, taking the gum between his teeth. "Just chew a few times?" he asked.

"Just like that," Carrie said, reaching for a napkin. "Make sure you get it on both sides of your mouth. Spread that flavor all over the place."

Eubanks chewed, and when Carrie said that was enough, he bent forward and spit the gum into the napkin on the table. He picked up the glass, swallowed a mouthful of her mixture, and gagged, clutching his throat. "Christ, that's disgusting," he rasped, spitting the rest out of his mouth across the bar.

Carrie snatched the napkin holding his gum off the bar and ran to the other end of the bar. The man slumped over bounced up from his booth, throwing back his hood to reveal his shining bald head. Steve Auburn thrust a paper envelope toward Carrie, and she dropped the napkin and chewed-up gum inside it.

From his seat, Fred Eubanks watched this unfold in slack-jawed astonishment. Steve Auburn closed the envelope and stuffed it in his back pocket, eyes fixed on Eubanks, daring him to make a sudden move.

"Steve?" Eubanks said, blinking in confusion. "What the hell's going on?"

Carrie shoved the double doors open and stuck her head into the kitchen. "All done, Paul. You can come out now." She walked past where Eubanks sat and said, "Nice meeting you, Fred. By the way, I'm Detective Santero, and you'll be seeing me in a few weeks with an arrest warrant for the rape and murder of Hope Pugh."

"Who?" Eubanks said, laughing. "Rape and murder? What the hell are you talking about?" He looked at Auburn. "This is some sort of joke, right?"

"Is it, Fred?" Auburn asked. "We found semen from the crime scene, and you just gave us a DNA sample. Are they going to match?"

People moved back as Eubanks got down from his stool. He raised his voice so everyone could hear him. "Are you seriously accusing me of that crime? Do you realize I will sue you and everyone you know for even suggesting such a thing?"

"Come on," Auburn said, leading Carrie toward the exit.

"Anyway, you can't use that gum as evidence," Eubanks called out. "You didn't get it from me legally. That's called entrapment." He pointed at the other patrons. "You all saw that. You're all witnesses. They just tried to entrap me."

"You spit it out, genius," Carrie said from the door. "That's called abandonment. I can use that all day."

The door closed behind them, and reopened seconds later, with Fred Eubanks bursting through it. "Steve? Hang on," Eubanks said, racing after them across the parking lot. "Steve, come on, quit fooling around. You know me. Everybody knows I'm not the kind to hurt anybody." His voice broke as he said, "You can't do this to me! I have a family. I have a daughter. Steve, please."

"My god, Fred," Auburn whispered. "It was you. How the hell could you do something like that?"

"I was a kid!" Eubanks shouted. He sank to his knees on the asphalt and buried his face in his hands. "Just a dumb, stupid kid. It was an accident. I didn't know any better. Please, I'm begging you, don't do this to me."

"Your daughter, were you good to her when she was little, Fred?" Carrie asked. "You give her a childhood filled with birthday parties and hugs and stuffed animals?"

"Of course I did," Eubanks said. "All of that."

"So, she grew up happy, right?"

"Because she had a good dad. I am a great dad," Eubanks said. "Ask anyone."

"Here's what I wonder sometimes, Fred. When a little kid gets murdered, what are they thinking about? Are they thinking about all of the parties and hugs and stuffed animals, or is it just blind terror? Do those few moments of torment erase all of the good that was in their lives? Because we tell ourselves it doesn't. Whenever some kid gets killed, we tell ourselves they had great lives right up until then, that we'll try to focus on the good stuff. But in reality, they're not thinking about any of the good things when it happens. They die in fear, and torment, and that's it. You murdered Hope Pugh, Fred. We both know it. You raped her, then you killed her, then you hid her body out in the mountains. And you spent all these years pretending it didn't happen, hoping this day would never come, but guess what? It did. Now you're fucked."

Eubanks sobbed into his hands. His gold bracelet and watch jingled as his body jerked back and forth. "Oh my God!" he moaned between his fingers. "God, please help me Lord Jesus! Please, help me, I beg you."

Carrie leaned back on the hood of her car, folded her arms, and looked down at him. "You want help?" Carrie asked.

"Yes, anything," Eubanks said. "Please."

"Tell you what," Carrie said. "If you mean it, and you really want help, I will make you a onetime offer. Do not piss me off, and do not try to negotiate with me, or it's off the table. Ready? You give us a written statement tonight saying it was an accident. Saying you didn't mean to kill her. I'll even let you write a letter of apology to her family and say you were just a dumb, scared kid who made a mistake. I'll make sure the district attorney and the judge both see it, but you had better tell us every single thing that happened that night."

Eubanks wiped his face on his sleeves, leaving them dark and stained. "You'd do that?"

"As long as you cooperate," she said. "Do you agree to go back to the police station, not in custody, and give us a statement of your own free will?"

"I'll do whatever I can. I have to think about my family," he said, getting up from the ground.

"Get in your car and wait for us back at the station, then. You okay to drive? You want a coffee?"

Eubanks ran his hand through his sweaty hair and took a deep breath. "No," he said. "I just want to get this over with." He fished in his pocket for his keys and headed for his car. He stumbled as he walked, dazed like a heavyweight who has just been knocked into oblivion but doesn't have the sense to fall.

Steve Auburn leaned on the hood of Carrie's car, watching as Eubanks drove out of the parking lot toward the police station. "Let me get this straight," he said. "You're going to do him the favor of letting him make a written confession?"

"I didn't lie," Carrie said. "The first people I'm going to show it to are the DA and the judge. Right after I convince them to try him as an adult and send him to prison for the rest of his life."

"We'll have enough to arrest him tonight," Auburn said. "Soon as that confession is signed."

"Let's wait," Carrie said. "Do the forensics on his DNA sample. Take our time writing the criminal complaint. With a case like this, it's better to go slow and have all our ducks in a row."

"I can't believe it," Auburn whispered. "After all this time." He looked up at the night sky, staring deep into the cosmos. "You seeing this, Pop? We did it." He dug in his pocket for his cell phone and said, "I've got to make a phone call."

Carrie watched him press his phone to his ear as he walked away, going back across the parking lot to where his car was parked around front. "Mom?" Auburn said, his voice quivering with excitement. "You awake? I never thought I'd be able to tell you this, but I want you to know something. I closed Dad's last case." Carrie could hear him choking up, telling his mom, "The Pugh girl. The last thing he was working on before he passed. I just caught the man who killed her."

Carrie got into her car and sat, not turning it on. Her breath was cool against the windshield, fogging it as she breathed. A couple came out of the bar, hugging one another and laughing as they headed for their car. Carrie shivered and buttoned her shirt. She grabbed her coat from behind her seat and put it on. She started the car, turned on the heat, and let it warm her bare legs.

She drove past the couple as they were leaning against their car, kissing, their eyes closed, hands clasped, lost in one another. Carrie turned on the radio and sang to herself as she waited to turn out of the lot to go back to the police station. She didn't know the words to the song, but the sound of her voice filled the empty space in her car.

CHAPTER 28

*O*n the night before Hope Pugh's funeral, Fred Eubanks lowered his glasses and peered at the computer screen in his bedroom. He clicked on his My Seller's Account, his legs bouncing up and down as he waited for the page to load. "Come on," he whispered, then read the screen and shouted, "Two sales! That's what I'm talking about."

Both of his gold Rolex watches had sold. It was no surprise. They were his most valuable items, worth thousands of dollars apiece. He'd almost strangled the We Buy Gold assholes for the price they offered him for his bracelets and rings. Fucking junkie enablers is all they were. He clicked on the sales page and froze. They had to be the wrong numbers, he told himself. He took off his glasses and pressed his face close to the screen, wanting to read it with his own eyes.

Three hundred fifty for the first Rolex, and five hundred dollars for the second. "No way," he said. "Fuck that." There was no button to cancel the sale. He clicked around until he found the Customer Service page. There was no phone number or e-mail address. Just FAQs that said nothing, followed by questions reading, *Was this information helpful?*

He bellowed and threw his keyboard across the room, smashing it against his wife Karen's assortment of perfume bottles, sending them scattering. He picked one up; it was a quarter empty and four years old. A $180 bottle of Chloe bullshit he couldn't sell. Next to it was a $585 bottle of Tom Ford bullshit he couldn't sell. You'd think she'd fucking use one up before buying four new ones, he thought, hurling both bottles at the dresser mirror. Shards of glass flew.

Her spending had them so overleveraged he couldn't even take a loan out to pay his attorneys' retainer. They'd been all smiles when he met with them the day after he'd been formally charged, telling him they'd get right on it, and he assured them the check would clear. It didn't. He'd managed to get a little more work out of them in the ensuing two weeks, but now they weren't returning his phone calls.

Eubanks sat on the bed, holding the sides of his head.

The phone rang on the nightstand. Wiping sweat out of his eyes, he picked up the receiver and said, "Hello?"

"It's your brother. How are you?" Ritchie asked.

"I'm fine. Everything's great," Eubanks said.

"That's good to hear, Fred. I wanted you to know we prayed for you at my congregation tonight. We prayed that the Lord will deliver you from the hands of your accusers. We prayed that the light of God's mercy will shine on our entire community."

"Sounds good," Eubanks said. "Listen, I have to get going."

"We'd like you to come to the house tomorrow during the funeral. We'll pray for that poor child and her family, and you will feel the blessing of Jesus himself when you surrender yourself to him."

"I have to meet with someone about my case tomorrow," Eubanks said. "But I appreciate it."

"Another time then, brother. Remember, the Lord is here for you when you are ready for him."

"Thanks," Eubanks said, and hung up the phone.

He went back to his computer and clicked New Message. He typed in the names of his attorneys and wrote: Guys, just letting you know the sales went great! I will have your money as soon as it comes through. Not sure how these things work, I never sold anything online before haha. Glad to still have you on my side. Let me know how things are proceeding.

Eubanks picked up the phone again and dialed his mother-in-law's house. It rang five times and he hung up. He called it back, letting it ring longer, and it went to voice mail. He called again. His wife picked up and said, "I told you I'd call you. My mother doesn't want you calling here."

"Karen, I need to talk to Jesse. It's important."

"She's busy right now," she said.

"Yeah, does she like having a cell phone? Because I pay for that. Does she like driving a car? Because I pay for that, too. Tell her to pick up the goddamn phone."

Eubanks rocked back and forth, waiting for his daughter to pick up. When she did, she didn't say anything. "Hey, sweetie," he said. "How's it going over there? Your grandmom driving you nuts yet?"

"It's fine," Jesse mumbled.

"Listen, I just need to set a few things straight, okay? I know you heard a lot about this in the news, but I want you to hear the truth from me. From your dad. Can you listen to me for a minute please?"

There was no response.

"I didn't kill that little girl," Eubanks said. "I never touched her. I was never anywhere near her. That's the truth. I swear it on my life. I'll swear it on a stack of Bibles. Those cops, they set me up. First, they got me drunk, and then they conned me into signing some bullshit statement. I didn't even read it before I signed it. My mistake, okay? I trusted the cops to be good people, and now I gotta pay the price for it. It happens to people every day in this screwed-up country, but this time, it happened to me."

"The news said the police have evidence it was you," Jesse said.

"Of course that's what the fake news says! All they want is to make money. Nothing else happens around here, and I'm a big name, so as long as they keep doing stories about me, people will keep watching." He bit his lower lip, hoping she'd say something. "Listen, you believe me, don't you?"

"I don't know, Dad," she whispered. "Grandmom said—"

"Forget what she said. That crazy old bat's had it in for me for years. All I care about is me and you. What you think, and whether or not you believe me. Do you?"

"I guess so," Jesse said, keeping her voice down.

Eubanks clenched his mouth together to keep her from hearing him sob. "That's all I needed to hear. I love you, baby. I'll talk to you soon, okay?"

"Okay," she said, and hung up.

He hung up the phone and lowered his face into his hands.

The lights from the office of Eubanks Insurance spilled out onto Auburn Street. An occasional car drove past, its headlights reflecting off the dark windows. Inside, Fred Eubanks was crouched on the floor, pulling everything out of his safe. Protected documents for his clients. Social Security numbers. Bank account details. Everything had value if you knew how to find the right buyer. It might take him some time, but he'd figure it out. He heard the office door open and stuck his head up above his desk. "We're closed," he said.

The shabbily dressed, bearded man standing in the entrance didn't move. Eubanks was about to open the desk drawer where he kept his pistol when the man said, "Hello, Fred. Been a long time."

Eubanks dropped the papers and stood up, squinting to see better. "Do we know each other, friend?" He moved around the front of his desk and leaned back against it, better able to make out the details of the man's face. "Holy shit," he said. "Piss Face?"

Jacob Rein sat down on one of the chairs and folded one leg over the other. He pressed his fingers together under his chin, revealing the wide, circular scar that wrapped around his left wrist.

"Wow, you look like hell," Eubanks said. "I guess time hasn't been too good to you. I heard you were a cop, then you got locked up. How was prison?"

"I don't recommend it," Rein said. "How are you?"

"I'm good," Eubanks said. "I'm great, in fact. I guess you heard about this bullshit case the cops are trying to put on me. I just got off the phone with my legal team, and man, what we are going to do to them in court is going to be disgusting. They're going to be begging for mercy. I'm going to sue the shit out of every single person involved in this. They'll have to rename Auburn Street to Eubanks Street. You'll see."

"Wouldn't surprise me at all if they did," Rein said.

The way Rein's eyes stayed on him was infuriating. The calm way he sat there, staring, was enough to make Eubanks want to pull out the pistol and shoot him on the spot. "You just come to stare at me or did you have something you wanted? I'm a little busy, and don't really have time to shoot the shit, even with an old friend like Piss Face."

"I just came to see whether or not you were the kind to make it through this," Rein said.

"What the fuck is that supposed to mean? Of course I'm going to make it through this. I just told you my attorneys are—you know what? Just get out. I don't have time to talk to you."

"You asked about prison. I'll tell you. It can be hard in there, for anyone," Rein said. "The isolation. The loneliness. Being cut off from the ones you love, not being there to protect them or provide for them. I was only there a little while, but the time I lost and the things I missed, I'll never get back."

"Well, I'm not going to prison, so I don't have to worry about that."

"It can be especially terrible if you've done things to children," Rein continued. "The men in prison might be criminals. Killers, drug addicts, gang members. But even they have children. They tend to take out their frustrations on child predators. The guards, of course, look the other way. The only thing they'll do is put you on suicide watch. Keep you from ending the pain. Making sure it goes on as long as you're there."

Eubanks felt his legs trembling with a rage that ran all the way up into his throat. "I told you to get out! Stop talking about that shit!"

"To be honest, Fred," Rein said, "by the time you get that far, it won't mean anything. By then, you'll have already endured the worst human misery possible. You'll have been exposed. Not just in front of the public, but in front of your family. Your daughter. All your lies and bravado will be cut down by irrefutable forensic evidence. Lab reports that say your DNA matches the semen found at the crime scene and the fingerprint on the knife you left behind. Your little girl will spend the rest of her life knowing her father raped a twelve-year-old, right before he strangled her to death."

Rein stood up. "By the time you finally wind up in prison, you'll be so hollowed out inside you won't even care what the inmates are doing to you. Everything about your life, even this conversation, will seem like a distant dream. So keep telling yourself you have this under control, that there's a way out. But we both know the truth. You are caught in the jaws of the beast, and it's just getting started on you."

He leaned closer, speaking into Eubanks's ear. "Do you know why I never came after you myself when I was a detective? I was afraid. I knew I'd kill you before I got the chance to watch you suffer." Rein stepped back, grinning. "Then again," he said, eyes shining with cruelty, "I still might."

Rein pushed the door open and stepped out onto the sidewalk, taking a deep breath of the fresh night air. Inside the office, Fred Eubanks slammed his fists on his desk and thrust himself into his chair, sending stacks of paper flying. Rein stood there long enough to listen to the cries of anguish erupt from inside the office. They were like sweet music. He smiled, and then he walked away.

CHAPTER 29

*C*ameras and news vans were setting up around the cemetery hours before the burial. One of the cameramen saw Steve Auburn's police car approaching and turned to film it. A few of them tried flagging him down, wanting him to give a few comments, but he kept driving. He went past the church, and there were news crews there too. At least they were leaving the Pughs alone. Auburn was paying a few of his officers overtime to take shifts sitting in front of their house, making sure nobody bothered them.

The speaker on his dashboard crackled, followed by, "Chief, you on radio?"

Auburn picked up his microphone. "Affirmative, Paul. You need something?"

"Meet me at Eubanks Insurance, sir. Step it up, please."

Auburn snapped the microphone back in its holder and groaned. What could possibly be happening now? Somebody had probably vandalized the place, he figured. The townsfolk were pretty pissed off and someone probably threw a brick through the office windows. He aimed his Crown Vic toward the cemetery's exit and drove.

By the time he pulled up behind Paul's police car, he realized nothing was wrong with the office. The windows were intact. Nothing was smashed or broken. It hadn't even been egged.

"Steve, come on," Paul urged, looking up and down the street. Passing cars were slowing down to look at what the cops were doing. Paul waved and smiled at them, calling out, "Hey, Bob," and "Morning, Mrs. Kline," as they passed, but he looked pale and sweaty despite the cold November chill. Whatever it was that happened, it had been too important for the idiot to remember to put on his hat, Auburn thought.

"What the hell's going on?" Auburn said, shutting the car door.

"I got a call from Fred's wife this morning," Paul said. "She said she went home to get some things, and the bedroom was all smashed up. When she couldn't get him on the phone she called dispatch and asked us to check on him here." He cocked his head at the insurance office's window, pointing at what was inside. "So I did."

Auburn pressed himself against the smoked glass and cupped his hands to the sides of his face, trying to see in. Fred Eubanks was splayed across his desk, his pistol still gripped by his rigid fingers. His eyes were permanently wide and vacant. Chunks of his skull and brain matter were splattered across the wall next to him. Thick, gelatinous blood pooled beneath his head and spilled over the desk's sides, forming dark puddles on the carpet below.

"Son of a motherfucking whore," Auburn said.

"I figured you'd want to know right away, before any of them news people show up," Paul said.

Auburn reached to pull the door open, finding it was locked. "Get the crowbar out of my trunk and bring the camera. We need to take photographs and get that body out of sight before the press shows up."

"Yes, sir," Paul said, hurrying for the police car.

"And, Paul?" Auburn said, halting the man in his tracks. "Put on your damn hat."

Inside Ruby's Diner, video footage of Pastor Richard Eubanks appeared on the TV set over the cashier's counter. "God will ensure justice is done in this matter, as in all things. I have faith that my brother's name will be cleared, and the true murderer will be revealed," Little Ritchie said, waving a Bible at the camera.

"Turn off that horseshit!" shouted one of the truckers seated next to Carrie.

"Frederick was never a violent person. He is a loving father and husband and founding member of this congregation," the pastor continued. "The people looking to tear him down are doing so for political reasons, I believe."

"Cut this off!" another trucker yelled. "They should fry that lying son of a bitch in the electric chair with his damn brother."

Carrie ate the last of her eggs and wiped the corner of her mouth with a napkin, then took a sip of her coffee, careful not to spill any on her new blouse. The people inside the diner that morning were all dressed better than usual. The truckers had their hair combed. The waitresses were wearing their church shoes and skirts under their aprons. A handwritten sign on the door read, CLOSED FROM 10–3 TODAY FOR FUNERAL.

The door opened behind her and she heard someone say, "Morning, Chief."

"Morning," Steve Auburn replied. Carrie glanced over her shoulder to see Auburn dressed in his uniform, his cowboy hat fixed atop his head. "You got a minute?" he said, coming up alongside her.

Carrie tossed a ten-dollar bill on the counter, then waved good-bye and followed Auburn out the door. The wind was soft and calm. It was an unusually warm day for that time of year. Auburn's face wrinkled behind his sunglasses. "Fred Eubanks is dead," Auburn said.

"You're shitting me."

"He shot himself in his office last night. We just found him a little while ago."

Carrie rummaged in her purse for her keys. "I need to see the body. Where is it?"

"Coroner already took him," Auburn said.

"Were there any signs of forced entry?"

"No, the door was locked from inside," Auburn said. "What, you think someone killed him and staged it? There were notes spread out all over the desk for his wife, his daughter, his brother. I can't give you any of them yet because there's blood all over the damn things. With the funeral today, and all the press, I guess he just couldn't take it."

Carrie stomped her foot in frustration. "Son of a bitch!" she shouted.

"It looks like he took the easy way out," Auburn said. "I say good riddance."

"Not the right way," Carrie shot back. "I wanted to see him dragged through the courts and sent off to rot in prison."

"If it all went through, sure," Auburn said. "If the court let us try him as an adult, and if his confession held up, and as long as there weren't any other loopholes or technicalities, maybe we'd get a conviction. That's a lot of ifs, Carrie. This way, it's nice and clean. Case closed."

Carrie looked at him, searching for his eyes behind his sun-glasses. "Did anybody go with you to that crime scene, Steve?"

He raised an eyebrow at her. "You asking me if there was any-one else who can corroborate me saying what I saw?"

"Is there?"

"Paul was the first one on scene. He could see Eubanks slumped over on his desk and he waited for me to get there be-fore we busted the door open together. Any other questions, De-tective?"

Carrie laughed, trying to pass it off. "Hey, lighten up, Steve. I was just kidding around with you."

"No, I don't think you were," he said. "I think you're doing the same thing to me you did to Eubanks the other night. You smile at people but that's just a mask, right? What's behind it lies some pretty dark shit."

"Well, I've seen some pretty dark shit," Carrie said.

"I don't doubt it," Auburn said. "You ought to come up for air every once in a while before it keeps you there permanently." He tipped his cowboy hat at her. "It's been quite an experience work-ing with you. Don't mind me saying I hope we never do it again."

She watched him walk off, another cowboy heading off into the dust, and was brushed aside by several people coming out of the diner all at once. "Funeral's about to start," one of them said. "Hurry up or there won't be any parking spots left."

The crowd at the cemetery was too large to see who all was there. Carrie had searched faces at the church and left her seat early and stood on the steps as the door opened and the people flooded outside. A dozen cameras flashed, fodder for the news sites covering the funeral, and she realized the person she was looking for wasn't there. Not with all that press. Never in a million years.

She found herself at the front of the crowd, near the casket, before they lowered it into the ground. People she knew from around town were nearby, but they were too far away to talk to. Across from her, Adam Kraussen was dressed in a black suit and tie, his leg free of its cast, but he was still using crutches. Carrie held up her finger to him, trying to get his attention, to tell him she needed him to wait for her after the ceremony. He lowered his face into a handkerchief in his hands, balancing himself on his crutches as he blew, wiped his sleeves on his eyes, and never looked back up.

Mrs. Pugh let out a cry of despair, clutching her husband and burying her face in his chest. She moaned, "No," over and over. No tears streamed down Mr. Pugh's weathered face, but he did not look away once from his daughter's casket.

A handsome woman with frosted blond hair stood to Carrie's side, sobbing. She stumbled on the uneven ground and was forced to reach for Carrie's arm to keep from falling. Carrie held her steady, keeping her right hand wrapped around the woman's bony fingers, telling her it was fine as the woman apologized. "Did you know Hope?" Carrie asked.

"No," the woman said, wiping her face and seeing her hands were soaked with tears. "I'm afraid I didn't. I was the dispatcher who took the call when her parents reported her missing. I was always hoping they'd find her. When I heard about the funeral, I just had to come." She looked around. "I've probably spoken on the phone to most of the people here. Heard them fighting with their loved ones, talked to them when they wanted to hurt themselves. I could tell you more about their lives than anyone else, and yet, I don't know any of them, and they don't know me."

"I'm Carrie," Carrie said, patting her on the arm.

"I'm Gloria," the older woman said.

"Do you want me to walk you to your car?"

"Actually, I have to visit someone buried here first. Someone I should have visited a long time ago."

Carrie stayed with her, helping her search. They knew the number of the plot, somewhere toward the rear of the cemetery, but it wasn't until they came upon it that Carrie realized what she was looking at. Oliver Rein, buried February 1981. Vietnam Veteran, US Army. Police Chief of Patterson Borough. "Were you Ollie's dispatcher too?" she asked.

Gloria nodded. "I was the last person to speak with him before he went into the woods. I've thought about that conversation a million times. What else I could have said, or what made him decide to do that." She bent down to touch the headstone, laying her hand flat on its cold, rough texture. "It wasn't until after he died that I saw his picture. They had it in the paper," she said. "He really was a handsome man. At least I got that part right."

She stood up and clasped Carrie's hand in hers, patting it before saying good-bye. Carrie watched her walk around the other graves, taking the long way, so as not to step on any of them. Carrie bent down to look at the grave marker. She placed her hand on it and said, "We did it, Ollie. We got the guy. Me and you. Rest easy, now."

"You two would have gotten along," a familiar voice behind her said.

Carrie spun around so fast she almost toppled over. She cocked back her fist and punched him in the arm. "Rein! You son of a bitch! Don't sneak up on me like that. Where the hell have you been?"

He was clean shaven, wearing black sunglasses and an oversized black coat with the collar flipped up, something he could lower his head into. His hair was cut shaggy and short, like he'd done it himself. He looked past her, down at his uncle's grave site. "I never visited his grave," he said. "I was gone by the time they buried him."

She put her hand in his, and he let her. She rubbed his forearm with her thumb, feeling the soft skin there. She touched the hard ridge of the scar that wrapped around his wrist and raised his hand to look at it in the light. "The scar is fading," she said, squeezing his fingers and feeling him squeeze them back. "How does it feel?"

"Like anything else that's been cut off and reattached. Sometimes all right. Sometimes like it doesn't belong there. But never the same."

Carrie laid her head against his chest, feeling his warmth. Rein stroked her hair and said, "If you're going to arrest my father, you'd better do it soon. He won't be alive much longer."

"Arrest him for what?" Carrie said. "All I heard were the ramblings of a dying old man."

They walked across the cemetery toward the gated entrance at the end of a curving brick path. "I heard you met Adam," Rein said. "He was shocked you figured out I was there so fast."

"Were you shocked too?" she said.

"Only that it took you so long," he said, smirking. She cocked back her fist like she wanted to hit him again and he put his arm around her. They exited through the gate onto the sidewalk, walking along Auburn Street toward the center of town. The factory's old abandoned smokestacks loomed over the trees, the skeletal remains of the past when the town was still alive.

"Is this your first time back here?" Carrie asked. When Jacob told her it was, she said, "And you haven't seen your dad in all these years?"

"We didn't part on good terms," he said. "I realized a long time ago that he thought he was doing me a favor sending me away, but he didn't have to do it like that. The truth is, by the time I ran away we were better off apart."

"He told me he tried to make amends, but you refused," Carrie said.

"A few years ago, he called me up out of the blue to tell me I should come see him. I offered to meet him for dinner somewhere. I didn't want to sit in his house and watch him get drunk. He told me he'd get back to me. I haven't heard from him since."

"You should go to him," she said. "Before it's too late. He loves you. He misses you, so stop being so damn stubborn about it."

"That doesn't sound like him," Rein said.

They kept walking. "Did you know it was Fred Eubanks all these years?"

"Of course," Rein said.

"So why didn't you ever go after him?"

"Fred would never have let me interview him. We have too much history. I couldn't have done a proper job and couldn't bear to see anyone else do an improper job, either, so I let it sit. What the case needed was a real detective. And then one came along," he said, squeezing her hand.

"Some detective. I almost set my hotel room on fire with a bug zapper trying to use it as an alternate light source," Carrie said. She reached up and rubbed her hand along his smooth chin. "I like you without the beard."

"It was time for a change," he said.

That evening, Adam cooked dinner and opened a bottle of wine that he retrieved from the cellar. "Germans aren't known for their wines," he said, setting the bottle on the table. "But the Riesling is well respected. My father got into collecting wine at one point, but he never drank any of it. I've got a few cases downstairs that I've been saving." He looked at both of them and said, "Well, I figured this qualifies as a special occasion."

He poured three glasses and passed the first one to Carrie. She raised it to her nose and inhaled, smelling its jasmine and honeysuckle fragrance.

"Dinner smells wonderful," Carrie said.

"I hope you like it. I've gotten into cooking over the past few years, but never get to do it for anyone else." He finished his glass and moved to refill Carrie's before pouring more for himself.

She stopped him and said, "No more for me. I have to drive back tonight so I can file my report in the morning."

"Just you and me tonight, then, old friend," Adam said to Jacob. "I have a surprise for you. I got the Betamax player working, and thought we could watch *Excalibur*, for old time's sake." He clasped his hands together as if holding a sword and intoned, "In the name of God, Saint Michael, and Saint John, I give you the power to bear arms and dispense justice."

"It's Saint George," Rein said. "The dragon slayer."

"That's probably similar to the vow you both took when you became police officers," Adam said. "In the olden times, knights enforced the chivalric code. Honor. Protection of the innocent. In fact, that's the reason police badges are designed to look like shields. You shield the rest of us from harm. Pretty interesting, isn't it?"

Jacob set his glass down on the table, cupping it with both hands. "Actually, I can't stay tonight, either. I have to meet my son in Harrisburg first thing tomorrow morning."

"Is everything all right?" Carrie asked.

Rein glanced at her with uncertainty. "I didn't want to say anything at the diner, because I hadn't decided to go through with it yet. Jacob Junior has been hounding me since law school to take on my case. He's convinced he can clear my name. I'm meeting with him to get the paperwork started."

Carrie was stunned. "I can't believe it," she said. "Do you think it will work?"

Rein swirled the last remaining drops around the bottom of his glass. "I suppose it's time we found out."

CHAPTER 30

"*I*'m not letting you walk all the way to the bus depot," Carrie said, tossing Rein's bag into the backseat of her car. It was so worn out that it's zipper came loose when it landed, sending paperwork flying. Carrie collected a large, folded piece of paper from the car's floor and saw it was a map of Vieira County. There were circles drawn in the deeply wooded sections. "What is this?" Carrie asked, holding up the map.

"Nothing," Rein said, reaching to take it from her.

Carrie moved out of his reach, examining the markings. One of them was labeled *Monica Gere* and the date of her rape. He'd highlighted main roads leading in and out of each targeted area, which the suspect would need to escape. Rein had drawn lines between other circled locations, forming wide-ranging vectors, showing the suspect's most likely path of travel and what areas he might potentially concentrate on next. "Rein, this is incredible. Can I hold on to it?"

"It's not done yet. I will work on it and let you know," he said.

"You should have shown it to Harv Bender and let him know where to start looking."

"Harv helped me draw it," Rein said. "We've been working on the case together."

"You're kidding me," Carrie said.

"Sometimes, detective work is all about getting people to do what they want to do, even if they don't think they want to do it."

"If you're going to get all Zen on me, you need to grow the beard back," Carrie said.

It was dark by the time they arrived at the bus depot. It was crowded with confused-looking travelers hauling suitcases, trying to make sense of the station's terminals and where they were supposed to be. Homeless people picked through the trash cans, or sat slumped against the depot's wall, muttering to themselves.

"I can drive you to Harrisburg," Carrie said. "This place looks disgusting."

"It's fine," Rein said, reaching into the rear of the car to grab his bag. He clutched the top part, trying to keep everything contained as he set it on his lap. "I'll call you in a few days, once I get settled at my son's house," he said.

"Rein," she said, touching his wrist before he could get out. "What changed your mind? Why are you letting him work on your case?"

"I've been thinking a lot about the people who died to make me what I am," he said. "I still owe."

Rein let himself out of the car, and Carrie sat watching him for as long as she could before he vanished into the sea of people. As she went to leave, she saw the folded map lying on the floor where it had fallen from his bag.

She picked it up and unfolded it, studying the circles and where they were set against the rest of the map. There was one only a few miles away, she saw.

What the hell, she thought. It couldn't hurt to take a look.

The woods felt strange and lonely as she drove. The sky was covered with clouds, only letting the moon emerge briefly to reveal its pale, full roundness, before being enveloped in mist once more. At least she could see the road, Carrie thought. A long empty stretch of backwoods with nothing but trees all around it. But it was straight, and flat, and she was traveling within the circle Rein had marked on his map. She needed music, if only to fill the emptiness of the land around her. She wished, more than any-thing, that Rein had stayed.

She checked the road to make sure no other cars were coming and picked up her phone and scrolled with one hand as she steered with the other, eyes glancing at the road and back, search-ing for something to listen to. It was a strange night that called for strange music, she thought. Something spooky to drive to.

A song began playing through her phone, and she tapped the screen with her thumb until it stopped. She shut down the app, scrolled to her settings, made sure the Bluetooth was connected, scrolled back to the app, and restarted the song. It played through her phone again. When she looked up, her car had drifted into the oncoming lane. She cursed, righted the car, and tossed the phone into the passenger seat. It was a good thing the road was empty in front of her. She'd have plowed into someone for certain. Stupid technology. The more complicated they make things, the less they work.

Red and blue lights flared to life in the mirror behind her, fill-ing the dark woods all around with their brilliance. The police car on her tail toggled its high-pitched siren.

"You have got to be kidding me," Carrie said. Okay, think, she told herself. Her heart was hammering in her chest. She was out in the woods looking for a would-be rapist who used a police car. Now there was a police car behind her.

I was swerving, she thought. Maybe it's a real cop. If it's a real cop, I'll just show him my badge and explain what I'm doing out here. If it's not, I'll show him my badge and stomp the shit out of him.

The car zoomed forward, nearly crashing into her rear bumper, jamming on the air horn on top of the siren now.

"I'm pulling over, all right?" Carrie shouted. She yanked the wheel to the right, trying to get a look at the man sitting in the car behind her. It was too dark. She rolled down her windows, want-ing to hear if he was using a police radio or not. "Come on," she whispered, wrapping her fingers around the handle of the pistol strapped to her waist.

Won't this be something if it really is a ticket, she wondered. If it's a cop, he saw me swerving, and will probably give me a field sobriety test, whether I badge him or not. It occurred to her that she'd had wine with dinner that night. Holy shit, how much did I drink? It hadn't even been a full glass. She wasn't tipsy. Was she?

Either way, she was going to have to call Harv Bender as soon as it was over. She'd rather be the one to tell him she got pulled over than for him to hear it some other way.

The car's spotlight switched on, filling Carrie's sideview mirror with light, aimed directly at her face. She raised her hand to shield her eyes.

She heard him approaching, and as she turned in her seat to look, another light appeared in her eyes. He was holding a flashlight, pointing it straight at her so she couldn't see him.

Totally standard procedure, she thought. She'd done the same exact thing to everyone she pulled over at night.

She squinted into the light, able to see a silver badge pinned above the man's left breast pocket. That looks real, she thought. She unbuckled her seat belt and sat up, reaching around to pull her police ID out.

"You were swerving, ma'am," the man said.

"I know that, hang on a second," Carrie said, her right hand stuffed in her back pocket, still digging for the ID.

He thrust his hand through the open window and snatched Carrie by the throat. His gloved fingers clenched around her larynx so quickly that the oxygen seized inside her chest with no way to escape, threatening to burst her lungs.

In that instant, he had her door open and was ripping her out of the car, hurling her onto the road at his feet. Carrie hit the loose asphalt stones and gasped, feeling it cut into her palms and knees. She'd caught herself in time to keep from cracking her skull, but even as she tried to roll away, the man reared back his heavy boot and kicked her in the side. "You dirty fucking whore!" he shouted. "Out here swerving all over, trying to kill somebody!"

Carrie rolled with the kick and tried to scramble to her feet, but the world was spinning. He ran up and kicked her again.

He dropped down on top of her, pinning her arms to the road

and lowered his face over hers. "I'm going to teach you what happens to cunts that break the law."

He grabbed her by the throat again, cutting off her air. Carrie watched him raise a clenched fist high in the air, ready to cave her teeth in. With his body blocking the light of his car, she could make out the words printed on the badge—SECURITY GUARD.

He was about to swing when he felt the hard imprint of Carrie's gun barrel pressed against his sternum. He looked down at the gun in wide-eyed surprise, still choking her. Carrie was trying to pull the trigger, as if from a thousand miles away. Her fingers were going numb. She could feel tears streaming down the sides of her face. Her entire left side was on fire from being struck, but she was pulling with all her might. Even as her life slipped away she was pulling it as hard as she could. He let go of her and spun away just as the gun fired.

The bullet struck her car, shattering the rim of her front tire, and sending sparks flying through the air. She never heard the gun go off. She'd doubled over the second he let go of her, retching as she instinctively sucked in more air than her body could hold. From the road, she could see the man running for the driver's-side door of his car. Metal handcuffs draped around his belt at the center of his back, flapping as he ran. He was going to try to run her over, she realized, so she could never tell anyone what happened. He was reaching for the door when Carrie raised her gun again, gagging and sputtering as she tried to aim with shaking hands, and she fired. The glass window shattered above his hand and he reeled back from it.

Carrie staggered toward him, wobbling, but keeping the gun aimed steadily enough to make him raise his hands and back up. She got a better look at him then. He had the right look at first glance, but it was missing details. His black shoes were shined but his white socks were a giveaway. His cheap nylon belt with no pouches or holster was a giveaway. His polyester uniform supply shirt with American flags on both sides was a giveaway. It was all cheap imitation.

The car was an older model police vehicle, stripped of its decals and emblems. The vehicles were sold at auction all the time, and most came equipped with the door-mounted spotlight, because it was too expensive to get them removed. He'd probably bought the light bar online, she thought. The goddamn holes were likely still drilled in the roof when he went to mount it.

She leveled the gun between his eyes, gripping it with both hands. He moaned and dropped to his knees, hands held high in the air. "P-please, don't shoot me! I didn't do anything wrong! I was just trying to help!"

Carrie tried to speak, but needed to swallow and clear her throat, trying to force it to work right again. She wrenched her badge free and draped its chain around her neck, letting him get a good look at it. "Get down on the ground, facedown, you piece of shit. You're under arrest."

"I'm on your side, can't you see?" he moaned, clenching his eyes shut. "I just wanted to help the police and show I could protect people. You don't understand." He lowered his head, sobbing until spit bubbles popped between his lips. "Please don't take me to jail. You'll destroy my entire life."

Carrie circled to his left, going around back of him, keeping the gun aimed at the center of his head. She kicked him in the center of his back, as hard as she could, knocking him forward on his hands and face, his rear end raised high in the air.

"Now put your hands behind your back, or so help me God, I will shoot you if you move a single inch."

Carrie kept the muzzle of her gun pressed to the base of his skull with one hand, while she checked his pockets for weapons. She found a wallet in his back pocket and flung it open. "Stewart Gates," she said, reading his driver's license. He was even wearing his uniform in his driver's license photo.

I could kill you, she thought. It would be easy. *Just have him roll over and shoot him in the face. Tell them how he came at you, and while you were struggling, you got on top of him and fired off a lucky shot. End this, right here, right now.*

"Please, don't arrest me," Gates moaned. "I think I might be sick or something. I need help. I can't control myself. Can you please help me?"

"Shut up!" Carrie shouted, grinding the front of her gun's barrel against the base of his skull.

Kill him. It's what he would do to you.

She could hear Ben Rein's voice in her head, telling her how he'd systematically eliminated everyone involved in Ollie's death when he told her the truth about war.

You don't spare the ones who plead for mercy. In war, you kill every fucking one of them.

Even Fred Eubanks had understood his part in everything was to die. To spare the system and the public the agony of enduring his presence any longer. Was this piece of shit any different? She'd killed before. The gun shook in her hand, her finger wrapped around the trigger so tightly its serrations were biting into her flesh.

Kill him. For Monica Gere and Hope Pugh and all the countless other victims of men just like him.

"Son of a bitch!" Carrie shouted and jammed the gun back into her holster. She pulled out her handcuffs and snapped them around his right wrist and bore down on him with all her weight. She pinned his neck and arm to the street, twisting the cuffs against his wrist until he yelped. "Give me your other arm!" she said.

He rolled just enough for her to grab him by the other wrist, yank it behind his back, and get it cuffed. Carrie sat on top of him, knees wedged in his back and neck, catching her breath. She wiped sweat from her face and stood up. "Get to your feet," she said.

"I can't walk," he sobbed.

"Walk or I'll drag you," she said, pulling him upward by his handcuffs until the muscles in his shoulders threatened to tear. He staggered to his feet and Carrie steered him toward her backseat. "Get in and lay facedown," she said. "Watch out for the roof of the car. Duck your head." She watched him lie down like he was told.

Carrie picked up her car's radio microphone and said, "Detective Santero to County."

The radio dispatcher answered, "Go ahead for County."

The moon had emerged once more, bathing the woods in its full blue light, falling on the creatures who hunt and the ones who are hunted alike. "I have one in custody," she said. "Assault on a police officer."

Her badge's golden shield reflected the car's swirling lights as she leaned against the door, clutching her side and wincing. Sirens in the distance, growing louder. The road dogs were coming, and the traffic cops were coming, hell, probably even a few bosses were coming, and she would be glad to see every single one of them.

ACKNOWLEDGMENTS

Of course, first and foremost, the kids. They know that. To all my friends and family with all my love.

To Adam. I have been, and always shall be, your friend.

To Sgt. Dennis Raftery of Baltimore Homicide. In 2002, Dennis took me into his home and let me work with him at one of the most elite investigative divisions in the world. We didn't stay in touch often, but that experience helped shape me. When I wrote "The Fuming Chamber" a few months ago, I looked him up, because that story was based on our time together. I wanted to send him a copy of the first book. Turns out, Dennis passed away in 2016. God damn it.

To US Army Technical Sgt. Bernard Samuel Schaffer Sr., whom I did not know very well during his life, but who really did capture a Nazi officer single-handedly and brought home some interesting trophies.

To Steve Zacharius, Lynn Cully, Lulu Martinez, Darla Freeman, Susie Russenberger, Adrianne Bonilla, the art department, and all the incredible staff at Kensington Publishing. Your hard work makes all this possible. There's a huge Frederic Remington sculpture in Kensington's lobby, and they've been dedicated publishers of Westerns for decades now, keeping the genre going. I said I was going to write Kensington a Western someday. Hope you all enjoyed it.

To John Gilstrap, for setting me straight about what writing a book series is all about. I've spent many an hour with him at the bars of various writer's conferences, asking him how to make sense of all this. He's a good sensei and a good friend.

To Lisa Scottoline, J. A. Konrath, David Morrell, and Lee Child, for their time, guidance, and kind words about *The Thief of All Light*. David Morrell, in particular, had a big hand in the final outcome of TOAL, and for that, I'll always be grateful.

My writing exists because of the love and support of women I've known throughout my life. My mother used to take me to bookstores as a kid and encouraged my great love of literature. My aunts, Donna Laing and Paula Lipp critiqued and edited my earliest work, although it was awful and unworthy of their time. The editors who guided me during the majority of my independent career, Karen S. (The Angry Hatchet) and Laurie Laliberte, were instrumental in helping me develop as a novelist. And now, I have the pleasure of working with the two ladies I'll mention by name below. There's another group I haven't mentioned, and don't feel fully comfortable talking about, but they are present in my mind and deserve recognition. During my twenty-year police career, I've worked with women of every age, from little girls to elderly adults, who have been victims of crime. They've been brave enough to come to the station and describe the most horrific, embarrassing events of their entire lives with me. They've been strong enough to go to trial, and face down their abusers and molesters and rapists and attackers. They've been good enough people to carry on after it was all over and keep marching forward. I owe a lot to all of these women. It's my name on the cover of the book, but it's their spirit you feel within the pages. During the writing of this novel there has been a lot of conversation about women and the way they are treated in this world. It took a lot to get to this point where powerful abusers are afraid and being held accountable, now it's our job to make sure it never goes back to the way it was.

And finally, to the Magnificent Two. Michaela Hamilton and Sharon Pelletier. You are my favorite readers and the best collaborators anyone could ask for. Let's do this forever.